STEALING THE HEIRESS

SARANNA DEWYLDE

Corvus Cocax

Published in the United States of America by Corvus Corax © 2019

Cover Art by Rebecca Poole

Stock Photo: Dreamstime

ISBN: 9781948001168

𝕾 I 𝕾

Warner Woolven had been built for war.

Instead of snakes and snails and puppy dog tails, he'd been forged with brutality, cunning, and—well, maybe a puppy dog tail. War was a werewolf after all. Even his nickname marked him as the weapon he was. In any case, times of peace were unnatural for him.

That wasn't to say he didn't long for them. He'd spent his life in service to the Woolven pack, his family. He'd not made his Alpha's claim, instead letting that go to his brother Sterling, who needed it so much more. He'd stepped aside when Arianna, his one true mate had been torn between him and Sterling. When Sterling had been murdered, instead of then making his Alpha's claim, Warner had allowed the mantle of Alpha to pass to Blake.

When the time had come to fight yet again, Warner answered the call. He'd gleefully separated the wolf who killed his brother and the love of his life from his head and this plane of existence.

When he'd realized he would die of those wounds he'd incurred in that war, he'd accepted it as his fate. It was a good, honorable death. It served his pack. They were safe.

It was okay to rest.

It was okay to sleep.

It was okay to surrender to that dark ether of silence and stillness.

Most of all, it was finally his turn to lose himself in the sweet, cold, chill of Arianna's specter who'd come to greet him, to take him wherever the spirits of dead wolves went after their time on earth was over. To lay his head on her breast, be wrapped in the fiery rose-scented shroud of her red hair.

And he'd been ripped from her arms by his beloved nephew's sacrifice.

Warner was ashamed to admit, he hadn't wanted to come back. He'd done enough.

Only, like in all things, Warner lived to serve. Literally.

Except things had changed since he'd come back. A shadow loomed long and terrible at the edges of his awareness. He could see it just out of the corner of his eye, sense it swinging like the Sword of Damocles over his head.

Something had come back with him from that shadowland between the living and the dead.

Warner, for everything he'd given up, for all the scars he bore as a testament to his purpose, had never felt like an outlier amongst his pack. Sure, he spent most of his time in wolf form, but they'd always accepted him for who he was and never asked him to be anything but himself.

Yet, as he sat among his family under the clear blue sky with a warm sun hanging overhead, everyone eating and talking, he'd never felt more different.

Separate.

They were eating BBQ and roasted corn, baked beans loaded with bacon, and strawberry shortcake graciously provided by the sugar fairy Gin Goodwich. Everyone was laughing and bonding over the good memories they chose to give breath and life to wipe out all the darkness they'd recently faced.

This was what peace looked like.

Once upon a time, War had been able to let go of the awful things they'd had to do in the name of the pack.

Now, all he could think about were haunting tableaus of ripping and tearing of flesh and fascia, the hearty crunch of bones between his teeth.

The taste of blood and meat on his tongue.

Nothing like the meat that lay before him. The pig. The cow.

His massive jaws and predator's teeth had always been a weapon he used to his advantage in battle. It was never any more than this. He didn't like the taste of his own kind on his mouth, but now he feared that's all he could eat.

He slavered, thinking of the last battle.

To his shame and horror, Warner Woolven hungered for the flesh of his enemies.

He feared that it was all that could sustain him.

But more than that? He feared that he'd start to hunger not just for enemy flesh, but for something more awful.

He was thrust from his dark spiral of thoughts by Maribella's small hand curling around his, and he turned to look at her.

By the goddess, she deserved better than this.

They weren't True Mates, but she'd stood by him like a True Mate would. Had nursed him while his body healed, and had even held him while strange nightmares of monsters held him fast in their unforgiving grip.

He had to protect her.

He had to protect all of them from whatever abomination was growing inside of him.

"You okay?" she asked him.

No, he was the farthest he'd ever been from okay.

"We can probably sneak away. We're still basically newlyweds after all." Mari smiled at him, offering him the escape he needed, but couldn't take.

He squeezed her hand. "I'll stay a bit longer. After all, this is a celebration."

Noah, Emmie and Drew's son, was home from Academy for the weekend and he'd appeared with the kind of stealth magic that only little children seemed to have.

"Can we run now, Uncle War? Can we? Please?"

"Noah Phelan Woolven, will you leave your Uncle War alone?" Emmie chided. "He's trying to eat."

"Mama, is that a question or when you say it like a question, but I have to do it anyway?" Noah asked.

War couldn't help himself. He laughed. "I'm done eating, Emmie." He hadn't actually touched anything on the plate. He couldn't get it down. The idea of running with young Noah was what his heart needed, but he didn't trust himself. "But I'm sorry, little Alpha. I'm still recovering from my wounds. But soon, okay?"

The disappointment in young Noah's eyes quickly turned to compassion. "Can I help, Uncle War? What would an Alpha do?"

This kid was going to be a magnificent Alpha. "Nothing at the moment. But it was right to ask."

Noah nodded solemnly and wandered over to the sugar fairy who slipped him a box of truffles. They were his favorite. In fact, he'd gotten in trouble a few times for launching himself into the display case in Gin's shop and making quite the pig of himself. He was still learning self-control.

As it seemed so was Warner himself.

Mari's hand was still in his, and he wanted to let go, to be an island unto himself, but he found he couldn't. Something about her tiny hand in his massive paw and it reminded him of all that was good. It grounded him in the here and now.

David Rutger, Randi's father, was seated on the other side of him. He was slathered in a sunscreen of his own making that made it possible for him to walk in the sun without bursting into flames, which was always a good thing.

Except he'd suddenly gone on alert. He stiffened and sniffed the air, his incisors elongated out of his mouth.

War felt it too.

It was like a siren's song. It smelled fucking delicious.

Something bad had come to Aphelion, and he was afraid he was about to show his pack exactly what he'd brought back with him from the dark.

Then Noah howled with delight. "Lennie! Aunt Lennie!" he screamed and darted for the figure who was walking up the hill.

Dear Goddess, please don't let it be the hunter that smells like food. Please don't...

Behind Lenore Breslin, two beings followed. One smelled like wolf and the other, Warner didn't need a scent to identify.

It was a thing that had crawled straight out of a human nightmare.

He was the Watcher, the Guardian. A bone fairy named Kasadya. He wore the skulls of his enemies, his victims, like armor. Even on his wings. He was a giant, even compared to the Woolvens.

On his back, he carried a pack and whatever smelled so delectable was inside that pack.

Horror clawed at Warner's awareness, but he refused to consider what he knew to be true. If he didn't think it, if he didn't acknowledge it... not speaking its name could keep it from becoming real.

At least that's what he told himself.

Noah barreled at Lennie full speed and she caught him up in her arms and put him up on her shoulders and she continued to close the distance between her little hunting party and the Woolvens.

Mari released his hand and went to stand with Gin. All of the women did. Randi, with her much-swollen stomach, Emmie with her arms crossed and Mari, ready to defend Gin against the bone fairy. Except Gin didn't hide behind her army of valkyries. She moved to the front. Warner could sense this bone fairy was different for her somehow. She wasn't afraid of him. (She'd been kidnapped by them as a child and forced to use her power to hurt people. To rot teeth so the bone fairies could collect them and raise their strength and power.)

Warner assumed it was probably because he'd gifted her with the heads of her enemies.

The bone fairy, for his part, slowed his approach.

War laughed. He'd seen this enough times to know what was going to happen. It had happened with Randi and Blake. Emmie and Drew. Even Belle and Parker.

"What are you laughing at, Grey Tail?" Parker teased him.

"Oh, you'll see."

"Gin and... the scary bastard thing sitting in a tree, K-I-S-S-I-N-G..." Parker cackled.

"Yeah." Warner laughed.

Their witch, Eleanor Westwood appeared with an armful of more BBQ and seemed to take no mind of the bone fairy or Lenore.

Warner knew better.

Their witch knew basically everything.

As if she'd heard his thought, their eyes met over the long table and she nodded.

We'll talk later. She whispered in the back of his mind.

Yeah, she'd know what to do.

"Greetings, Woolvens! I return victorious." There was a light, teasing tone to her voice, but it held an undercurrent of sadness and resignation.

The group of women around Gin closed around Lenore, and Noah slipped from her shoulders and squirmed away from the crush. They held her close and it was almost as if they were working some kind of magic.

Somehow, Lenore Breslin, one of the most feared, yet noble hunters had become part of their pack.

Westwood eyed the bone fairy and Gin, before giving them some space.

Well, fuck that.

Warner got up and walked quietly over to stand behind Gin. He didn't want to interfere, but he wanted her to know that he was behind her if she needed him. He also had to get closer to that pack.

Kasadya acknowledged him and the unspoken boundaries with a nod.

"You've returned." Gin spoke first.

"Yes, I have. I would've brought you more enemies to lay at your feet, but his bones are nothing. He is only meat." Kasadya seemed to look right through Warner as he said this last.

"This is good." Gin's voice was soft. "You are... not hurt?"

"No, little one. I am not hurt."

"That's good. Do you want to join us?"

Warner could smell her fear, and her hope, and the proof of what he suspected: the sugar fairy had the hots for the "scary bastard," as Parker called him.

"I don't eat as you do."

"What do you eat?" The smell of Gin's fear spiked.

"Bad things." Again, Kasadya looked at him. As if acknowledging their sameness.

Warner had never wanted to flee anything as much as he wanted to get away from the knowing in those otherworldly monster's eyes.

Because he didn't want it to be true.

"You can still sit with us. Rest after your long journey. Let us welcome you as a hero," Gin said and turned to look at Westwood. Obviously, to make sure she hadn't overstepped.

Westwood nodded. "There is much still to discuss. Kasadya, whose gift is death, be welcome at our table."

He moved to sit down, but did not use a chair. His massive form would've crushed it to splinters. Instead, he sat on the grass and the sugar fairy sat next to him with her food.

Then, the bone fairy removed his pack and held it out to Warner.

"This is yours."

Warner knew in his bones that the words were true. Whatever was inside that pack, it belonged to him. His teeth had elongated in his mouth, and the Change raged to take over, but Warner fought it back.

With the pack in his arms, he struggled not to run, to fly away to the dark woods to be alone with whatever was inside.

The scent was unlike anything he'd ever smelled. He'd only dreamed of it. His stomach rumbled and he couldn't fight it any longer.

He ran.

He ran as fast as his legs would carry him. In the past, he'd been able to run as he Changed. It had been seamless, painless, and natural.

There was nothing natural about what happened to him now.

His bones were breaking to reshape. His body curled in on itself, twisted and cracked and pulsed. Even the wind on his skin that had once brought sweet relief was agony.

He didn't know what he looked like.

He didn't want to.

Warner managed to drag himself to a distant cave where he completed the surrender to the darkness that began when he'd died.

He arose something new.

Something awful.

Something that devoured what was inside that pack with a glutto-nous, orgiastic glee.

When Warner came back to himself, it was dusk and instead of lying of a cold cave floor, he was lying in Eleanor Westwood's lap.

She was singing and stroking his hair like she had when he was a pup.

Warner did something then that he hadn't done since he put Ster-ling and Arianna in the ground at Den Hollow Cemetery.

He cried.

She continued to pet him and to hum the tune that had rocked him to sleep as a pup.

"Put me down," he begged. "Put me down before I hurt them."

"You won't hurt anyone that doesn't deserve it, Warner Woolven. I know you."

"How can you? I don't know me. I'm something else now."

"I know, lovie."

"I ate what was in that bag. I ate him," Warner confessed.

"As you must. Nature requires balance. When the world is out of balance, she strives to make it right. You have always been a protector and that is what you will still be. With the rise of this new threat to both humans and wolves, something just as horrible must rise to fight it. I've seen in the runes that a dark champion will be born."

"I can't live like this. I'm no champion. I'm becoming a Berserker."

Berserkers were a horrible fate. Mad with bloodlust, they were nothing but killing machines with no hope, no light, no family, no pack. It was only about the blood. The meat. They were almost unstoppable.

"Your pack needs you, Warner. Blake is waiting."

Warner Woolven pulled himself up out of the witch's lap bloody on the outside and broken on the inside to answer the call of his pack one more time.

2

"We've got a serious fucking problem," Blake said when Warner entered their war room.

Warner would've laughed if not for the direness of the situation. His nephews sat around the table and they were all still munching on Gin's sweets. Other faces were present as well. Tirigan, the ancient Sumerian vampire who'd helped them win the war. Parker's father-in-law, if he wanted to get technical, Lenore, the wolf who'd come with her, and Westwood.

His nephews each chewed with violent purpose and it amused him to no end.

"I know, right?" Parker said, obviously knowing exactly what had War about to laugh.

Blake narrowed his eyes. "Now is not the time."

"Oh, it's never the time. Come on. I laughed when I was dying. I think I'm allowed to laugh now. You guys look so stupid. I mean, look at Drew. He's making his serious face and chewing those cookies like it's the worst thing he's ever had to do and he just keeps shoving them in his face." Parker ate another cookie.

"Back to the serious fucking problem at hand?" Lenore prompted. "By the way, what did you do with Peter?"

9

Bile rose in the back of his throat. "What do you mean?"

But he knew damn good and well what she meant. It had been Peter's boneless, still living remains in that pack.

"He's taken care of. Just trust me on that," Warner replied.

"I figured. His head started screaming and then it turned to ash," Lenore said.

Another surge of bile rose in the back of his throat.

Blake gestured to the unknown wolf. "We've been honored today with the presence of Luchtaine."

Holy fucking shit. It had to be serious. Luchtaine was a story, the monster under the bed. The oldest living wolf, if he was who he claimed to be. Older even than the Rommulus and Remus Alphas.

Maybe he was the answer to the darkness blooming rancid inside of him.

Luchtaine nodded at him, but then cocked his head to the side, appraising him as a fellow predator. He seemed for a moment as if he would speak, but he didn't.

Blake nodded to Lenore. "All present and accounted for. I'll give you the floor."

Lenore stood and braced her arms on the table and made eye contact with each of them in the room.

She was quite the magnificent creature for a hunter. In modern terms, a badass. He wasn't ashamed to admit he admired her. He admired all of the women who were part of the Woolven pack. They were fierce, devoted, strong and powerful. His heart surged with love for his pack.

"So, you all know I accepted the Council's contract to hunt down my brother. Our plan worked, as evidenced by the remains I brought back with me. In short, with an immunity to silver, I had to find another way to neutralize him. Luchtaine was strong enough to fight him, but he could match him blow for blow. It would've been an endless battle. We utilized the bone fairy's Watcher to liquefy his bones. It worked on all of his body except his head. I had to use a blessed blade to sever his head." She turned to fix Warner with a hard stare. "And you and I need to speak with later about how you finally killed him. Nothing worked. I even tried dropping his head in acid. The fucker was almost invincible."

"Which brings us to the real problem," Luchtaine said.

"Fuck. That wasn't the real problem?" Tirigan groaned.

"It was the beginning of the real problem," Lenore said. "He infected others before we could take him out. He started his own pack of creatures just like him."

Tirigan sighed. "Well, at least this won't be boring."

"Goddess fuck." Drew shook his head. "If it took all of that to take down Breslin, and granted he was an Alpha, what's it going to take to deal with this pack?"

"There's a snowball's chance in Hell that they won't be a danger. We need to determine that their infection is the same as Peter's. Because Marchessa Rommulus was infected similarly, but she has no madness. And David is working on a serum to replicate her immunity to silver for us," Blake said. "We need to send a scout."

"That needs to be you, Warner." The witch pointed at him.

"You know I'd do anything for the pack, but I can't in good conscious agree to this without presenting all the facts. I'm not—"

"—going to talk about this now," Westwood interrupted him.

War didn't usually argue with Westwood. He questioned her now and again and together they'd wrought brilliant strategy with their Alpha that had seen the Woolven pack through the worst of times.

But Warner couldn't think of anything worse than this.

"Yes, I am."

The room seemed to have gone dead silent. As if no one had dared breathe after his declaration.

Westwood sighed. "You'd think you little shits would've learned to trust me by now. But fine." She shrugged and sighed again.

"Keep sighing like that and you're going to deflate just like a tired old balloon," Parker teased.

"I'm sick, Blake. I'm in no position to represent the Woolven pack."

"What do you mean?" Blake prompted.

"I think you're going to have to put me down." He looked down at his hands. "For the pack."

"Berserker?" Blake's face was solemn, his jaw set.

This time, Parker didn't have anything witty to say. Instead, he said, "Like hell."

"There's something wrong with me, boy. Something dark came back with me."

"Is it my fault?" Parker looked to Westwood.

"Of course not. The runes say differently. The runes say a dark champion will rise and I think that champion is War," the witch countered.

"Some champion I am. Do you know how I dealt with Peter's remains? I fucking ate him."

Parker's snark was back. "The runes did say "dark." He coughed and ate another cookie.

Luchtaine stepped in. "Maybe you're the dark champion. Maybe not. The facts we have to go on say that whatever has happened to you, you are the only one who can kill them. I would take that from you if I could, Warner Woolven. But that gift didn't choose me. It chose you. If it brings you any comfort, you don't smell like Berserker to me."

Warner growled. "No, it doesn't bring me any fucking comfort. At least if I was going Berserker, then I'd have the relief of forgetting. Of being consumed by the rage and the hunger. Whatever has happened to me? There's no forgetting. There's only a need I can't control that puts everyone around me in danger. What happens when I run out of bad things to sate this cursed hunger? Huh, what then?"

"One thing at a time, Warner. The pack needs you," Westwood whispered the magic words that had driven him for the whole of his life.

He looked to Blake. His nephew, who was more like a son. His Alpha.

"Please, Warner."

"Of course." He scrubbed a hand over face and then through his hair. "If that's what you think is best."

"We'll figure this out, Uncle. We won't leave you alone in the dark. I swear it." Blake's words carried the irrefutable, undeniable promise of an Alpha. The words might as well have been carved in stone.

"Where am I going?"

"You know where," Westwood said.

"Minnesota was where we took Peter," Lenore offered.

And Minnetonka, Minnesota was where he'd been dreaming of blood and death.

He didn't say anything else. Instead, he left the war room and headed straight for Den Hollow Cemetery and Arianna Woolven's grave. He asked her advice on raising her sons often. Of course, the only answer he ever got in return was silence, but it made him feel like he was doing the right thing.

Even if it was stepping in shit.

He'd done his best for the boys and the pack. His chest puffed with pride at the thought.

Warner had buried her and Sterling together beneath an old oak on a small hill that overlooked the Hollow and had a straight view to Aphelion.

The sun shone down, still bright and warm. The sky somehow was still clear. The air smelled of green growing things. Nothing seemed to betray that fact he'd fallen down the hole to Hell.

He sat down at the foot of their graves.

"I've done my best," he began.

But had he?

"Blake's a strong Alpha, Sterling. He's more than you or I could ever have been. You'd be proud of him. I'm sure he's come to talk to you, what with Randi round with pup. He led us to war and negotiated peace. He did it for all the right reasons."

Warner stopped and inhaled deeply.

"Drew. Goddess, Drew is the kind of Beta that all Alphas need. Parker is ever the little shit, but he makes my heart swell with pride. They've all been matched with mates we'd never have expected, but who make Woolven that much stronger."

He looked at Arianna's side of the stone as if he were talking to her. "I know I swore you a promise, I'm not sure if I can keep it this time. At least not in the way you'd want me to. They've got so much faith in me, and Goddess, if this were anything else, it wouldn't be unwarranted. This is different and I just don't think I can fight this while I'm breathing."

"Warner?" Mari's soft voice interrupted. "I don't mean to intrude, but Westwood said you needed me."

His first instinct was to say that Westwood was mistaken, but that would've been unnecessarily cruel. He did owe her an explanation, if nothing else.

She sat down next to him. "Is this where she's buried? Your mate?"

Warner studied the delicately beautiful woman sitting next to him. Everything about her seemed so fragile, so breakable. From her fey features, the high cheekbones, the large ice-blue eyes and her white-blond hair to the grace with which she moved. Her fingers were slender and seemed to have been made for magic, not the earthy paws they became when she Changed. Even her voice was melodic and soft, but he knew she had strength and fire.

He didn't know if he would be so calm and curious if the situations were reversed. If she had a True Mate who'd never claimed her, who died, and he'd found her sitting at the foot of his grave, talking to him about things she should've been talking to Warner about. After all, he'd taken her to mate. They were partners now.

She didn't deserve any of what had happened to her. She deserved a True Mate. She deserved everything good the world could give her.

"You don't have to tell me if you don't want to," she said.

"Sorry, Mari. I was lost in thought."

"If you'd rather be alone, I understand."

He should tell her to go back. He should tell her to stay far away from him. He should tell her that she's free.

But he couldn't make the words come out of his mouth.

Instead, he said, "I don't want to be alone. But it's probably best if I am."

"That seems to inform all of your choices, Warner. You are always alone, but you don't have to be. You have an amazing pack, but you spend all of your time on the fringes."

"Is that how you see it?"

"How do you see it?" she asked.

No one had ever asked him that before. "Doing my duty. I stay on the fringes so Blake can be the best Alpha he can be. I guard the pack in ways no one else does. I'm always watching so my pack and my family are safe."

"That means staying in wolf form? Sleeping in the woods?"

He didn't expect her to understand. They were cut from very different cloths. She never Changed unless she had to. She spent all of her time as a human. Warner preferred the wolf. At least he had, until the darkness came.

Now, he didn't know if his wolf could be trusted.

She didn't wait for an answer. Instead, she said, "Westwood says you're going to Minnesota. Wasn't that the same place you'd been having nightmares about?"

"Yeah. It's also where I met Arianna. The boys' mother."

"Tell me about her. How you met."

"Why?" He'd never really talked about her. He left those stories for Westwood to tell the boys.

"Why not?"

"Okay. I mean, you're right. Why not?" *Why not? Because talking about her was still like ripping open a half-healed wound.* Except he found he wanted to rip that wound open. Maybe just once more. "I was sent to investigate reports of a rogue wolf who'd been terrorizing the pack there. It was a fall evening and the leaves had turned crisp. The moon was high overhead, a witch's moon with three blood-red rings. I was patrolling the woods when I saw her. She was naked, singing the songs of invocation and dancing around a fire."

Mari sighed. "That's pretty perfect. Then what?"

He found himself laughing. "Then she took me down."

"You?"

"Well, I let her."

Mari crossed her arms over her chest. "That's not romantic. I would never want a man to just let me take him down. Gross. I'd want to do it on my own."

"Really?" He tried to imagine her taking him down and it just didn't happen. The images wouldn't form in his brain. Not even a little.

"You say that like it couldn't happen." She pursed her lips.

"I'm not saying it couldn't happen, but the likelihood..." He realized his mistake. "Listen. It's not that I think you're not capable. I know you are, but physicality doesn't seem to be your strong suit."

"Is that why you won't complete the mating?" Her voice was small, as if she had been afraid not only to ask the question, but of the answer.

The question punched him in the gut. He prided himself on duty. On loyalty. By not completing their consummation, he realized he'd done her a great disservice. Whether she was his True Mate or not, she deserved more than he'd given her.

He supposed he knew that.

"I didn't think you wanted to. I figured you already got the shit end of the stick being forced to marry me."

"Hold on. I wasn't forced. You asked me if you could bite me after you stole me from the limo. You think I couldn't get away? I have teeth and claws just like you, War. But I said yes."

"I have to ask why you said yes. Duty?"

"For being the great Warner Woolven, you're really not as bright as I expected."

"Ouch. Damn, woman." He clutched his chest.

"Well, I've been as obvious as I can." She took his hand. "Come back with me to the cabin before you leave."

Her invitation was sparklingly clear.

His cock surged at the thought of taking her. Of burying his nose in the champagne and strawberry scent of her hair. Of being given the care of something so precious as Maribella Woolven.

But he couldn't.

It wasn't safe for her.

If he hurt her, he'd never forgive himself.

"Mari, I can't."

"Because you don't want to? Because of Arianna?"

"No, that's not it. I..." he struggled for the right words. She was right, he wasn't very bright. At least not when it came to things like this. Talking about his feelings. It wasn't that he'd been taught feelings were bad, but he'd pushed them down for so long because his feelings didn't serve the pack.

So he drowned them. Smothered them. Hid them away. Now that he was trying to bring them into the light, he didn't know how.

Although, it didn't matter.

He had to do the right now.

"This can't happen. You're not safe with me, Mari."

She put his hand on his face. "I've never felt safer than when I'm with you."

Her words were the arrow he needed.

"That's changed. *I've* changed. Something's happened. I'm not right. It's not just you who isn't safe. It's everyone."

Looking up into her wide, guileless eyes, he knew what he had to do.

"I release you, Maribella. From our marriage, from our bond, with no dishonor. The fault is mine. You'll still have access to all things Woolven. Especially your accounts."

And that was when he realized he'd seriously misjudged her physical abilities.

The hand that had been resting so lovingly, so reassuringly on his cheek had become an anvil.

She slapped the feeling out of the right side of his face.

3

"What the hell was that for?" Warner rubbed his cheek.

Mari was furious. More than furious, she was hurt. His words had wounded her in a way like she hadn't let anything cut her since she was thirteen.

She knew it was wrong to hit him because it sure as shit wouldn't have been okay for him to hit her.

"I have done nothing but what was asked of me. I haven't asked you for much. Nothing beyond what you owe a mate. I nursed you after you healed. I tried my best to be your partner. I've even come up here while you worship Saint Arianna, and have I judged you or asked you to be anything other than who you are? And this is what I get? *I release you?* Are you fucking kidding me?"

Warner seemed genuinely confused. "I said you'd still have your accounts—"

Which was precisely the wrong thing to say. "Do you think I give two bits of a damn about money? I have my own. I'm a freaking heiress. *HEIRESS.* Even without the mineral rights my father granted the Woolven pack, I could buy Woolven ten times over."

Her fury fizzled as quickly as it had ignited because it gave way to

19

sorrow. To pain. To the ugly truth that no matter what she did, no matter how hard she tried, she was never going to be good enough.

Not for her father.

Not for her pack.

And not for Warner Woolven.

She sank back on the ground. "I did everything right, didn't I?"

"Of course you did," War reassured her.

"And you still don't want me. Still too pretty to be of use?" She threw his previous words back at him.

"Oh hey. That was a two-way street, if you'll recall. You said I was too old to be of use." He eyed her with obvious censure.

She swallowed hard. "I guess you're right there. I didn't mean that. You just made me angry."

He leaned forward. "I didn't mean it either. I didn't know what to do with you."

"What to do with me? Like I'm some sort of present you didn't want?" Then she wilted. "I guess that *is* what I am."

"Mari, no. You're young. You're beautiful. You look like you should be a fairy instead of a werewolf. And I'm... old. Scarred." He shrugged as if that word encompassed all of their problems.

"I like scars." She hated herself for admitting it to him. For giving him that leverage by admitting she liked how he looked. Although Mari supposed it didn't matter now.

"Why?" Warner seemed genuinely perplexed.

"Because scars show you've fought a battle and won. You're strong. You're fierce. All good things to have in a mate."

"And so are you, but I'll hurt you."

"You're already hurting me." She pressed her lips together. "But you can't help how you feel. I was going to ask you to take me with you Minnesota. Let me help. Let me be your partner in all ways. I thought I could convince you that I could handle it. That *we* could handle it." Tears burned behind her eyes and it was hard to swallow, but she wasn't going to beg. She may not have a mate, but at least she could salvage a remnant of her pride.

She got up, but he grabbed her hand again.

"Before the darkness, we would've made a great team. We would've had this conversation and I'd have hauled you back to the cabin and taken you every way you'd let me."

His words caused desire to wash over her in heady waves. She wanted every part of that sentence to be a prophecy of things to come.

She didn't understand why they couldn't be.

"This isn't fair, War. You can't offer me everything I want in one hand and take it away in the other."

"I know. That's why I have to let you go. It's because I want you."

"No, you don't. You're just trying to hide a fuck-you-sundae in sprinkles. No thanks." She pulled away from him and put her hands on her hips. "You talk about this darkness. I haven't seen it. Where is it? Show me."

"You really don't want that."

"Don't tell me what I want. Furthermore, stop trying to push me out of this pack. You know what my life was like growing up. Remember that Christmas my family hosted yours in Tahoe?"

"I remember all the other wolves were outside playing. All we could see from the great room window were tails sticking up out of the snow."

"Where was I, War?" she prompted.

He didn't say anything.

"You probably don't remember, so I'll tell you."

"I don't need you to tell me, I remember. We sat quietly, reading by the fire and drinking cocoa."

"I loved you a little then for not abandoning me like the rest of them. I've never fit in anywhere. Except here. Except as a Woolven. Here, it's okay for me to be exactly who and what I am. Please don't take it away."

"You're still Woolven. I'm trying to do the right thing here."

"Well, stop it. Because you're screwing it up." She swallowed her tears and what was left of her pride.

She should leave him there in the cemetery clinging to memories of the dead saint and take all that he offered. Take her freedom and make some kind of life for herself. She wouldn't be anyone's property, asset, or chattel. She'd go somewhere and buy herself some peace.

Except that wasn't what Mari wanted.

She wanted what all the other Woolven brides had and she wanted it with Warner Woolven.

Mari looked down at him. At the questions in his eyes and the earnest expression on his scarred face.

Yeah, she wanted him for exactly the reasons he tried to send her away.

"What is the right thing, then? Tell me."

"Can't you just try?" she asked.

"What does that mean to you?" He pushed his hand through his hair. "Shit, what am I doing? Fuck. I can't let you risk yourself."

She cocked her head to the side. "And when did that ever work for your nephews' mates?"

"You're different, Mari. You know that."

"You mean I'm not strong enough. Not good enough. Just not enough."

"That's not what I said and not what I meant."

To her shame, she couldn't stop thinking about the answer to his question.

What does that mean to you?

What was her idea of Warner trying? What did it look like?

Damn it, she could see it all as if it played on a drive-in theater screen. He'd take her in his arms right there on the hill underneath leafy arms of the oak tree. He pushed her down in the soft grass and it wouldn't matter that Arianna was buried there. He'd let her go and embrace what he had right in front of him.

Literally.

He'd make love to her. He'd fuck her. He'd mark her for real. It would be enough.

Mari would be enough.

Only that was just a fantasy, wasn't it?

She remembered his broad, scarred hands on her flesh when he'd stolen her out of that limo. When he'd ripped the roof off with his bare hands. His eyes flashing amber with the power of his wolf.

He'd made her so wet.

Yet to her eternal disappointment, he didn't seem inclined to do anything about it. Just like now.

He'd closed his eyes, breathed deep. She watched as his chest rose and fell with the mechanics of breath.

"You smell good, Maribella."

Goddess, but she felt like a shit. She wanted nothing more in that moment than to seduce him right here. She'd even shed her human skin and run with him. She wanted to know what it felt like to run through the dark woods by his side. She wanted to know what it was like to be his in every way. She wanted it so much she thought the ache of it would kill her. She'd never wanted anything like she wanted Warner Woolven.

She swallowed hard. "What do I smell like?"

"Like hot, wet female and strawberries and champagne. I bet that's how you'd taste too."

His voice had dropped an octave. Lower than any human could go. It made her shiver with desire.

"So why don't you taste me?" she dared.

"That's not a good idea."

"We do lots of things in this pack that aren't a good idea. It seems to work out," she taunted.

He didn't move. He didn't accept what she offered, but that didn't stop her.

Maybe it should have.

"Unless you really don't want me." Her voice wasn't small and soft, it wasn't the utterance of a woman who was unsure about her appeal. It was sex-kitten sultry. It was like she was under some kind of spell.

She leaned in toward him, some polarity pulling her forward, guiding her. His eyes burned with the amber light of his wolf and he narrowed his intensity on the fullness of her lips.

Mari would swear she could feel them swelling under his scrutiny, plumping to welcome his mouth on hers, to entice his body into hers.

Oh yes.

Her desire spiked and his nostrils flared.

Part of her began to understand why it was good to be a wolf.

She could scent his lust too.

It was like caramel and burning leaves. There was a scent underneath it all that was different. Wrong. It smelled like no natural wolf or were. It was different. It was other.

It was darkness.

It was blood.

Instead of frightening her, or even setting off her warning bells, it made her that much hotter. The darkness and blood called to her like nothing had ever before.

Maybe because it was wrapped up in Warner Woolven.

Whatever the case, she couldn't get enough and her intrinsic need to devour the beast that bore that scent—and be devoured by it in turn—would not be denied.

It was as if every wolfy instinct she'd had and ignored for so long had been magnified on a quantum level.

There was only War.

Only this pulsing need between them.

"You don't know what you're doing, Mari." He worked his jaw as his teeth fought to elongate and he crushed the animal inside of him with an obvious iron fist.

"Maybe I don't, but my wolf does. I can't control her, War. And I don't want to. It's been so long since I wanted to let her out."

"Don't say it's for me." His growl was low, lower even than she'd ever heard it before. Even when he was fighting to the death.

"Not for you." She licked her lips. Their mouths were almost close enough that she could've tasted him, had she dared. "Because of you."

She wanted to touch him everywhere. Trace her tongue down over the brutal mesh of his scars, she wanted to give him another scar. On his throat. She wanted to tear at the flesh there, to mark him as her own.

Mari had never had feelings this intense before.

She'd never felt so connected to her wolf.

She never knew she could.

And she wanted him to do the same to her. To tear into her throat with his long, sharp teeth and brand her as his own.

To really belong to Warner Woolven, body and soul.

The very idea caused a strange spasm between her thighs that she felt all the way to her toes. It wasn't quite an orgasm, but it wasn't a stab of desire either. It was like both the question and the answer at the same time. A yearning, and fulfillment both.

"The way you smell right now," he confessed, "makes me want to do things to you, Mari. Things you can't possibly want. You want a kiss in a graveyard and I want to tear open your throat."

Another of those delicious shudders wracked her body at his words and she tilted her head to the side and tugged the sleeve of her dress down to give him complete and total access.

He slammed her to the ground and his face was buried in the tender crook of her neck, his breath was hot on her skin, but he didn't bite.

Dear Goddess, why didn't he bite?

Her breath came in ragged gasps and she put her arms around him and pulled him closer.

His weight pressed her down into the soft grass beneath her back and she could feel the thick bulge of his cock against her thigh.

This mating might kill them both, but she knew it would be worth it.

Every cell in body vibrated with a hollow frequency, that awareness before the strike. And the longing for the sharp pain, and the pulsing sensation that couldn't be distinguished from pain or pleasure.

He pulled back from her neck and looked down into her eyes.

Holy Hecate, but he was a fearsome beast. His beautiful amber eyes had gone blood-red and they were no less beautiful. Mari could see the shifting skin and bones sliding around beneath the surface of his human façade and it too was horrifically beautiful.

War was still holding back and Mari, secure now in his desire for her, wasn't going to tolerate his denial any longer.

She arched up and pressed her mouth to his.

When he kissed her back, the whole world changed. It was as if she'd only been seeing the world in faded memories of color and every sensation, every moment, every breath was brought to stark and effervescent life.

Just like the champagne bubbles she'd had to use to induce her Change as a kid.

Warner's kiss made everything champagne.

Mari knew then this was exactly where she was supposed to be and this would be no half-assed mating.

Warner was her True Mate.

He might not know it, might not be ready for it, but she belonged to him, and he to her.

His hands began to move over her body and she drowned in a haze of sensation and pure, animal lust.

Until he had her writhing and aching beneath him, and then he took it all away. He pulled back from her, no longer touching, tasting, or grinding his hard body against her heat.

She opened heavy-lidded eyes to gaze up at her mate and what she saw didn't make sense in her brain.

The thing that was above her was not Warner Woolven.

Yet, somehow, it still was.

He was misshapen, wrong. She didn't have the words to describe his new form. Everything about him was other.

It seemed that even the dirt beneath them screamed in agony at his nearness. His wrongness.

Those red eyes that burned like the fires of hell had focused on her.

Specifically on the pulse in her throat, but for some reason, she wasn't afraid.

Maybe because beneath all that "other" she knew he was still Warner. Still one of the strongest, noblest wolves to breathe air.

Westwood had said he was a dark champion.

Well, she'd be damned if she'd leave him alone in the dark.

Mari was strong enough to do this. Strong enough to be his mate.

She turned her head to the side, once again exposing the full, creamy expanse of her neck to his elongated jaws with their bear trap of razor tusks.

With a roar, Warner opened his death maw, but his jaws never closed around her throat.

Instead, with a terrible otherworldly howl, he tore off into the woods as if the very hounds of hell were on his heels.

Leaving Mari alone with her lips swollen, her body aching and unfilled, and her heart battered.

4

Warner ran through the trees. He didn't know where he was running to, or when to stop. If he could stop. Ever.

He couldn't distinguish between the wrenching hungers that twisted up his guts. He couldn't separate them—the need to devour, to consume and his need for Mari.

He should keep running.

He should run until his legs fail, until his bones break, until there's nothing left of him but meat for the carrion.

It was the only way to keep them all safe.

To keep her safe.

What about the Pack of Peter Breslins roaming free in the north? What about the shadow you feel inside you falling over the world?

The thought was inside his head, but it wasn't completely his own.

Something other whispered in the back of his head, growing there like an oily cancer.

Just then, he caught the scent of blood on the breeze and his hunger wouldn't be denied. Blood was the only thing that would satisfy the raking claws through his guts.

It won't help you.

Nothing can help you, except the flesh of the cursed.

Pictures of the animal built a slideshow in his mind.

He knew where it was, knew all of his injuries, and yes, he even knew the gender.

It had never been like this... hunting. He would catch a scent and his mind would pour through what seemed like mental files to find the animal it belonged to. It was a very human way to think—a meld of his wolf brain and his human brain.

This was... this was like he'd tapped into some kind of magic.

He was at war with himself.

Warner needed to make this pain, this raging hunger be silent, but the darkness told him it wouldn't be the release he needed, he wouldn't be sated.

Was this what it was going to be like? A never-ending insatiable hunger?

He didn't want this.

Couldn't live like this.

His new sharper, longer teeth elongated in his mouth and the Change hit him hard.

Warner's bones all broke at once, shattering inside his skin and he heard a sound like a howl, or was it a scream? All he knew was the sound was awful and it was coming from his own throat.

The bones knit themselves back together, faster now than the last time, and he was once again bipedal.

Somehow, the hunger had intensified. He didn't have the words to describe it.

The bear lumbered about, just beyond the creek, leaving a trail of blood behind him.

And Warner's faint control disappeared.

He was no longer in the driver's seat. The dark thing was.

Suddenly, it wasn't about eating to feed his physical body. It was about the violence. The depravity.

The thing he'd become was rage personified.

When it was finished, when the darkness was sated, all that was left of the bear was a pile of oozing muck.

When Warner came back to himself, he was still hungry.

Naked and bloody, he lay face down in the grass and screamed into the earth below him.

Then, he inhaled the scents around him that were not blood and death. The green grass, the loamy earth, the trees...

He knew what he had to do.

For maybe the first time in centuries, Westwood was wrong.

He was no champion, dark or otherwise. He was a vessel for something that had hitched a ride back from the other side and it needed to be returned before it wreaked this kind of devastation on his pack.

It wasn't fair, but life often wasn't. Warner knew that better than anyone.

He wasn't going to rail against what he couldn't change.

He would do what within his power to do.

Warner would go to Minnesota. He'd kill this infected pack, and wipe it from the earth.

Then, he'd do the same to himself. It was the only option.

He only had one regret. In a long, preternatural life filled with so many sorrows, not being able to give Mari the things she deserved and wanted was the one thing he wished he could change.

Not Arianna's or Sterling's death, they'd made their choices. He wouldn't take that from them.

Not even stepping aside so Arianna could be with Sterling. Without that, he'd never have his wonderful nephews. The pack wouldn't have blossomed as it had under Sterling's and now Blake's rule.

And they'd been happy.

That was enough for Warner.

But Mari.

As he thought of her, his breathing slowed and agony still shooting through him began to subside.

He remembered her words. How she'd reminded him of that Christmas. Warner knew she'd spent most of the holiday alone, being unable to transform to share in the wolfy festivities. She was so delicate. So very human.

But fierce too, the darkness reminded him.

He agreed. In the cemetery, when he'd been Changing, it was awful. He didn't know how he looked, but he knew it was wrong.

She hadn't been afraid of him.

His first instinct had been to think that maybe she didn't know enough to be afraid, but Mari was smart, and definitely capable. She knew.

She simply had faith in him.

By the goddess, the way she tasted.

His cock throbbed to life and he had to roll on his back. He tried not to think about her. There was no point in obsessing over what he couldn't have.

You could have her.

Remember, she offered herself to you.

Was hot and desperate for you.

Take her.

Bite her.

Mark her.

Taste her...

That was exactly why he couldn't have her. He wouldn't take the chance that he'd hurt her.

Although, she hadn't seemed like she was in any kind of pain except the kind induced by his refusal to do his duty.

Even in this state.

Her mouth tasted like summer and her skin, like strawberries. He wondered if her cleft would taste the same. He wanted to lick her until she came on his face, screaming.

Warner didn't know where this was coming from—this need for her. It wasn't like this when he'd claimed her.

Sure, she was beautiful. But she wasn't The One. His True Mate. And it would've been no hardship to bed her. In fact, he would've made sure they both enjoyed it immensely, when the time was right.

Something had changed between them and the only thing it could be was this new shadow inside of him.

Of course it would want her. She was soft, and sweet, and—

It's more than that.

She is us.

Warner had a brief vision of gouging that voice out of his head with his own claws.

"No, she's not," he said aloud.

Laughter echoed in his ears.

You'll see.

"No, I won't. And neither will you." Determination flooded him and he wasn't going to let himself anywhere near sweet Mari every again.

Doesn't matter. She'll come to us. She must.

And you want her to.

His hand had closed around his cock and while it felt so good, he didn't want the thoughts in his head.

They were all about Mari.

About licking her. Tasting her. Touching her.

About tearing her tender throat with his dark bite.

About how she fucking loved it.

His stroke moved faster, harder and his hips thrust in time. He should stop, he wanted to stop. He didn't want to come thinking about hurting her.

And the visions changed.

She was the one infected with the darkness. She was the one running him down in the woods to tear at his flesh.

Goddess Above, when he imagined her marking him with the same hell-teeth like his own, that's what took him over the edge, and he spilled his seed in his hand.

The grass died where it touched, and if Warner had harbored any hope that he'd ever touch her, they died in that moment.

The natural world was so offended by his existence, the vehicle with which he could reproduce was poison.

This was all he could have of her.

He knew he could never see her again.

But he didn't think it would be a problem after Minnesota.

He dragged himself to his feet and began to make his way back to Aphelion.

Normally, he'd just Change and run. In his wolf form, he could cover the distance in a short time, but he didn't want to Change. He didn't want that devil face anywhere near his pack.

And he wondered briefly if he was in that form if Aphelion's ward would rip him apart. They were magically keyed to destroy anyone who passed the boundaries with ill intent toward any of the residents.

He'd say that his hunger for Mari was definitely ill-intended.

His cock had begun to throb again and now his teeth along with it. They both ached to be inside her.

But he wasn't going to allow that to happen, was he?

The darkness inside him was quiet now, but he wasn't under any illusions that anyone was safe. It was simply biding its time like a master predator would.

It took him an hour to run back to Aphelion using only his human form.

And it felt surprisingly good. He liked feeling the way his body worked, the press of his feet against the ground, the way his lungs expanded and contracted with effort. He even liked the discomfort that verged on pain. He ran harder, wanted to feel more of it. Because that meant he was still Warner.

There was a kind of numbness in darkness, a toxin to make him more amenable to all the awful things it wanted him to do.

When he stepped inside Aphelion, it struck him that it would be for the last time.

This was his home.

Where he'd helped raise a family, and a pack.

This was where his heart lived and where it would stay long after his flesh was gone.

He leaned against the stone column and pressed his forehead to the cool surface for a long moment before heading to the armory.

Unfortunately, when he got to the armory, it was already occupied by one Miss Lenore Breslin.

She was sitting with her legs crossed, swinging her leg impatiently while sipping a coffee.

Various bits of hiking gear and supernatural self-defense detritus lay spread out on the prep tables, along with two backpacks and camping gear.

"Took you long enough. I thought you'd have tried to sneak out hours ago."

"You're not coming with me."

"The hell you say." There was no rancor in her tone. It was as if she were telling him about the forecast, which smelled like rain.

"Lenore—"

"Warner?"

"I know you're a big girl. I know you can take care of yourself. But this is different." He didn't want to see anything happen to the hunter.

Like he'd thought earlier, yeah, somehow she'd become part of their pack and he wanted to protect her.

"I'm not going to say it's not different. I know that it is. But you don't need to do this alone."

"I ate him, Lennie. You want to come with me knowing that? Or will that make it easier to take *my* head when the time comes? Is that why you want to come?"

"Don't be a dumbass, Warner. I'm not taking your head."

"Then I don't need you."

"Yes, you do." She rolled her eyes. "Look, I get it. You're noble and shit. You're the champion. But in all the stories we've ever heard either in our own lore, or human lore never has there been The One who didn't have a team. Who didn't help them reach the final battle they were meant to fight. So you're The One. And I'm the team, 'kay? Good."

He put his hand out on her arm and she arched a brow at him.

"Listen to me. You know what else happens? Those team members die. They sacrifice their lives and I couldn't take it if something happened to you. Noah couldn't take it either."

"That's not fair."

"No one said it would be."

"Okay. You got me there, Gray Tail."

"You're pack, Lenore. I know that you're a hunter. I know that you're always in danger, but I can keep you from this danger. It's my responsibility, and my honor."

Lenore sniffed and blinked. "I love you, too, you grumpy old bastard. Which is why I'm still coming. Pack means no one left behind. And if you want to protect me, I guess that means you just have to stay alive to do it."

He closed his eyes

"Goddess damn it, Lenore."

"I'll make you a promise. If you're not the wolf I think you are, the wolf Westwood thinks you are, then I'll do it, okay? If you become a threat, I'll take your head."

"I don't think I'll be able to let you."

"None of the wolves let me, War." She hugged him tight. "But it's not going to come to that. I know it."

He let himself rest in her embrace for just a moment. He wasn't only hugging Lenore. He was hugging Noah. Drew. Blake. Parker. Emmie. Randi.

Mari.

A low growl started in the back of his throat as he thought of her, but Lenore didn't pull away. Didn't tense up. She simply kept hugging him.

He wanted to live up to the picture she—all of them—had painted of him. He wanted to be what they thought he was.

Wanted to be the wolf he'd always believed himself to be.

Which was why he had to get away from them. All of them.

Even Lenore.

But he knew he wasn't getting out of Aphelion without her.

He pulled back from her. "Fine. But it's not because you hugged me," he grumbled.

"No, it's because I'll tranq your ass if I have to and you know it." She grinned.

"That I do, Lenore."

"Glad that's settled. Do you want the Sig or are you just going to use your teeth?" She held up the modified Sig Sauer P226.

"Might as well take a few of those, but I don't know that the silver nitrate bullets are going to do any good."

"Well, I had an idea. I got some empty rounds from David and we're going to fill them with your blood. If your saliva is toxic to them, your blood will be too."

"You're not worried I might make more like me?"

"Nah. Westwood said whatever is happening to you is to force balance. And hey, after the world is back as it should be, maybe you will be too."

Warner knew that was as likely as shit sticking to the moon and tasting like one of Gin's cupcakes.

But eliminating the threats to his pack and his family were all that mattered.

5

W arner was gone.

Mari knew it in her bones before she saw his motorcycle was missing from the row in the garage.

And she knew where he'd gone.

He'd gone to find the rogue pack and take them down.

With the hunter Lenore. Her motorcycle was gone, too.

A stab of ugly jealousy knifed through her that she was good enough to take with him, but not her. Lenore was a hunter, but she was human. It was her he'd chosen and not his own mate.

Mari swallowed hard, because it was indeed a bitter pill. If she could pick anyone to take into battle, she wouldn't choose herself either.

There had to be something she could do.

There had to be some way she could be of use.

Lifting her chin, she found her way to Westwood's labs.

A strange green smoke billowed out from under the door and she heard what sounded like the honest to goddess, legit wicked witch cackle.

She wondered if maybe this wasn't the best time to bother the witch. Who knew what was going on in that lab of hers. She could be doing important work. Like gathering eye of newt and toe of frog from some Prince Smarming gone awry.

"By the pricking of my thumbs, something heartbroken this way comes," the witch said when she opened the door.

"I'm not heartbroken."

"Didn't say it was you, my sweet little darkling." She held the door open wide. "Come in, come in. Cookie?"

A gingerbread man danced his way up to her and shook his little sugar booty at her.

She snatched it out of the air and crunched him, washing it down with the lovely steaming cup of tea that floated toward her after she was done with him.

"Another?" Eleanor asked.

"No. Yes. No." Mari sighed.

"Yes, another. I think it will be just the thing."

This time the gingerbread man booped her nose with his butt and she chomped. Surprisingly, Mari felt marginally better.

"Better, then?"

She nodded.

"I assume it's Warner troubles that bring you to my door?"

"That obvious, is it? Am I that pathetic?"

"No, of course not. I just know Warner. I'm guessing he's fucked off to Minnesota on his own with some noble, but misguided, idea about saving us from his darkness or whatever."

"Yes, but he's taken Lenore."

To Mari's extreme irritation, the witch cackled again.

"I don't see how this is funny."

"He didn't take Lenore. Lenore took him." The witch shook her head. "You know that there's nothing but pack between them, right?"

"I know. But she was good enough. I wasn't."

"Oh, honey." Eleanor pulled her into a grandmotherly embrace. "It's not that you're not good enough. He wants you and so does the dark champion inside of him. It doesn't want Lenore. He doesn't doubt you. He doubts himself."

"I must be crazy to not be afraid of him—it."

"Have you seen it, then?"

Mari nodded.

"That bodes very well. I think there's part of you that knows something that the rest of us don't."

"Part of me that knows something you don't? That would be a miracle, wouldn't it?"

"Not at all, Miss Mari. There's a strength inside of you that's wholly your own, but you've been cut off from it."

"You mean my wolf?"

"Hmm." Westwood studied her, eyes narrowing. "Yes, I see now. I suspected as much."

Mari suddenly felt like an odd little bug pinned with her wings spread under a microscope.

"What?"

"Ah, yes."

"I... for the love of the Goddess, what?"

"Hmm."

"Okay, you're freaking me out." Mari squirmed under the witch's scrutiny.

"Yes, that would be normal in this situation."

What. The. Actual. Hell.

"So, you're telling me I'm really an alien or something, right? Something awful is going to tear out of my stomach and tapdance stage left?" Mari was only half kidding.

"Kiddo, all I can tell you is that you need to trust yourself. Listen to your wolf. Let her speak to you."

"That's just the problem. I've never been able to hear her."

Mrs. Westwood put out a hand and let it rest on her shoulder. "Have you ever wondered if there was a reason for that?"

"Besides the part that I'm a freak who isn't wolf enough for the supe world and not human enough for the rest of the world? No. What possible reason could there be? My genes are just too diluted, I guess."

"Oh, child. It's nothing like what you think. This generation of Woolven Wives have all been just like you. Randi was human, but when she was Turned, she became more than just a werewolf. You know the story."

Yes, everyone knew how Randi had taken out a pack of Berserkers on her own.

"And Belle," Westwood said.

"She was already a vampire before she met Parker."

"She was, but she's basically a living goddess."

Mari couldn't argue with that.

"And Emmie... she's become a whole new kind of wolf that's half-demon, but all badass."

She didn't quite get what Westwood was getting at. Her logical brain connected the dots, that Westwood was saying she was more than the little wanna be wolf who failed at everything but shopping.

But Mari couldn't bring herself to believe it.

"And then there's me. Who couldn't transform unless she had a bowl of champagne to lap at."

"Yes, Mari. There's you. The draw you feel toward Warner is not one-sided. Nor is it a mistake."

"He thinks it is."

"Warner Woolven is a good wolf, but when it comes to matters of the heart, he doesn't know his ass from a hole in the ground. Trust in the balance. Trust in the natural law. And most importantly trust in yourself."

"That would be stupid."

"Oh really? Why is that?" Westwood arched a perfectly groomed brow.

Mari just realized she'd told the terrifying witch that her advice was stupid. Yeah, maybe not the best choice she'd ever made.

"Uh..."

Westwood laughed. "No, I genuinely want to know why you'd say that."

"If I could trust my own instincts, I'd go after Warner. But what can I do?"

"I don't know what you can do. Only you know what you can do."

"I can't do anything. Warner is becoming something else. Something more powerful than anything I've ever seen. What do I have to offer him that will help him? Nothing. Just me."

Westwood handed her another cookie. "Why haven't you ever considered that just you is enough? Just little Mari is all he needs."

"Because that's laughable."

"Blake needed Randi before she became what she is now. Drew needed Emmie when he thought he could never give her his mark. Parker and Belle needed each other when they thought it was impossible for them to actually be together."

She supposed all of those things were true, but it didn't mean that the same formula was meant to work for her.

But why couldn't it?

This question wasn't something she'd dared ask or hope for in the past. Yet, it remained, loud and determined in the back of her head.

What could she lose by trying?

Her life? Yet, even as she answered herself, it was so far out of the realm of what she believed. She knew with a certainty that Warner wouldn't hurt her.

Couldn't.

Not because of who he was, but because of who she was.

But that was stupid because she was no one. She was just an heiress with mineral rights the Woolven Pack wanted to acquire.

She wasn't fierce like Randi, strong like Emmie, or damn near invincible like Belle.

But looking in the witch's ageless eyes, she saw a reflection of herself that she wanted so desperately to be true.

The witch saw her as capable, strong, and an asset to the Woolven Pack and her beloved Warner.

All of the other Woolven Brides wouldn't think twice about joining their mates if they thought they were needed. Even before they became icons of badassery.

Lenore was out there with him, and even though she was a trained hunter, she was still human.

Not that Mari thoughtless of humans, but Mari realized she'd completely discounted herself and she'd been doing it for years.

"I guess I'm going to Minnesota."

Westwood nodded. "Yes, you are. You should call your father before you go. I have a feeling there's something he'll want to tell you."

Mari knew her father loved her, but his love language was actions, not words. Sending her to Woolven when he knew they'd be on opposite sides of the conflict had been an act of love. He knew that no matter what, Woolven protected its own. And he knew Woolven would win, but because of old promises and ancient alliances, he'd been forced to side with Remus.

So she really did know.

But her love language was spoken, and maybe he'd speak her language, just once.

"Well, go on. Get packed. Call Daddy. And haul ass. Time and Destiny wait for no man. Or woman." Westwood shooed her toward the door. "The keys are in the Vette."

Mari let the witch guide her toward the door and out of her lab.

"How will I find him?"

"Your bones will tell you."

When the door closed behind her, she supposed if Westwood could have so much faith in her that maybe she could summon a little faith in herself.

The witch knew things, after all.

She pulled out her phone as she walked toward the garage and dialed the number.

"Alpha DeVaughn isn't taking calls," a rough voice answered. It was Rodrigo, her father's Beta.

"Put him on, Rod."

"I said he's not taking calls."

Rodrigo knew damn well who she was and it cut like a knife that he had permission to deny her the chance to speak to her father.

But the pain gave way to anger.

No, he didn't actually have that right. Who the hell was he? She was the Alpha's daughter. He was Beta. Not Alpha.

Something strange and new stirred in her chest. "Put my father on."

Her voice was not her voice. It was deeper, and it sounded like it had echoed from the depths of hell instead of her throat.

Rodrigo howled in pain.

"Maribella? Are you alright?" Her father's voice came on the line.

"Yes, Papa. I just wanted to hear your voice."

"What did you do to Rodrigo? His ears are bleeding."

"I'm not sure. Things are changing. Something's happened in the north and I'm going."

She waited for her father to tell her she shouldn't go, that she should stay safe in Aphelion, to leave the fighting to the warriors, but he didn't.

"Oh, my little princess. It's happening."

"You know?"

"I wish I could help you. I wish I could tell you, but I'm magically bound. All I can tell you is that you must listen to your wolf."

"Papa, I've never been able to hear my wolf."

"I know. You didn't need her until now. But when she's ready to come out, you trust her. You give her the reins. It'll save your life." He sounded so full of regret.

She wanted him to say it, so she had to ask for it in the only way she knew how. "Westwood said I should call you before I left. I wanted to tell you that I love you and I hope you can be proud of me."

"I've always been proud of you, princess. Always." He was silent for a moment that seemed to stretch into eternity. Until he finally said, "I love you."

Something unwound inside of her and tears pricked the back of her eyes.

"Thanks, Papa." She sniffed. "Tell Rodrigo not to deny my calls anymore."

"He and I will speak on this. I would never allow him to deny your call. Has he done this before?"

"He has."

"Why didn't you tell me?"

She swallowed hard. "You have responsibilities, I'm not unaware of that."

"There is no responsibility more sacred to me than that which comes with being your father. I hope you'll understand that in time."

Yes, she knew he loved her, but it was something altogether different to hear him speak the words.

"I know," she whispered.

"Then believe me and the voice inside of you."

"I've got to go."

"Call me when you return. If the magick binding has been broken as I believe it will be, I'll tell you everything then. If you still want to hear it."

"I will."

She hung up the phone.

That was when her skin began to burn.

And she knew that she had to get to Warner.

His presence was the only thing that would soothe the fire, the volcanic heat that bubbled in her marrow and the raging beast that now clawed at the edges of her mind

❧ 6 ❧

Not for the first time that night, a strange premonition skittered down his back and something whispered inside the shadows that Mari was coming.

Except she wouldn't do that.

She'd stay where she'd be safe.

I'm coming.

It was louder this time and it wasn't only a fey whisper, it was as if Mari stood in front of him.

He perked his head up and his ears twitched. Warner scented the air, but the only creatures in this part of the forest aside from him and Lenore were small woodland animals. There were a few hikers several miles away, but they were no threat and they weren't Mari.

"What's up?" Lenore asked. "We got company?"

"Not yet, anyway." Warner sighed. "I think Mari followed us."

"Why do you think that?"

"I just... it's a feeling."

"You know how those Woolven Mates are. You can't keep them out of the line of fire."

"Lenore, you know this is different."

"I'm sure that Blake thought it was different with Randi, too."

Lenore had him there. He for sure thought the same thing.

"Maybe I should call Tirigan and see if he can catch up to her and take her back to Aphelion."

Lenore made a disapproving face. "Why would you do that? You don't get to make her choices for her. Just like she can't make yours for you."

"It's different."

"How?"

"It just is."

"So, you know I have a wolf mate."

"This is news to me."

"Well. I keep it on the DL. But I thought all immediate Woolven knew." She suddenly became very busy with her camping gear. "Anyway," she continued, not looking at him, "if he tried to keep me from what we're doing, I'd skin him alive."

"You're Lenore Breslin." As if that was all the answer anyone needed.

"My name didn't always inspire fear and awe. I had to earn my cred. Just being Diana Breslin's daughter and Peter Breslin's sister didn't earn me anything I wanted." She looked up to meet his gaze now. "And if you'll recall, you tried to protect me, too. You tried to keep me from coming with you. What if I was your mate? What would you do to keep me from this threat in the north? Especially if you weren't you. You're here with me. You can defeat these things. What if you were... say... Luchtaine? What if you were the oldest and your power had gone unchallenged for millennia? What if you were the demon wolf who died only to be reborn with a human mate you couldn't protect?"

"I'd..." he began. Warner had been about to say that he'd wrap her in bubble wrap and chain her to the wall. But he wouldn't. He'd want to. But he wouldn't.

Then the deeper meaning behind what she'd said kicked him in the balls.

"Luchtaine is your mate?"

"Yeah. I mean... it's not really a big deal." She folded, and refolded her sleeping bag.

"Mari is soft and sweet. And utterly breakable."

"I'm sure that Luchtaine sees me the same way. Utterly breakable, even though I bested him. Don't you think the Goddess knows what she's doing by now? Do you think you'd be given a mate who couldn't match you?"

"She's not my—"

"Yeah, totally not." She rolled her eyes. "That's why you know she's coming. That's why your skin is on fire and your teeth are getting too big for your mouth. That's why you think about devouring her in every way you can."

"Lenore, don't trespass where you don't understand."

"But I do. Luchtaine has told me about all the darkness inside of him. He's told me how it wants me in... I guess you could say 'unholy' ways, if you subscribe to that way of thinking. How it wants to taste me in every way. Devour me. Sound familiar?"

Warner scrubbed a hand over his face. "Too familiar. But again, you're Lenore Breslin."

"And you don't know who Mari is. Not yet. She hasn't had to prove herself. Can you imagine who I'd be without my training? Without being tested in the Dark Woods at the age of sixteen? I'd be... I don't know. I haven't even thought about what I'd be if I wasn't a hunter. If I had the kind of resources DeVaughn has, maybe I'd be a lot like Mari."

"I have a hard time imagining that."

"Which is why you have a hard time imagining that Mari could be a strong wolf. Strength isn't born without strife, Warner. It's like your muscles. You can't build them without tearing them apart. You have to work them. You have to give them something to push against before they rebuild and grow."

"There's logic in what you say. I understand this, I really do. But my gut refuses to accept logic. It refuses to allow that this darkness will do anything but destroy."

Lenore reached out her hand and put it on his shoulder. "This darkness in you was born to destroy. It's why it was created. To eliminate the unnatural threat of Peter's get. You will be an unstoppable force of destruction, but I fully believe it will be only to those who need destroying. You won't hurt her. Trust yourself."

Warner wanted to believe the hunter's words more than anything. They were the easy answer to the rift inside of him. They soothed his fears and made it so much easier for him to surrender to the dark beast.

"I wish I could believe that."

Lenore studied him for a long moment. "Okay, Warner. If you're all darkness and terror, tell me, what does your darkness want right now?"

"Mari. Blood. Bone. Flesh. Mari."

"Mmhmm. Look at me."

Suddenly, Warner, who'd never really been afraid of anything in his life was terrified to look at Lenore. He didn't want her to see underneath his skin. Didn't want to show her what he knew she was looking for with her too keen eyes.

But he was never one to cower.

So he looked at Lenore, met her gaze and let the chips fall where they would.

Not wanting to look at the monster inside him didn't make it any less real. It didn't take any of its power. It didn't save anyone.

Except Warner's own idea of self. His pride, honestly.

"What do you see when you look at me?"

He hadn't been expecting that question. Warner didn't know what she hoped to gain from this little game, but fuck it. He'd play. He stared at the hunter. He saw that she was a woman, a beautiful woman. A strong woman. A human who walked two paths. A human who was pack.

"I don't know." He shrugged. "You're Lenore. You're my great nephew's aunt. You're my friend. You're my family."

"Are you hungry?" she grinned.

He scowled. "I'm always hungry."

"You know what I'm asking. Does your darkness want to tear me to pieces? Do you want to eat me?"

"Don't ever say that to a werewolf," he growled. "Especially one you know has eaten more than animal flesh."

"Answer the question."

"No. I don't want to hurt you that way and neither does whatever is inside of me."

"I think you're still adapting to this. Your brain is rewiring. You don't know the darkness yet. What it wants. How it wants. It's going to be okay."

"Or maybe my darkness knows better than to express any dark desires for you, Lenore."

She snorted. "An ancient so-called evil isn't going to be afraid of little ol' human me. Regardless of whose ass I've kicked."

"I don't know. You've got bone fairy backup."

She laughed. "If it'll make you feel better, I can consult the Three. They have volumes of Old Lore that might bring more clarity to the situation."

"I don't know. I'd rather eat my own tail than go to other witches after Westwood."

"You're not going. I am. But if you trust Westwood so much, why do you doubt her word on this?"

Warner didn't have an answer.

"I think you're afraid of being special. I think you've been in the shadows so long, you don't know how to be anything else. You've never wanted to be anything else. I know you always said that Sterling needed the mantle of Alpha more than you did, but I think you never wanted it. I think it was a relief for you to abdicate to him."

Warner roared. "I did what was best for the pack."

"Of course you did. It just also happened to be what was best for you, too. No shame in that, Warner. And don't roar at me, for fuck's sake. We're trying to be stealthy."

"Don't piss me off."

"Uh, no. You have control over your actions. Regardless of what I say or do."

He huffed. "You're right. About a lot. Stop shining lights on things better left in the dark."

"Can't do it, my friend."

"Damn it," he grumbled.

Lenore laughed. "But listen, if you can hang out here, I'm going to the witches. I shouldn't be gone very long. I spotted a fairy ring of mushrooms not too far back."

He briefly considered forging ahead on his own. This would be the perfect way to keep Lenore out of the line of fire.

"I know what you're thinking and if you ditch me, I will kick your ass."

He laughed. "No."

"I thought wolves couldn't lie?"

"We can. We just don't. But no could mean any number of things."

"Jesus Fucking Christ, Warner. Will you just accept the help? We've all been through some shit. You think yours is bad? All of us have shit we have to deal with. You suck it up and work through it and go forward the best you can."

"Yeah, but you didn't eat—"

"I've had enough of this. If eating my brother's head would've helped me defeat him, I'd do it in a second. If your gift came to me, I'd fucking take it. Because this is what we do. So you ate a bad guy. Big fucking deal. I did too."

"What?"

Lenore coughed, after she seemed to realize what she'd said. "Yeah, I mean... whatever. No big deal. I ate the demon wolf in a stew. I didn't know it at the time, but I did it. So whatever. Shit happens, Warner."

"I don't know this story."

"No one does. Not really. And I don't care to tell it. But here we fucking are. So can you please get on board."

It wasn't actually a request.

And Warner realized that he'd been wallowing. He'd been hanging himself up like some kind of martyr when no matter the cost, he had actually been given a gift.

It wasn't a gift he wanted.

But it was one that he, his pack, and the world as they knew it needed.

So for all of his posturing, it was time to suck it up.

Although, he reserved the right to do what he needed to do to protect the people he loved. He still thought the beast was a threat, and he'd continue to treat it that way until it was time to loose it on the world.

And hopefully, those he loved would be far, far away.

Maybe the witches would have some ideas for that.

"Alright, Lenore. I'll wait for you."

"You better. Warner Woolven's word is gold. We all know that."

"Yeah, yeah."

"Try to get some sleep. We've got some long days ahead and who knows what this is going to take out of you. And before you argue, a good night's sleep is just as important as any weapon you could take into battle. My mother said that all the time. So if you don't listen to me, listen to her. She's the Hunter of Hunters, after all."

"I'd rather listen to Lenore. Diana isn't half the hunter you are."

Lenore swallowed hard and stuffed her hands in her pockets. "I mean... okay. I'll be back soon."

She darted off into the woods, leaving Warner alone.

Without Lenore's presence to distract him, he couldn't stop thinking about Mari.

She drew ever closer and every cell in his body demanded he run to meet her. That he Change and cover every inch of ground between them until she was in his arms.

And his jaws.

The beast burned beneath his skin, demanded to be freed, but somehow, he locked it down.

There was still a chance Mari wouldn't find him. Although, the very idea sounded hollow to him. She'd find him as sure as the sun would rise in the east.

But he still had this idea that he could protect her from all of this.

Especially himself.

Fuck, but he wanted her. He wanted to be inside of her in all ways. His cock, his teeth, he wanted to taste her blood with his mate's mark and he wanted her to taste his.

His body began to twist and contort into the unnatural Change.

Agony stabbed through him as muscle and sinew stretched and snapped, but he dug his claws deep into the rich, dark earth and demanded his body obey him.

Demanded by the powers of the Goddess above, and the earth below. He called out to every power he could think of and none answered.

But he didn't expect that any would.

He knew that this was a matter of will.

And he locked it down without mercy.

As his body returned to his control, he knew at some point, he would have to let it free. And he promised himself that he would.

Only when it was time.

Only when utter destruction was the only answer.

He lay there, in the dirt with the night sounds of the forest echoing around him—something that surprised him.

Usually all the night animals went quiet in the forest when a werewolf walked in his warrior form or something unnatural stalked the area.

Yet, the frogs still cried out for their mates, the crickets sang their songs, and foxes and owls still darted about.

Perhaps it was because they knew he was no threat to them.

He clenched his hands in the dirt, loving the feel of the cool earth on his skin. Warner wanted to bury himself in the reprieve it offered and he found himself digging deep and fast until he burrowed underground like some kind of vampire.

The comparison revolted him, but not enough to make him crawl from his nest.

Here, the darkness was safe.

Here, the darkness was comfort.

And he slept.

Warner Woolven did not find the respite he needed.

In his dreams, he walked a desert landscape with red and orange ridges and deep canyons. Where clean, sweet streams should have been were rivers of blood cutting through the rocks and gorges.

Packs of wolves roamed—no, they didn't roam. They fled. They ran from him in great, stampeding numbers but he ran them down like deer. He ate them like he would any other he'd run down.

He devoured them all.

That wasn't the worst part of it though.

It was that he wasn't alone.

Mari ran not only at his side, but her appetite was as ravenous as his own. Perhaps more.

And he ran her down, too.

She let him.

When he caught her, he fucked her hard and slow and they reveled in the sensations of flesh, blood, and the utter destruction of all life that stood between them.

7

ari drove faster than what could be considered sane.

For the first time, her wolf senses had come to her when she needed them, allowing her to navigate the twists and turns of the road with superhuman ability.

It seemed to her as if she'd driven into some kind of wormhole because she never doubted for a second she would catch up to Warner and Lenore.

Even if they traveled as the crow flies and she was bound to back-roads and highways.

She let her body guide the path she took, not using her wolf sense, or even common sense. She didn't scan the highways for a sign of him, she didn't look for their motorcycles. All she did was drive. Even when darkness fell. Mari simply kept driving.

Until it was time to stop.

It hit her out of nowhere. She was on a heavily wooded, abandoned state highway. She hadn't seen another automobile for hours. Nor were there any streetlights to guide her way. It was just her, the headlights, and the endless sky above and the road that stretched out before her in a gray ribbon.

But she knew the place.

This was it.

Her skin itched and burned, and Mari would swear she was about to crawl right out of it. Yes, right out of her skin. She wanted to shed it like a dirty shirt and leave it far behind.

This wasn't something she'd ever felt before.

She left the Vette by the side of the road and Mari had to stop and breathe, to find her center before she did the same with her human form. Mari didn't know what she was walking into, or what she was becoming.

She knew that it was different.

It was darker. And Warner needed her.

She trod through the dark forest, her wolf eyes burning as she began to see things not in their whole, real form, but as only heat signatures. And she was hungry for everything. She was driven to feel every sensation, fill every emptiness, to glut on anything she could dig her claws into.

Mari sensed him before she scented him. Before she saw him. Some extra sense more than human and more than wolf recognized him.

And suddenly, all of those feelings she thought she couldn't control receded and she was grateful. She needed to be in control so that she was a help to him instead of a hindrance.

"Warner?" she whispered.

A dark shape moved through the trees. "You shouldn't be here."

"I shouldn't be anywhere else."

For every step she took forward, he took one back.

"Where are you going, Warner? I can see you."

"I was hoping you wouldn't follow."

His words, in other circumstances might've been hurtful, but she wasn't fazed. "Really? Then why aren't you running? I'm sure I can't catch you."

"But can't you? You're here now."

She caught scent of something that slithered inside of her and seeped into her bones. It made her want. It made her hunger. It made her need.

"Stop that," he said.

"Stop what?" She took another step forward.

"Stop making that damnable scent."

"I could say the same thing to you."

"There's no way this can end well," he swore.

"Then I guess we have to put that part off as long as possible then, don't you think?"

"I've been trying, woman."

She laughed. "I know. But there are forces at work here that are older and stronger than we are."

He took another step back. "That's why we have to fight it."

"I don't want to fight it."

He growled.

"Especially when you do that."

"I'm scared, Mari."

She stopped her advance. "I know. Me too."

"Everything I know to do to keep you and the pack safe is wrong."

He looked so lost. Not helpless, but... alone. So very alone. With no one to give him aid or succor.

Yet here she was and that was all she wanted to do.

"So maybe you should try something else. Something that goes against everything you thought you knew." She licked her lips. "Maybe you have to surrender."

He'd stopped backing away now. "I know how to surrender, Mari. How can you think I don't?"

"Oh, I don't know. When have you ever surrendered?"

"Let me count the ways. When I abdicated for Sterling both with the pack and with Arianna."

"That wasn't surrender, Warner. That was a sacrifice."

"What's the difference?"

"You knew the consequences. You knew exactly what lay on the other side of that."

"What if I hurt the people I'm trying to save?"

"What if you hurt the people you're trying to save by resisting? I guess it all comes down to you. You can only do what you believe is the best thing going on the information you have."

"The information I have tells me that everything I know to do is wrong."

"So let me help you, Warner. The information I have told me I needed to be with you. It told me how to find you. Because you need me."

He sighed and his shoulders sagged. "I do need you, Mari. I need you more than I know how to say. I need you to be safe."

"And I need you to be safe. So stalemate, eh? Or you can just stop fighting it and let me be with you. So I can keep you safe and you can keep me safe."

"I think you might be the Devil."

"We don't believe in that."

"You said I should start something new. This. Here's proof of the Devil," Warner said dejectedly as he took a step toward her.

"How's that?"

"I can't stay away from you."

Mari wanted to say that the surrender she was talking about wasn't surrendering to her, but she wanted that, too. No point in lying to herself, or to him.

"I think you could if you wanted to, but you don't want to." At least, that was what Mari hoped.

"You're right. I don't want to. And that scares the shit out of me. It should scare you."

"I'm not afraid. Maybe I should be, but I can't ever seem to do anything I'm actually supposed to do. Even my marriage of convenience is highly inconvenient."

His eyes began to change like they had in the cemetery, going from amber to a deep, blood red. Her heart began to beat faster.

"Is that fear?" His question was more like a plea.

"No." She bit her lip for a moment, but then she couldn't seem to catch her breath. Her mouth fell open and she breathed deep.

"I want you to run, Mari."

"To save myself?"

"No. Because I want to catch you."

She was poised to burst into a sprint, but something told her that this wasn't the right time. If he ran her down and ravaged her, even if it was what she wanted, he'd never forgive himself.

So she held out her arms. "Come to me, then. Come to me now."

To her absolute surprise, he did. Warner closed the distance between them and they sank together to their knees. He buried his face in her neck and she could feel the tension still flowing through his body. He was a live wire and she knew he needed to be able to let go. At least for a moment.

"I'm here. You're not alone."

He turned his face farther into the crook of her neck and she stroked her hands through his hair and down his back, soothing him.

She wanted to touch him and be touched, but right now, this was all for him. This was what she could do.

"Mari," he whispered. "Maribella."

Hearing her full name on his tongue sent delightful shivers coursing through her. She tugged him closer, offering him anything he could think to want from her.

"It's okay, Warner. It's all okay."

The stubble on his chin had gotten longer, sharper. He was getting closer to Changing. Mari was too enraptured to care. She was dizzy with lust, lost in a haze of desire just from his nearness and his touch was almost more than she could bear.

The animal inside of her wanted to feel it too.

It tore at the edges of her mind, ripped at the bonds that held it back. Mari didn't want to share this with her wolf. Not a second of it.

Her wolf had never come to her when she needed it, so why should it get to bask in the spoils of flesh? It had never had to endure the taunts, the failure, the absolute and utter loneliness of being Maribella DeVaughn. It had stayed hidden, had locked itself away.

It wasn't fair.

And Mari wasn't going to let it away this one thing she wanted for herself.

Except as Warner pulled her tighter, as the low grumbling growl she knew to be a kind of purr seemed to be able to touch her physically, as the languid heat of desire became desperate, she began to wonder if she had a choice.

Her skin was too tight, her teeth too large, and her hunger grew. Even as he stripped her bare, and the friction between their bodies drove them both higher, she wondered if it could be enough to quench the fire that raged within her.

The more he touched her, the more her human thought receded. If anyone were to come upon them now, Mari would be hard-pressed (hard, oh so hard) not to tear them to pieces for interrupting their interlude.

And to whatever it was in Mari's skin right now, that seemed a perfectly rational, reasonable response.

"I want you naked," she growled.

"I am naked," he said, as he pulled her to sit astride him.

"No," she demanded, using that same voice of power she'd used on Rodrigo. "I want you *naked*. Take off your skin, Warner. Shed it all."

He moaned into her ear, his cock swelling even larger against her wet, hot cleft.

"I'm a monster," he whispered.

"I need a monster." She looked into his red eyes and rolled her hips. "Goddessdamn, but I need a monster."

He roared as the beast inside rose to meet her demands. And as he Changed, so did she.

But their Changes were not agonizing and alien or strange, they were seamless. They were all power and flame.

His teeth sank into her shoulder and a searing pain that quickly became bliss shot through her. She didn't hesitate to crunch the meat of his shoulder between her jaws and they moved together in an ancient dance. Connected to the earth below by their paws kneading the forest floor, the sky above by the air moving through their lungs, fire was the spark between them, and water was mingling of their blood, but it wasn't until their spirits touched when the heady orgasm took them both that some kind of bond had been sealed, stitched into the very fabric of time itself.

Yet, as the moment faded, Mari became aware of something else.

It wasn't just her contrary beast.

It was darkness.

A darkness unlike any other.

No, that was wrong. It was similar to Warner's darkness, this other thing that lurked inside of her.

As she lay on the bed of leaves, she put her hand to her shoulder where Warner had bitten her and when she drew her hand back, it was covered in blood.

Warner, still in his Changed form, padded closer to her. His nostrils flared, and he nosed the air.

The blood.

But she wasn't evil. Was she?

His eyes narrowed and he focused on her with a singular intensity. She'd never been able to imagine what prey felt like, until this very moment.

Mari couldn't help but wonder if that's why her wolf had been locked down. Because it was something different. Something evil.

She moved slowly, deliberately. Mari reached for her clothes but found herself crushed to the ground by the giant snarling beast.

He growled right in her face and his spittle dripped on her chin.

"Damn it, Warner. That's nasty."

The beast, looking momentarily confused, as he wiggled his snout and licked his chops that she laughed.

He mashed his face against hers, growling again, and she laughed harder.

She supposed the sensible thing to do would be to be afraid. This beast that was atop of her, he didn't seem to be Warner at all.

While that was okay when she was a beast, she was just little Mari now.

But it was funny.

"Get off. I have to get dressed."

He growled again.

Then, pictures began to dance through her mind's eye on a reel. She realized he was growling at her clothes. The wolf was mad at her clothing for daring to cover her body.

His long, purple tongue dragged over her wound where he'd bitten her. He lapped at her there and Mari wasn't sure it was the best idea, but it did feel so good. She felt every swipe of his tongue not just on her shoulder, but right between her thighs.

In for a penny, she figured and she lay back and spread her thighs for him.

He growled while he tasted her, while he lapped at her and it was decadent to keep her human form while he was Changed.

She felt like a girl in a fairytale and while she knew fairytales weren't real, it couldn't hurt to let herself have it just this one time.

Mari had promised Warner she'd help him. Easing his body and his beast was help, right?

She shuddered with pleasure as Warner continued to lap at her. She kept waiting for her beast to try to resurface, but it was quiet. Mari might've thought strangely quiet, but she hadn't heard from the bitch on the regular since... ever.

And yeah, she thought. It was a bitch.

Literally.

She giggled, and the beast stopped its ministrations, and she rose up on her elbows to look at him.

He growled at her again, and used one, massive paw to press her to the ground while he finished his meal.

Her last coherent thoughts were that this Dark Champion stuff didn't seem to be so bad after all.

While they wouldn't agree on meals, it wasn't like he was Hannibal Lecter.

She giggled again. Or maybe it was.

He growled.

"Don't growl with your mouth full."

8

The dawn came quickly and with it, the harsh truth of what he'd done.

Mari bore a gigantic, puckered, angry scar on her shoulder. It spread from the ball of her shoulder all the way up into tender lines of her throat.

It was a mating mark.

He bore its smaller twin on his own shoulder.

He thought it was supposed to feel different. More.

Although, he wondered if maybe they'd broken each other. Maybe they'd felt all the sensations that there were to feel last night. Maybe their wolves felt everything for them.

Except the pain.

His whole body hurt. Even deep inside his bones.

Everything creaked and ached.

Normally, after a night sleeping wild, he'd run down breakfast. In his current state, Warner wasn't running down shit.

And he wasn't even actually hungry.

Which concerned him.

Mari stretched and reached for him. He lay back down and held her close.

This thing that had happened between them, he didn't know if it was good or bad. Probably bad, given the state of things, but he couldn't bring himself to regret it. Even though he knew he probably should.

She'd come to him.

She'd offered herself to him.

She'd wanted it as much as he had.

He remembered Lenore's words about how he had to let her choose for herself. It didn't matter if Warner thought he knew better. Or if he actually did know better. He couldn't take away her agency.

He remembered last night when she'd demanded he give her the beast.

His cock stirred to life as he thought of it.

"Shut up and lie down," he whispered. "Now is not the time."

"Hmm?" she murmured.

He stroked her face and kissed the top of her head. "Shh. Go back to sleep. Everything is fine."

But it wasn't fine, was it?

Except when he looked down at her, sleeping so peacefully, looking like a delicate little frost fairy curled up on a pile of holly, he wanted to make it fine.

That's really what Warner was wired for.

Not just War.

He was a fixer.

And he couldn't fix this.

His ears perked as he picked up the sounds of something—no someone, in the forest. He lifted his nose to the air and realized it was Lenore.

She was back.

Hopefully, she had the answers they were looking for.

He was grateful when he found he hadn't shredded all of Mari's clothes. Her shirt had a rather artful slash across the back from his claws.

Although the jeans, he guessed, when he saw the shredded denim, those were going to be a problem.

"Mari, love. We have company."

"No."

"Okay. Be naked if you like. I'm sure Lenore won't care." He pushed an ice blond lock of hair away from her forehead. "I know I don't mind."

Bleary-eyed, Mari reached for her shirt and when she saw the slash, she arched a brow, but shrugged it on.

The jeans? She just looked at them, looked at him, and looked back at them with a sigh.

Seeing her sitting there in that shirt that he'd torn through like a candy wrapper to get at the tasty treat inside, well... it had him all kinds of hard again.

He'd hadn't wanted a woman like this in... he couldn't remember ever feeling like this. Ever being such a slave to his cock.

She sighed again.

"It's really too bad we don't have more time." She raised her eyes to meet his.

She wanted him again, too.

He was starting to wonder if that's all it would take to keep his darkness in check. If he could just lose himself in a haze of pleasure with Mari. If that was the key. If it was, he'd never complain about this gift again.

Mari crept over to him and crawled into his lap.

"Don't start something we can't finish," he warned her.

She laughed. "We can always finish it. It's just a matter of when and where," she teased.

But that was when she did something even more devastating than not fearing what he had become.

She reached up and cupped his cheek while looking into his eyes.

He'd have been tempted to say that was just soft, sweet, Mari. There was something new in her eyes. A kind of knowing that wasn't softness or sweetness. She saw him.

She really saw him.

And she still wanted to touch his face like that. Still wanted to be his mate.

He didn't understand it.

Warner could hear Westwood in the back of his head telling him not to look a gift horse in the mouth, but if the Trojans had bothered to look inside their gift horse...

Was that what Mari was? A Trojan horse that once he let her inside, she'd break down all the walls?

She splayed her hand on his chest and leaned her head on his shoulder.

He knew she wasn't made of spun glass, but she still seemed so delicate here in his arms. He hadn't broken her last night, he reminded himself. And not for lack of trying. They'd tried to break each other.

He couldn't remember too many details from the night before. He remembered the pleasure. Goddess, the pleasure.

He remembered when he Changed with her, there hadn't been as much pain. It had been more natural. More streamlined.

Or maybe his body was becoming accustomed to this new form?

Except, the more he thought about it, the more it seemed like there was something different about her Change, too.

She hadn't become the pretty white wolf he knew her to be. It had been her warrior form, but...

"You usually remember what you do as a wolf, don't you, Warner? What about in the beginning," she went on. "Your early Changes. Did you always remember?"

"I suppose since we're mated, it's not unusual for you to read my mind. I was just trying to remember last night."

Lenore emerged from the trees into their camp.

"That's just rude, Warner. You spend the night with a lady, you damn well better remember," Lenore teased. "Kick his ass, Mari."

"I can't really remember much of it myself."

"Oh. Should I fuck off for a few hours?" Lenore grinned. "I could go catch some big boy bass for breakfast. Learned how to do it with my hands when I was a kid. Keep the reflexes fast."

Part of Warner, mainly his cock, thought that was the best idea he'd ever heard, but he knew they needed to get down to business.

Not that business.

Mari laughed. "No, it's all good. Although, if you had an extra pair of jeans I could..."

"I don't do jeans. I do have a pair of leathers, though." She grabbed her pack from the ground and tugged out a pair of leather tactical pants.

Oh Goddess. No. No way could he handle Mari's ass in those pants. Nope. Nope. Nope.

And worse, wrapped in leather, she'd smell like food.

Or at least, she would have. Before.

"Thanks." She disengaged from his lap and took them gratefully.

"I'll make some coffee if you two want to take a quick dip in the river. You should both be present for what I have to say."

That didn't bode well. Not at all.

About an hour later, they convened around a small, contained fire. Lenore had a magically enchanted, foldable fire pit she carried in her pack. Westwood made is especially for her. It was guaranteed to be forest-safe. Never a stray spark would escape it, and with a single word, it would extinguish itself and fold up into a small square. Leaving no trace. Warner thought it was pretty brilliant and he thought it spoke to the kind of person he knew Lenore to be. She cared about what she left behind, how she impacted the world around her.

It occurred to him then that if Lenore believed in him, if Westwood believed in him, if Mari believed in him, then maybe he could believe in himself, too. Maybe it was time to learn a new way.

He guessed maybe you could teach an old dog new tricks.

Although, that shit wasn't easy. They needed lots of help.

And treats.

All the treats. He was thinking of Mari's breasts. The way her nipples puckered in the cool night air, the texture of them on his tongue...

He had no problem remembering that.

Lenore poured steaming cups of hot, black coffee.

Mari sipped hers and wrapped her hands around the mug, and Lenore did the same.

"Okay. So." Lenore exhaled heavily. "The Three did know what was happening. And they promised not to tell Westwood we asked them either."

"I didn't ask them not to." Warner sipped his coffee.

"We didn't have to. Apparently, the Three have concerns about how much power Westwood has at her disposal now. The Three were queens in their own right and since Westwood married the goblin kind... but that's neither here nor there."

"What did they say?" Mari asked.

"There's a prophecy," Lenore began.

"Well, that would've been nice to know before all this shit with your brother blew up," Warner grumbled.

"Right? There's a prophecy about me, too. They wanted me to wash their glass eyes with my tongue before they'd tell me that one. I said fuck it."

"Fuck it, you did it, or fuck it, it's not worth it?" Mari questioned.

"It's not worth it. Not a chance. I think they just wanted to see if I'd do it. Which... no. Anyway, back to the prophecy at hand." Lenore took another drink. "A darkness will rise in the north blah blah... a Dark Champion... blah, blah." She shrugged. "We know all that. Oh, by the way. The Dark Champion can only be born into the world by the best of us, the witches said. Only the best of us can channel that kind of power without being corrupted by it."

Warner snorted. "It's like..." he struggled for the words he wanted. "Distilled corruption. Like evil nitroglycerin."

"Damn it, will you just take the compliment?" Lenore grumbled.

"I didn't know I was avoiding it."

"You always do," Mari said. "It doesn't feel out of the ordinary, because it isn't."

"Listen, we don't need a Warner's Awesome Party. We need to—"

"Why not? I'd love a Mari's Awesome Party."

"Hey, me too. I'd love a Lenore Rocks Party. We should do that."

"Like herding cats. Goddess Above." Warner sighed.

"Oh. Right. Sorry. Anyway." Except Lenore didn't say anything else. She looked back and forth between Warner and Mari.

"Holy Goddess, woman. Spit it out. It's not like not telling us is going to change it."

"Stop taking her name in vain, Warner. She's going to smite you," Mari teased.

"Look, either I'm her favorite or I'm not. There should be some perks to this Dark Champion garbage."

"Fair enough. Before I go on, I have to ask something personal. Mari, is that a true mating mark on your neck?" Lenore looked worried.

"Yes. Why?" She bit her lip.

Whatever Lenore was going to say, Warner knew that it was going to hurt his Mari. Goddessdamn it. Why? Being with him had only brought her pain. She deserved so much better.

"The Three say that whence the Dark Champion rises, so too does his mate."

Mari closed her eyes for a long moment. "What does that mean? Aside from the fact that we all know it's not me."

Warner hated the surety in her voice, but he couldn't argue. Being with him had made her darker, but she wasn't—

"She will be a Wendigo." Lenore took a breath. "She will rise from the dead to join her mate in the fight. Wendigo are monsters. They're the source of a lot of human lore about werewolves. They're... insatiable."

"And they feed on their own." Like me, Warner thought.

A small voice inside of him said he wouldn't have to be alone. To rejoice. That he wouldn't have to hold back with this mate. That she would be his equal in every way. He couldn't hurt a Wendigo.

Not like he could hurt Mari.

"Oh. I see," Mari said aloud.

He was afraid that she did see. If he could've saved her this pain, he would've. And damned if he hadn't tried. He'd tried to leave her, he'd tried to stay away. He'd tried not to touch her, but she'd demanded he surrender and so he had.

"It's going to be Arianna, isn't it?" Mari continued flatly. "She was meant to have been Warner's in life, now in death, she will be. She'd come back to fight for her pack and her family."

Lenore reached out and squeezed her hand. "We don't know who it is. The Three tried to scry to see, but her face was shrouded from them."

Warner opened his mouth to speak, but Mari turned fiery eyes on him. "If you even think about telling me to go back to Aphelion, I swear by all that's holy you won't make it to your next mate. She'll have to raise you from the dead, too."

That had been exactly what Warner was going to suggest, but he'd since thought better of it.

"Uh, no. Nope. I was just going to ask if you wanted more coffee."

"No. I don't. I'm ready to head north and find these fuckers."

"A woman after my own heart," Lenore said.

"It's probably the leather pants. They make me feel like a badass."

"You are a total badass. You're brave and smart and strong," Lenore said.

Warner looked at Mari and saw her in a new light. He knew that she was all of those things, but somehow, it hadn't clicked in his head.

Of course she was brave and smart and strong. Mari was amazing.

Which was part of why he didn't want her anywhere near where they were going.

Warner's ears pricked. Gooseflesh raised across his body and all the hairs he possessed stood on end. He realized he probably looked like an agitated cockatoo, but it hit him hard and fast.

Their time was running out.

Something had happened.

"What is it, Lassie?" Lenore teased.

"Eat a dick, Lenore." He snorted. "But seriously, we need to go. And we need to go fast."

"What's happened?" Mari asked.

"I don't know, only that something has. We need to run." He turned to look at Lenore. "I'll carry you. I don't want to hear any complaints."

"You won't get any."

"I might after you see what I look like when I Change." Christ, but he hoped he could keep it together long enough to carry the hunter as far as they needed to go. He prayed the beast would keep his shit in check and realize how much they needed the hunter.

He Changed.

To Lenore's credit, after she whispered the magic words that cleaned up the camp and made their supplies small enough to pocket and she simply climbed onto his back and held on.

It wasn't long before they were running so fast it was like flying and Mari kept pace beside him.

9

Utter devastation.

That was what they found when Warner finally stopped running.

Mari didn't know how far they'd run, but she knew it had to be quite some distance. Mari, for her part, was rather amazed she was able to keep up.

It was probably the mating bond.

The one she'd wanted, gotten, and was going to lose to some dead girl who decided to come back and stake her claim.

It broke her heart.

Although, her heart, even as it was breaking, it knew, too, that Warner needed a mate who was his equal. Not someone like her.

Because for all of her wishing, hoping, and trying, she would never be his match. Even though she wanted to be.

A woman who was a match for Warner wouldn't be thinking about her own loss right now.

She'd be thinking about that poor, small town that had been reduced to... meat and gore.

That's all that was left.

Mari smelled it before she saw it, but that was all she needed to know not a single living thing was left in the town.

This was why Warner was needed.

A Dark Champion who had the power to save these people.

And why she'd step aside when it was time.

She swallowed hard.

"We're too late, aren't we?" Lenore said as she slid to the ground and Warner, still in his new warrior form stretched and paused just at the edge of the forest that surrounded the town.

He charged forward and Mari followed, with Lenore behind her.

Everywhere they looked, there were bits of meat left that used to be werewolf. These were all someone's mother, father, sister, brother.

These bits had all been *someone*.

Bile rose in her throat.

And that's when it hit her.

She'd seen all of this before.

Memories she'd stuffed down as a child, hidden behind lock and key in the deepest recesses of her mind were of this moment. It was as if she'd walked in a place out of time and had watched all of this unfold.

This was why she'd been afraid to transform.

This was why she'd locked her beast away and hadn't been able to hear her. She didn't want to. This was what lay on the other side of this.

The bile she'd been holding back surged up and she turned away as she vomited.

A comforting hand was on her back. It was Lenore. "Me too, dude. This is... I can't even."

"What if I did this?" Mari choked out after she wiped her mouth with the back of her hand.

"What? Why would you think that? It was Peter's pack. Obviously."

"I... know this scene. The name of the town is Morning Lake."

"How do you know this?"

Mari looked up and watched Warner running through the various shops, and buildings, searching for signs of life.

She knew he wouldn't find any.

"I dreamed about it when I was a child."

"All of it?"

"Down to the muck under your foot."

Lenore looked down. "Goddamnit. I hate it when I get it on my boots."

"Yeah." Mari sniffed. "I'd... I'd forgotten. This scene used to make me wake up screaming. This was why I never wanted to Change. I knew I'd do this."

"You didn't do this. Stop that."

"How do you know? You weren't here last night. Maybe Warner and I did this together."

Lenore grabbed her by the shoulders. "Don't even think that. But never say it. Never. Warner has enough doubt without yours too."

"The truth is right here, Lenore. Why else would I have dreamed it? It was surprisingly easy for me to run this far. I've never done that before. And there's a darkness in me that's changing me. Like Warner."

"Shut up with that too. He's going to blame himself. I get it, this sucks. But he needs your support now more than ever. Have you ever stopped to think that maybe the Wendigo is you?"

"Of course not. I'm not dead."

"That could change at any minute, couldn't it?"

"No, it's not me. It's the love of his life. Arianna."

"And you're a witch now? A prophetess?"

"Maybe. I did dream of this," Mari said.

"Maybe you dreamed of it so you could help Warner. There are all sorts of reasons the powers that be might've sent you that dream. It doesn't always have to be the worst thing."

"Doesn't it, though?" Mari realized how hopeless and pitiful she sounded. What did it matter if it was always the worst thing? There were very few things that were within her power. So it was up to her to do what she could with what she could. Instead of complaining like a spoiled child. "You're right, Lenore. I'm sorry."

"Hey, I know it all looks like shit, now. And I don't mean to blow sunshine up your asshole, but you gotta get that Vitamin C somehow, amiright?"

Mari snorted. "You're right."

"I carried around a lot of guilt for a long time for something that wasn't mine to carry. But I picked that bitch up and carried it anyway because I thought it was mine. It wasn't. Neither is what happened here. That's not your fault. But if you can, think back to your dream. Can you remember anything else? Any small detail you might've seen then that we can't see now?"

Mari took a deep, shaky breath.

"So, normally in these situations, I'd say it's just a dream. It's not real. It can't hurt you. Only it is real, but it's already happened. It can't hurt you. But it might hurt someone else if we don't catch this pack."

She began to open herself to the dream. To allow it out of the box where she'd locked it and to let it play before her mind's eye. Mari watched in horror as the carnage unfolded.

"In the dream, Lenore, it's me."

"Step back, then. It's not you. You know it's not. Breathe."

Mari did as Lenore instructed, but she couldn't change the perspective. "I'm sorry, I can't..."

"It's okay. It might take some time."

"That we don't have."

"Tonight, when you sleep, if you can sleep, try to ask it to show you what you need to know."

"I'll try," Mari agreed.

Warner came back to meet them, as a man.

"We're too late. In the time it took us to run, they obliterated this town," he said.

Mari was still picking at the tangled threads of the dream when it hit her. While she'd been allowing that awful thing to play, she remembered in the dream she wanted—no, needed—to head north.

And there were survivors from the town.

A whole... herd. Yes, they'd been taken as livestock.

Mari wanted to vomit again.

"Mari?" Warner asked. "You're so pale."

"I know where they're going. I mean... not precisely. Like, I don't have coordinates. But they're still moving north."

"I saw some tracks in the mud on the far side of town that seemed to be headed north as well. Not enough for a pack, but..."

"I dreamed about this, Warner. This scene right here is why I couldn't transform as a child. In my dream, I'm one of them."

"I will never let that fucking happen," he swore.

"Men," Lenore snorted. "That's not the point. The point is, in her dream, she has to go north."

"Just saying," he grumbled.

Mari wanted to say that she didn't need him to protect her, but maybe she did. Or maybe she just wanted him to. She wouldn't be able to enjoy the perks of being mated to him much longer.

Maybe she was selfish and spoiled, but she was going to make love to him again as soon as she got him alone. She was going to give him every bit of pleasure she knew how and she was going to take some for herself too.

"There are some survivors. Warner, they took them for livestock."

"We have to save them, if we can. But we can't leave the town like this. We need to cleanse it with fire. We don't know what their venom will do the animal life around here. That's all we fucking need is infected squirrels or something."

Lenore half-laughed. "That would be just our fucking luck, wouldn't it? Listen, I can get a crew of witches in here and stand guard until they get here. We need a controlled burn to protect the wildlife and the forest. Then I'll catch up with you, if you text me."

"It looks like we're about to move out of Woolven Territory. I should probably call Blake so he can make sure no one's tail gets in a knot."

"These new bags that transform with you are pretty great, huh? I don't know what we'd do without Westwood," Lenore said.

"I'd be naked in the woods without a phone, I guess. Which doesn't always sound terrible." Warner shrugged.

Lenore hugged Mari. "We've got this. All of us. Right?"

"Yeah. Thanks, Lenore. You know, it's crazy. I never thought I'd get to meet you, let alone be your friend."

"You're one of the cool kids." Lenore grinned. "I'm lucky to know you."

"For fuck's sake," Warner growled. "Come here." He hugged Lenore too. "Take care of you until we see each other again. Don't ever forget you're pack."

"No, you." She grinned and slapped his back. "And I mean that."

"I know."

"Good."

Warner took Mari's hand and was going to lead her around the edge of the woods, but she stepped forward, walking toward the town square.

"It can't hurt anything now," she said. "They're already dead and I've seen it at least a thousand times."

"Mari," was all Warner could say.

"What? I'm strong. I can do this. If I can't walk through the carnage, however will I fight those who are willing to commit it?"

"You shouldn't have to."

"If not us, then who?"

She walked, fighting nausea the whole way.

When they were on the other side of the woods, he pulled a sat phone out of his bag to call Blake.

"We're not too far from the border, so I thought I'd put in the call now. We're tracking these things into the Northern Territories. Beyond Woolven Borders."

Having supernatural hearing, she could hear the Woolven Alpha's responses.

"Shit. I was hoping to keep it contained."

"You and me both, Nephew. Damage is bad. Morning Lake is gone."

"Gone? As in..."

"Obliterated. We suspect they took some of the residents with them."

"Are they Turned or for food?" Blake's tone was flat, but Mari knew the Woolven Alpha felt all of this on a visceral level.

"Food."

"I'll put in a call. I'm sure I don't have to tell you to wait for my word."

"I'll do my best."

"Explain," Blake commanded.

"This Dark Champion doesn't answer to anyone. Not to you, not to me. I can't promise I won't, but I'll do my damndest."

"That's all I can ask for."

Warner ended the call.

Blake wasn't like any other Alpha she'd ever met. He didn't preen, didn't take every question or every snag as an insult to alphahood. She admired him.

"So we wait," she said.

"That's all we can do."

Suddenly, Warner growled and cracked his neck as his features began to shift like some kind of alien. It was an uncontrolled Change.

"Damn it."

"I guess the Dark Champion didn't like being told he can't do anything," Mari said, putting a hand on his. "It's okay. Stop thinking about it. We are doing something. We're ensuring that we don't start another war."

At this, Warner seemed to quiet, although when he opened his eyes, they were still red.

And Mari still found that incredibly hot.

"Do you like him? The Dark Champion, I mean?" Warner asked, after sniffing the air.

"Obviously. I can't help it."

"He likes you too. Obviously."

"Good. Since he's my mate," she said, but the teasing smile on her lips faded. "At least for now," she managed a faux bright tone.

She hated how she sounded. So needy. So pathetic.

"Not just for now, Mari."

"Oh, Warner. You know that's not true. Lenore told us—"

"What do those old bags know, anyway? Not a damn thing." He held up his hand before she could object. "No, seriously. They wanted Lenore to give their glass eye a tongue bath? What the fuck? No."

Mari couldn't help but laugh a little. "That doesn't mean they don't know what's going to happen."

"After all that you've done for the pack. For me. Do you really think I'd betray you like that?"

"Warner, being with your True Mate isn't a betrayal. Did you think Arianna betrayed you when she chose Sterling?"

"No, of course not. But she wasn't in the same set of circumstances that we are. You've walked through fire for me. I won't reward that with abandonment."

A lump formed in the back of her throat.

"I don't actually want your duty in this case. I know that doesn't make sense to you, but if you're with me, I want you to want me for me. Not because you owe me something."

"I do want you."

"That will change when the Wendigocomes. Please don't make promises you can't keep. Not only would it break my heart, but you'd never forgive yourself. You just told Blake you didn't know if you could obey him. That the Dark Champion doesn't answer to him."

"The Dark Champion wants you."

"Maybe now he does."

"I'm not leaving you, Mari. Unless that's what you want."

"How funny that only days ago we were having a similar discussion, but you were trying to get rid of me."

"I wasn't trying to get rid of you. I was trying to protect you. Like always."

"Yes, just like always," Mari agreed.

❧ 10 ❧

Warner didn't like the tone in Mari's voice. It was so resigned.

Why couldn't she understand that protecting her was his honor? His joy? His privilege?

He'd been about to tell her so when the sat phone rang.

"Turn around," Blake said. "They want to handle it themselves."

"Did you explain to them that they can't handle it themselves?" Warner began.

The Dark Champion stirred, stretched inside him as it became aware that it was being told not to pursue its prey.

"I did what I could, Warner. The answer is no. Come home."

Warner didn't say anything for a long while.

"Do you need me to command you?"

"I might, Blake."

"Warner Woolven, I command you to return home." His voice echoed with all of the authority of an Alpha. It resonated deep into his bones.

It should've been impossible to ignore.

It should've caused him agony to consider it.

But it didn't.

"Warner?" Blake asked. "It didn't take, did it?"

"No, I'm afraid it didn't."

"I've been grieving the loss of you since your death, Uncle. Even when you came back, I felt you'd been lost to us."

Warner's heart broke. He didn't know what to say.

Blake said it for him. "Come home anyway. Aphelion will always be your home. You will always be family. You will always be part of my pack. *No matter what.*"

Warner understood the words that Blake didn't say. No matter what he did, no matter what he became, Blake wouldn't turn him away. "I'll try."

"Good. This pup needs you. Just like the rest of Woolven. Uncle, I still need you."

A litany of words were born and died on his tongue. He didn't know which of them to say. "Nice of you to say, boy. But you don't. You're a fine Alpha. The best any pack could hope for."

"Not just for leading the pack. You're the only father I remember. I want my child to know you. Your wisdom, your stories, your ferocity. Your honor."

Warner couldn't breathe for a moment. "Even if I don't come back, all of that lives in you. Your pup will know it well. But I swear to you, I want to come home. I want to be there."

That seemed to be what Blake was looking for.

"Good. Check in when you can."

"Just tell him you love him, jackass," Randi called.

Warner chuckled. "He did. And so did I," he said back, before he hung up.

Goddess, he did want that. To go home. To see the pup. To run with Noah. But they weren't safe while this threat loomed. The one in the north or the one inside him.

He turned to Mari and he didn't know what to say to her.

Warner wasn't good with talking about his feelings. It wasn't that he was embarrassed of having them, he simply wasn't used to them being a consideration. He wasn't used to expressing them.

He wanted to tell Mari everything, but luckily, it seemed she knew.

As she would, being his mate.

No, he wasn't going to leave her. Not for anything.

She welcomed him into her arms, and again it seemed as if she were the one with all the strength. If he was being honest, and he always chose to be, even with himself, he didn't know what he'd have done without her.

"I'm glad you tracked me down. I'm glad you didn't let me tell you who to be."

"That's good, because it's not changing any time soon." She rubbed her cheek against his.

"I need you, Mari. Is it okay?"

He didn't know if he was asking if it was okay to need her strength, okay to touch her, okay to find solace in her body yet again when he had nothing to offer her.

Nothing but pleasure.

"Always," she said. "I need you too, Warner."

He was used to hearing that he was needed. That his pack needed him. The boys needed him. It was nice to be needed. It was nice to know that what he did made a difference.

Except hearing it from Mari's lips satisfied him in an altogether different way. It also made him need her even more.

Since he'd become this thing, he'd transformed into a raw nerve. He felt everything ten times as intensely from his hunger to his emotions, to his physical desire.

It was all so much.

Too much.

But still he wanted more.

Warner didn't understand how that was possible.

The Dark Champion surged, almost as if using its own existence to answer his question, but he didn't want that answer.

He knew the time was fast approaching that he'd lose himself inside the beast. So for now, for tonight, he couldn't obey his Alpha, but he could have this last time with Mari as himself.

No, the darkness said. *I am already you.*

He wanted it to be silent and he growled, but Mari liked it when he growled. Her scent grew more powerful, and the way she writhed against him more intense.

"I want this as a man, Mari. You'll get the beast soon enough if that's what you want."

"I want it any way you want to give it to me, Warner."

Another growl was torn from him.

"Goddess, but you're delicious," he said. "I want to devour you."

She sank to the ground and leaned back, spreading her thighs. "If you promise to be very careful, I'll let you take these leathers off with your teeth."

"I can do that."

"Good. Because I didn't know how else I was going to get them off."

"They suit you."

"I like them. You seem to."

He didn't answer with words, instead, he did just as she'd asked and peeled them down her body using his very human teeth.

But before he dipped his head between her legs, she tugged him up so that they were face to face.

"We're mated. Here in this moment. Whatever happens, right now you belong to me. And I belong to you. I love you, Warner."

He didn't know what to say. He cared for Mari, he wanted her, he needed her.

"It's okay. I don't need you to say it back. I didn't say it hoping to get something from you. I said it because my heart feels like it's going to burst. So kiss me. Kiss me like you'll never get to again."

Her words had a ring of truth to them. They echoed with the finality of prophecy and he wanted to argue, but since their time was so short, he wouldn't waste it arguing.

He'd do as she asked.

He kissed her.

It was a different kind of kiss, this one. It was full of summer sunshine and Elysian fields, but it was tainted with a lemon tang of regret, too.

She pushed her fingers through his hair and turned her face to the side so he could nose at her neck.

It seemed she'd had enough of lemons.

And regret.

As had he.

He moved down between her thighs and drank her in. Warner decided that this might be his favorite activity. She arched beneath him, inviting him to take more, to give more. Always more.

Which was what he wanted, what he needed.

But he was unhurried.

There wasn't nearly enough time to say everything that needed to be said, to do all the things that still needed to be done, but this— there was time for this. For her pleasure.

It took her longer to come with his human tongue and for a moment, he knew a stabbing, blinding irrational jealousy.

Which was stupid.

He was the thing with the long, powerful tongue. It was still him. And then again, it wasn't.

Warner growled against her, and that's what sent her over the edge.

His growl had her sweetness flowing over his tongue and her thighs squeezing his head.

Signs of a job well done.

He couldn't help but ask, "So you like the Dark Champion better, huh? When it comes to this?"

She gasped a laugh. "He is good at what he does. And I love it, but a lot of it is because I don't think I'm supposed to. I can't do this with him after, either."

Mari pulled him up to kiss her.

Warner had had lovers, but his numbers were nothing like his rake-hell nephews. He preferred it to matter. He preferred more than fingers and mouths in the dark which would be gone once the morning came.

He liked discovering her, the things that turned her on, the things that pushed her over the edge. The things she thought were intimate. Like this.

Warner kissed her and she was languid in his arms, soft and pliant.

Then she surprised him.

"Now, it's my turn."

She pushed him on his back and the position was so foreign to him.

Warner was used to serving, not being served.

When Mari flashed her playful smile, something uncoiled in his chest. A tight knot he hadn't known was there and it unfurled like the petals of a rose, opening so wide.

And like a rose, it was all tenderness and gentle things.

Even when her mouth closed around his cock.

Oh by the Goddess, it had never been so good.

The dark thing inside of him was content to be quiet, to let him have this, at least for now. Warner was sure it was some kind of trick to lull him into complacency. To let his guard down to make it easier for the darkness to take the reins.

But he couldn't think about that now.

All he could think about, all that mattered, were these moments with Mari.

Something told him that he'd never see her like this again.

Never touch her.

The worst part was, he'd never know what their life together could've been like. No, that was a lie. He knew what their life together could've been like.

It could've been... happy.

She took him deeper now, and her propped himself up on his elbows so he could watch her, look into her eyes.

He could see the same desperation there.

It awakened the previously slumbering beast. Even as his body began to change, he fought it.

"It's okay," she whispered. "I'll take you any way I can get you."

"No, I don't—" As he fought, agony blasted him in tidal wave after tidal wave. It hurt more when he fought it.

"Calm, Warner. He's a weapon. He responds to fear, stress, and aggression. That is, if you don't want to Change."

Warner tried to breathe. Tried to calm the desperation he felt. The sadness.

Like Mari suggested, the beast settled.

Could it be that simple?

He doubted it, but he would take it for now.

"Surrender to me," she whispered. "Don't just lie back and let me do what I want, surrender your body to the sensation. If Change, you Change. I don't care. He won't hurt me. *You* won't hurt me."

This was a secret desire he'd hidden so deep that he didn't even know it was something he'd wanted until she'd spoken it aloud.

"Yes, Warner. Give me all of you."

She took his shaft in her mouth again and worked all the way down the length and he realized that his surrender was no longer a matter of choice. She'd tamed him, at least for the moment and he wouldn't have it any other way.

Pleasure spiraled through him and he rode the waves as they carried out to a blissful sea.

He was lost in Mari and the moment.

After she brought him to culmination, and they lay sated in each other's arms, it didn't occur to him to put all of his armor, his protections back in place.

He didn't think he'd need them.

But he was wrong.

When he awoke with the first strange lights of pink dawn stretching over his skin, he realized something was horribly wrong.

Mari was still in his arms, but his muscles all ached and there was a smell. A scent of blood and death that permeated the air. He breathed deeply, trying to unravel the scents from the one another.

So much fear.

That would make sense with him in the forest if all the little woodland animals hadn't fled from his presence. There were no other living creatures in this part of the forest. No mammals anyway.

He tugged at the thread and the strongest scent after the fear was the copper tang of blood.

With an undercurrent of silver.

At one time, silver had smelled like poison to him. Something rotten.

It didn't bother him now. It simply was. It was another scent like any other.

He opened his eyes slowly, not actually wanting to see the scene that awaited him, but knowing he had no choice. Whether he looked or not wouldn't change anything.

His hands were sticky, in fact, his whole body was covered in some kind of—blood.

His eyes flew open and he realized that when he'd said there were no other mammals in the forest, he'd meant it. He hadn't sensed Mari's life force, but she was right here in his arms.

Dear fucking Goddess, if something had happened to Mari, may she smite him.

Except, her chest rose and fell with breath. He didn't understand what was happening.

Mari opened her pretty ice blue eyes. "What's wrong, Warner?" She gave a languorous stretch. "Mm, what's that smell? It smells divine."

Warner froze. "Does that smell like food to you?"

She nodded. "Mmmhmm." Mari licked her lips.

"We should go to the river. Close your eyes."

"I'm not closing my..." Mari turned in his arms and she saw the carnage strewn about them.

He realized she had blood on her mouth.

What had he done?

❦ 11 ❦

Mari knew their idyll in the woods couldn't last.

They were on borrowed time.

She knew it would end, but she didn't expect it to end like this.

Mari realized she now knew his horror intimately. She'd awakened to the scent of something delicious. Something she wanted to devour, only to discover it was wolf flesh.

Fear gripped her because she couldn't remember what happened.

But she stuffed it down because Warner would be able to smell it. Whatever had happened here, there had to be a reason.

"What have I done?" He looked up at her, his eyes haunted.

"We don't know that you've done it. I might've done it."

"You couldn't have," he whispered.

"I'm just as covered in blood as you are." She took his hand. "Come on, we need to get to the river and clean up."

"No. I need to be locked up. This wolf wasn't infected."

"How do you know? Because what's left isn't still squirming? Maybe Peter's progeny are easier to destroy than he, himself, was. First things first, though. Come with me."

He looked at her outstretched hand like it was some sort of long lost treasure, so she didn't understand why he wouldn't take it.

"Look what I've done. I understand that I have to do whatever it is I've been created to do. Run down those wolves. Destroy them. I get that. But I can't be around—"

Mari wasn't going to argue the point just yet.

Yes, he should go back to Aphelion where Westwood and Blake can help him. Where he could be surrounded by the pack that he loved. Where he could find a way to live with this.

A way to do what he'd been created to do and to be happy.

Mari wasn't going to push that. Not when he was covered blood and gore. Not when his hands and teeth were still bloody with guilt.

She just had to get him to the river.

If she could baptize him in a way, rinse it all away with the cold, natural waters, make him feel clean again and then wrap him in her love, she was sure she could save him.

Correction: She was sure he'd let himself *be* saved.

She knew if he wouldn't go for himself, he'd go for her.

"Please come to the river with me. I need to bathe too and the current is fast."

He looked stricken, but then he finally took her hand.

She led him carefully through the trees toward the river and away from the scene of devastation behind them.

"You don't really need me here," he said as she stepped one tentative foot into the water.

"Yes, I really do, Warner."

"You're a strong swimmer."

"I am. But I need you. What if one of those things were to find me? What if the current swept me downstream and right into a whole village of them?"

What if I let you run away and I never see you again? What if I'm the one Woolven Mate who isn't up to the task?

"It's unlikely." He turned haunted eyes on her.

She reached up slowly, carefully, with her palms cupped and began to scrub the evidence of what had happened from his skin.

He had so many scars. His body was covered in the proof of his strength, his ferocity and his loyalty.

Suddenly, anger blossomed in her chest like a poison flower.

His steadfast loyalty had earned him nothing but this. An existence contrary to everything he believed. He everything he'd worked for. Everything he was.

He'd done everything right, this noble wolf.

He'd sacrificed until there was nothing left for himself and still the powers that be decided he had more to give.

Warner didn't deserve this.

But maybe she did.

She'd never given up anything she wanted. Mari had never had anything in her hands that she'd worked for, bled for, and carved out a very piece of her to see it grow and thrive. Never.

Mari knew what she had to do if she wanted to help Warner.

She had to entreat the Goddess to take away his curse, but Mari knew that it would only come with sacrifice. If there was another to take his place.

She didn't have much to offer as far as Dark Champions went. Apparently, only the noblest wolves were chosen. Only those who were pure of heart could handle the beast.

Mari knew her heart was nowhere near as pure as Warner's, but her intentions couldn't be nobler. And maybe, just maybe, the Goddess would give her enough strength to endure this until the threat had been eliminated.

And Lenore could put her down, if that's what it came to.

Warner would be free.

Mari knew fear, but it was only the fear that she wouldn't be enough, that the Goddess wouldn't take her in his place.

She wasn't anywhere near as horrified at the prospect of devouring shitty rogue werewolves for dinner as she should've been.

She'd have eaten Peter Breslin herself if she thought it would've helped anything.

And she'd have had champagne with the meal.

Thinking of champagne reminded her why this plan was the stupidest idea she'd ever conceived. How would she ever control anything so elemental, so primal when she couldn't even call her own wolf?

Except maybe that was the key. She'd kept telling Warner to surrender, to be the weapon the Goddess wanted.

Warner suddenly grabbed her hand and pulled her out of her thoughts.

"What's wrong?" he said. "The look on your face is utter dejection."

The expression he wore seemed to beg her for an answer, any answer except that he was the source of her wound.

"I was just thinking about our little problem."

He laughed. "Little?"

"Meh." She shrugged and continued to sluice water over his body. Deciding to distract him, she pointed at the scar around his throat. "Surely, our current situation is not as serious as this."

He seemed to come back to himself. Enough at least to flash her a wry grin. "Well, I was pretty sure I was going to die."

"Yeah," she said, tracing it with her fingertips.

His eyes closed as he allowed her to caress the marred, puckered skin.

"And you were okay with it."

His eyes opened, his irises ringed in the red that she'd come to associate with his desire. "I was."

"Why?"

"I was tired, Mari. So tired. I was all used up."

"Was?" Her fingertips fluttered down to the bottom of the set of scars that sliced from his forehead, down across his eye and all the way down to his chest.

"Do you remember being dead?" She traced other scars on his body, following their path with the water and doggedly scrubbing him clean.

"Yes."

One word answers seemed to be his specialty, but in this case, she could hear the hard push behind the word. He remembered, but he didn't want to tell her. She could let it go, but she needed every weapon against the hopelessness that infected him.

Mari rather thought she knew what he was going to say.

He'd seen Arianna.

Been in her arms and he hadn't wanted to leave.

Warner looked down at her, his expression softening. "Mari..."

"Tell me. I know already. I just want to hear it. I want you to hear it."

"Hear what?"

"I'm not sure yet. Say it. Tell me about how you were with Arianna."

Warner looked like he'd been punched. "You don't want to hear about that."

"But I do. I need to. Tell me."

She grabbed his hand and cupped his palm, filling it with the cold water and guiding him to wash her the same as she'd washed him.

The water was ice cold, but somehow, she hadn't even felt it. Not since she first led him into the swirling, rushing, depths. All she felt was him. The heat of his nearness, the heat of his hand, the way his very presence filled up the world around her and stole her breath.

"I was in her arms. Drowning in the fire of her hair."

Mari girded herself against the pain to come, but no sharp stab of pain, or jealousy, or even her self-doubt.

"What did she say?"

"She told me to come back. That my work wasn't finished."

"And would she want you to finish this work?"

"Damn it, Mari. You're not playing fair."

"Oh Warner," she said, his hands moving over flesh. "This life hasn't been fair to either of us. We do what we can with what we have."

"I'm sorry all you have is me," he said quietly. "You deserve better."

"So do you." She put her hands on his, holding his hands still.

"I've tried my best to protect you, to give you what you need, but you wanted none of it. So tell me, how do I make things right for you?"

"You're not going to like my answer."

"I'm sure that I won't." Warner pulled her closer to him. "But tell me. I'll do it."

"Good. I want you to come back with me to Aphelion. Back to Blake. Back to Westwood."

"Westwood..." he trailed off. "Westwood."

"Yes. Obey your Alpha. Even if it's just to prove to yourself that you can. And before you say anything, I'll send word for Westwood to enhance the wardings. You won't hurt anyone you love."

"Okay, Mari. I'll do this." He sighed heavily. "I'll do it," he said again, as if trying to convince himself.

She tightened her arms around him. "Thank you."

"You're good at getting your way."

"Sometimes." She exhaled heavily and relaxed against him. "We're going to get through this, Warner. I will help you. I swear."

He didn't say anything, he just held her in the frigid water for a long time. Until they were both caught up in another spell that had them walking for the rocky shore at the same time as if some other power had decided.

"I don't think I have other clothes," Warner said.

"There's a bag in the Vette. I think we should drive back."

"I think you are correct," he agreed.

She took the lead and he seemed content to allow it. Mari, using her nose, led them around what was left of Warner's morning meal. They both knew it was there, but it seemed easier not to look at it again.

Naked, they approach the car. For the sake of expediency, they were lucky that the road was mostly abandoned and the car had yet to be towed, or broken into. Or stolen. Mari got the bag from the trunk.

It was then that a chorus of howls echoed stark and unnatural into the morning.

Warner froze.

At the stricken expression on his face, Mari knew something awful was about to happen.

He didn't speak, didn't seem to have the words.

Warner tried to take another step forward, tried for all he worth to go with Mari, but she knew as sure as the sky was blue that Warner Woolven would not be returning with her to Aphelion.

The beast burst from his skin.

Exploded from him like a rocket.

It seemed as if one minute, he'd been Warner, and the next, he was something else.

This was a new incarnation of the beast.

This was the Dark Champion in all of his wretched glory.

This time he'd been given, it had been a chrysalis.

He was bigger than ever before, standing nearly nine feet tall. His muscles were unnaturally large. His legs, she suddenly knew, would carry him distances that had once been unfathomable. Long, spikes protruded from his back all went all the way down to the tip of his tail. The spikes were all damn, seeming to be covered in something sticky. It was probably venom. When she looked into its eyes, she could see nothing of Warner. Nothing of the wolf or man that he was. There was zero recognition in its red eyes.

He nosed at her, finding the traces of blood she hadn't washed off.

Its lips pulled back from a mouth full of too many long, sharp teeth. His muzzle more like it belonged on a shark than a werewolf.

His growl was earth-shaking, but Mari stood very still.

The beast's long tongue slid out to glide over the blood on her skin and he growled while he licked her clean.

And it wasn't anywhere near as erotic as it had been the night before.

His ears pricked and he drew his massive head up and away from her as he listened and with one last look at her, he ran back toward the woods.

Back toward the howls.

And away from the only answer Mari had.

With shaking hands, she finished dressing and rummaged around for the cell phone to try to call Lenore.

They were going to have to activate the emergency plan.

Hunt him down.

Tranq his ass.

And drag him back to Aphelion.

Only, after seeing the Dark Champion she wondered if maybe he'd been right all along. Maybe he didn't belong at Aphelion.

But she had to try.

What if this started another war between the packs? They needed time to heal. Time to prosper again and build alliances.

For all intents and purposes, Warner was a Berserkr.

She didn't want to think about what that meant.

Mari hoped against hope that Lenore would pick up. Since she was overseeing cleanup, she could already be anywhere.

"Whatcha got?" Lenore answered.

"This is Mari."

"Not that it's not great to hear from you, but if you're calling, everything must've gone to shit."

"The Dark Champion has risen. Warner is gone."

❧ 12 ❧

Warner had zero control over his body.

It still felt as if he'd mutated into one giant, pulsing nerve that was made only of desire.

Desire for fucking.

Desire for meat.

For blood.

For ripping and tearing into soft flesh.

The darkness was in the driver's seat.

He knew this wasn't right. Dark Champion or not, these cravings were increasing in intensity and he refused to believe that the powers that be would unleash this kind of darkness with no way to stomp on the breaks.

He was as big of a danger to human and supe populations as Peter's pack.

It didn't make sense.

Be quiet.

Be still.

All is as it should be.

We will hunt them down and tear them apart.

No more pain.

No more hunger.

Stop fighting.

Westwood told him to stop fighting.

Mari told him to stop fighting.

Lenore and the witches had told him to stop fighting.

Maybe surrender was his only option.

He caught the scent of a small pack and he saw what was going to happen to that pack in his mind's eye. In this territory, they would be under Woolven protection, unless they managed to dark across the border.

The pack wasn't infected as far as he knew, but that wasn't the worst part. The worst part was that he didn't want to fight it anymore.

If he surrendered, he wouldn't have to bear witness to what this beast did.

And he'd finally be sated.

He tracked them now, using his superior predator's skills. He could pick up more scents at a greater distance, he could see more than just heat signatures in the dark, and he could move faster than he'd ever dreamed.

It felt good and right to use these skills. It was like stretching after a long, restful sleep.

He ran them down, these hapless wolves.

Ran them down and burst upon them like a lion would a herd of injured gazelles.

He tore through them easily and with great pleasure. War noted one or two of them escaped, but that didn't matter to him. In fact, it was good. Let them tell the story—his story. Let them carry it back to a hunter.

Or the council.

Then this would all be over and the rest of the pack would be safe.

The darkness pushed at his consciousness, and he realized it was locking him away. Pushing him down so he didn't have to watch what came next.

He was a coward.

Warner Woolven was nothing like the story said. He was nothing like the wolf he thought he was or the wolf he wanted to be.

That should've been a rallying cry, but it wasn't.

Instead, it opened a door to a deeper place where he didn't have to feel this shame or sorrow.

It opened a door to oblivion.

13

"I can't believe I'm tracking Warner," Lenore said out loud.

"Me either." Mari leaned against a tree.

"He told me it would go down like this."

"Hey, we're not putting him down," Mari snarled.

"Of course we're not. But we are going to have to contain him," Lenore warned.

"I know. Sorry about the growly thing, too. It's been happening a lot more lately."

"I have my suspicions about that. So do the Three."

"Lenore, I..." Mari wasn't sure how to say what she wanted to say. She trusted the hunter, she thought the witches knew what they were about, too. After all, they had a thousand years on her. But she couldn't stand the hope anymore.

Hope was a demon because it made her want. It made her think the things that were impossible had a chance to live and breathe.

When they didn't.

"I know you don't believe, Mari. But why else would you suddenly be going through all of these changes?"

"The prophecy said his one true mate would rise from the dead.

That has to be Arianna. I really can't think about that right now because it makes me a bad person."

Lenore stopped and looked at Mari. "How does that make you a bad person?"

"I'm jealous. I'm heartbroken. And I'm so goddsdamned mad. I'm basically having a pity party, table for one over here when we've got bigger fish to fry."

"That's a pretty normal response, I think."

"Would Warner worry about his own feelings, or would he just want the person he loved to be happy and safe? I think we've already seen the proof of his answer in Blake, Drew and Parker."

Lenore sighed. "I have thoughts on this that you won't like."

"There's a lot about what's going on that I don't like. So you might as well hit me with it. Tell me."

"I think that Arianna was never his True Mate. He was attracted to her. Intensely. He admired her. And I think it was the same for the mantle of Alpha. He didn't want it. Not really."

"He spent his whole life pining for a dead woman because she wasn't his True Mate? Yeah, I can't really reconcile that."

"He never felt anything like what he felt for Arianna. That much is true. But Warner isn't a wolf of high passions."

Mari raised a brow. The last few times they'd been together, he'd been a wolf of very high passions to say the least.

Lenore laughed. "No, really. It's different because it's you. You're his one. You both need to figure it out before the shit really hits the fan."

"I'd say that we're a little too late on that count." Mari scented the air. "I smell death. We're still in Woolven Territory, aren't we?"

"I believe so."

"Then I guess it's not as bad as it could be, although if word gets out that Woolven is ravaging their own people, that could be just as bad."

"Fuck," Lenore muttered. "What do you smell?"

"Death and a lot of it. Although, we'd been traveling through these woods and there were no other packs roaming here. So I don't know where they came from or why."

Lenore nodded. "Suspicious as hell. It might've been a distraction. Or a trap."

"I can't even think about who would be evil enough or insane enough to try to trap something like what Warner has become."

"Can't you?" Lenore fixed her with a hard look.

"If that's our only option, then yeah. But we love him. They're going to try to hurt him and all that will be left of them will be a smear on the ground."

"And would that be so bad?" Lenore gave her a half-grin.

"I don't think so, but Warner will. He'll feel so guilty."

"Maybe. Maybe not. I think we have to consider that when we get to Warner, and we will, he may not be the Warner that we knew."

"We'll find him. The real Warner. No matter how long it takes," Mari said, hating the almost innocent hope that filled her voice.

"Mari, sometimes the Dark Champions..." Lenore shook her head. "Listen, I'm not saying this because I want to give up on him. I'll never give up on him. He's part of my chosen family and I love him. But the Three told me that only the strongest, the noblest of wolves are chosen to be Dark Champions for a reason. They're the only ones that contain the darkness long enough to wield it like the weapon it was meant to be against evil. It feeds on goodness. On the insides of the very ones who channel it. It devours them from the inside out."

"He knows that, doesn't he?"

"He does."

"So what's our plan?"

"We're going to help him fight. Nothing has changed. Nothing at all." Lenore's mouth set into a grim line. "If not for my shithead brother, we wouldn't be in this mess."

Mari studied the hunter for a long moment. She'd never considered that Lenore felt any guilt for this. Any regret. She was a hunter. She was strong, infallible, almost. Mari knew no one was a monolith. Not really. "It's not your fault, you know that right?"

"I can't help but feel like it is. I bear some blame. After what happened to Emmie... I should've put Peter down before it came to this."

"You couldn't have known. He was your brother."

"I should've killed him when Emmie left him."

Mari knew the story well by now about how the cursed wolf thought she was a human to keep her safe. How Peter had been protective at first, then he'd shown his true colors and had been a waking nightmare for the woman who was now married to the Woolven Beta.

"Maybe you should've, but maybe not. You can't know what would've happened. Emmie might not be married to Drew now. She wouldn't have Noah. And she is happy. She's ridiculously happy. You can't undo the bad without undoing the good. No regrets, hunter."

"If I'd killed him, we wouldn't be here," Lenore sighed.

"Maybe not, but you can't change the past. You did the best you could with the information you had. You tried to do the right thing. That's what matters."

Lenore grabbed her and pulled her in for a tight hug. "It means the world to me that you think so. This will be okay. I'll make it okay. I swear."

"*We* will make it okay." Mari returned the hug.

She didn't know why both Warner and Lenore wanted to swear to her. It wasn't as if she was anyone of consequence. She didn't hold their fates in her hands. She wasn't any kind of judge.

Lenore pulled back. "You've got me for life now, too, you know. I mean, as soon as you married Warner, it was implied. But in case you didn't know."

Mari found herself welling up with emotion. She'd never really had close relationships with anyone, let alone other women.

Since she'd come to Woolven, she'd bonded with Randi, Emmie, Lenore, Belle and even Westwood. It was a sisterhood within a family, and the cords of love and respect bound them all tightly together.

"Thank you," was all she could manage. "I'd like to keep you."

"You sure?" Lenore teased.

"I mean, I guess. If I must," Mari teased back. "This may sound incredibly naïve, especially considering how absolutely defeated I was feeling earlier but I just have this feeling it's all going to be okay."

"Good. Let's hold on to that."

"As tightly as I can." Mari nodded.

"I know we'd agreed to let Warner do what he needed to in this situation. Dealing with the infected pack, but I think we'll have a better shot at... basically everything if we contain him first. We tranq him and airlift him back to Aphelion where David and Westwood can work their magick on him and find a way out for all of us. Including Warner."

Mari nodded. "I like that plan. Because honestly, say he deals with this threat. Then what happens to him? We owe it to him to help him not only with the task that's been laid on his shoulders but to see that he survives it."

"Glad we're on the same page. I want you to know, Mari, I couldn't do this without you."

"I'm sure you'd be fine. You're Lenore Breslin," she blurted.

"I am. Yeah. Last time I checked." Lenore grinned. "Stop doubting what you have to offer. You bring a lot to the table, my friend. When you discount yourself, you discount the rest of us who love and need you. Those of us who believe in you."

Mari had never looked at it that way before.

She'd never been needed before.

"I just don't want to let you down. I want your faith in me to be justified."

"That's for me to decide, isn't it? It's my choice to believe in you and ultimately, yours to believe in yourself. I really wish I could do it for you. You'd see how amazing you are. How bright you shine to the rest of us. Only you can do that for you, though."

Westwood had said something similar about recognizing what she had to offer. About herself being enough.

It was hard for Mari to imagine a world where this was true.

Except these people that she loved and admired said it already was the truth. It wasn't a someday, somewhere proposition. It was here. It was now.

And everything would somehow be okay.

Even when they crossed the line out of Woolven Territory.

"I guess I'm earning my keep now. I can scent him. He came this way."

"Did he cross the border?"

"He did. Right here." Mari sank down on her haunches to push away the underbrush and saw she stood in an impossibly large footprint that looked as if belonged to a werewolf.

But no werewolf stood as tall.

Except Warner when he'd become The Dark Champion.

"What the fuck is that?" Lenore was immediately down on her haunches as well. "Jesus Fucking Christ, that's huge."

"I told you he was bigger."

"I thought you meant warrior form bigger. Not... monster bigger."

"Yeah," Mari said. "Monster bigger."

"I don't know if I brought enough to tranqs to bring him down, Mari. He's that big with super strength and a supernatural rage problem? We might be slightly fucked."

"Only slightly." Mari shrugged.

"Well, we've come this far. You still in?" Lenore asked.

"Of course."

"We're also crossing into forbidden territory."

"I know that. I'm still with you. Whatever it takes."

"I figured, but informed consent is important to me. This could all go to shit in any number of ways."

Mari laughed. "It's quite likely to go to shit all around."

"You're not wrong."

Mari made it a point to step over the dividing line between the territories. "It's done now."

They forged ahead through the dense forest and Mari was aware of how the woods had gone unnaturally quiet.

The small birds and mammals had gone silent. The insects were no longer buzzing, no frogs sang for their mates. The wind disturbed no leaves. It was unnatural.

Small hairs on the back of Mari's neck stood up. Heat traveled up the length of her spine and settled on the back of her head.

The beast inside of her was silent.

"We're being watched. Maybe hunted," Lenore mouthed at her.

It wasn't Warner. Mari knew that for sure.

Although, since he'd already passed this way, they should've been safe. Or as safe as they could be with this new threat running free.

Or maybe Warner was herding them back toward the territorial border? Chasing them into Woolven lands so he could do as he pleased? That would make sense. That's what a smart predator would do.

Warner was incredibly strong and smart. He was a master tactician.

She and Lenore shared a look and it spoke volumes.

The continued to move forward, slowly, carefully. Very aware they were being watched by an apex predator.

Mari was tempted to Change.

Or at least to try.

The infected wolf would go for her before Lenore. From what she understood it seemed like they were most interested in increasing their numbers. It was possible the creature was unaware of who Lenore was, even though she carried the tools of the hunter.

She didn't know if while Warner was in this new state, this darker plane of existence if he'd still feel it if she were in danger.

He'd marked her, but his transformation to the Dark Champion wasn't complete. Would this thing feel—no, Warner. Underneath it all, he was still Warner. Would he feel her peril? Would he come to save her?

She could only hope.

"You're a long way from Woolven Territory, aren't you, pretty one?" A deep, gravelly voice sounded from behind them.

Mari turned to look at the creature that approached them.

"Not really," she replied. "Maybe a few feet."

He was big, but almost werewolves were. He stood on his hind legs to make himself bigger, taller, and much more terrifying. She wasn't normally afraid of her own kind, but he wasn't her kind.

His teeth were all like Warner's.

Except tipped in silver.

Dear Goddess, he was one of the Infected.

"So you know that you're out of your territory."

"The same way you knew you were out of yours, fiend." Lenore put her hands on her hips.

"No one was speaking to you, hunter." He said this last as if it were sour on his tongue.

"Oh, but weren't you? I have the power of the council behind me."

"Fuck the council. And fuck you, hunter."

"Fuck me?" Lenore laughed. "I mean... no. Since you're my brother's get, that would make this all a bit too incestuous for my taste."

The creature roared, and fought what seemed to be a physical battle to keep himself from charging them both.

Mari wanted to run. To hide. To do anything but stand there and wait for the cursed thing to make a choice about to do with them.

To do *to* them.

She knew he'd smell her fear and that pissed her off. Even though being afraid in this situation was just common sense. He was faster, stronger, and far deadlier than she.

"What's wrong? Don't know what to do without my brother pulling your strings?" Lenore laughed at him.

But Mari could see that the hunter was slowly and slyly preparing to fight. She had a gun, but Mari didn't know what good that would do against this thing, but Mari had faith it was more than a silver bullet because Lenore was smart and savvy. She knew that these things were immune to silver and she'd brought her brother's still talking head back in a sack.

Warner. Mari thought of him. Willed him to hear her. To feel her. To come to her.

A disturbance in the underbrush caught her attention and watched as the foliage parted and revealed the only thing more terrible than the beast before them.

Warner Woolven.

The Dark Champion in all of his horrific glory.

14

Warner was not completely lost.

His awareness and control had come back to him in waves.

He hadn't wanted it. He'd surrendered to the thing inside of him and perhaps that was what it had required all along.

His complete and total surrender.

Although, he was different.

He was not the same Warner who'd loped off into the forest, but nor was he only the Dark Champion.

He was more.

He was less.

And there was something else inside his body with him. Something *other*. It seemed more malignant somehow than this other skin her wore, and it seemed that only the Dark Champion could keep it contained and only when he surrendered.

Warner knew instinctively it was a zero-sum game and he was quickly running out of moves.

Luckily, he'd discovered why the pack in the northern territory hadn't wanted Woolven interference.

They'd become the thing he was hunting.

All of them.

The entire pack had been turned.

He'd been leading them back into Woolven Territory. So when he slaughtered them all there would be no interference from the council or anyone else.

Except he sensed other presences in the forest.

He felt Mari.

She should've gone back to Aphelion by now, but he'd underestimated her.

Again.

She was here and he knew she was here for him.

Her fear crawled up his back like a spider and he'd be goddess-damned before he'd led any creature on this earth make his Mari feel that way.

He didn't trust himself around her, but he couldn't let this threat to her go unanswered. Warner caught another scent and it was as he suspected: Lenore.

The Dark Champion stirred.

He didn't like that Mari was under threat either.

She belonged to him.

Warner didn't stop to think about what that meant. Only that he had to get to her. Everything inside of him burned to protect her.

And to destroy whatever menaced her.

He ran hard, covering a distance at a speed previously unknown to human and supe alike.

When he emerged into the clearing and saw that Mari was under threat, rage boiled the blood in his veins.

And he'd walked into the pack's trap.

But it didn't matter.

Not to him, anyway.

They could rip and tear at him all they liked and maybe he'd bleed, but they'd never be able to take him down.

Everything in him spoiled for a fight. His teeth literally ached to rip and tear. To devour. His claws itched to be buried deep in infected flesh.

"He comes," the interloper said.

Mari's eyes widened in horror and Warner didn't know if it was because of his new form, or if it was because of the group of infected that had started emerging from the forest to surround them.

Maybe a little of both.

Lenore pulled her guns and Warner hoped that the ammo she'd made from his saliva was would protect them.

But if he was honest, he didn't see how Lenore was going to survive this.

He wanted her to, but the Dark Champion wouldn't allow him to prioritize her safety over the destruction of the beasts that surrounded them.

Warner had thought his transformation complete. He didn't realize the darkness could go deeper.

Somehow, it had.

The Dark Champion was distracted by Mari.

Her very presence agitated him in a way that Warner didn't think he could fight. He wanted to sink his teeth deep in her throat.

Not to hurt her, but to claim her.

Change her.

But Warner knew his bite to be venomous. He'd kill her.

Only that's what the darkness wanted. To end her so he didn't have to fear her destruction.

She will be reborn from death.

She will rise Wendigo.

Except that was only the lie the beast told him to gain compliance.

To get him to trundle along down the primrose path without a fight.

Except Warner couldn't fight. He'd already surrendered to this thing. Already decided there was no choice.

He couldn't let Mari be a casualty of this war.

Of Peter Breslin and all the evil he'd loosed on the world.

"You've served your purpose," the infected wolf said. "Run, run away to Woolven lands and warn the rest of them what's coming. We're going to take down your champion."

Mari lifted her chin, her eyes blazing red. "No, you won't. And we won't run from you."

Red.

Her eyes were red.

He'd already tainted her.

Lenore raised her gun and fired, the bullet grazing the shoulder of the wolf who stood before them.

The flesh sizzled and crackled where the projectile entered him, but he didn't seem to feel any pain. He only smiled.

Lenore wasn't dissuaded in the least. She emptied the clip into his chest.

"Now I know what you say about Peter is a lie. You didn't take him down with these little pins." He laughed.

"No. I dissolved his bones from the inside out. And these will make short work of you in a moment."

"Not before I rend your meat from your bones."

He leaped at her, but Lenore saw it coming and had already dropped into a roll that positioned her out of the way of his strike.

"This is going to be fun," he said and gave the signal.

The rest of the beasts began to advance, but they avoided Warner. He knew what they were doing.

They were trying to distract him with Lenore and Mari so they could attack him as one, as if their greater numbers gave them any kind of advantage.

They'd soon learn.

He waited, watching their advance with cool indifference.

"You can't tell me you're going to let us have them. Your scent is all over the weak one," one of them said with a laugh.

That was when he launched himself at the wolf and tore his head right from his body.

And he stripped the bones clean within seconds. There was no chance for him to regenerate.

The other wolves saw this but they were still coming. He didn't understand why they'd do that.

They weren't stupid.

But maybe he was.

He'd never stopped to think they might have a reason for luring him there. Might have some agenda. He couldn't think what it could be and the harder he tried, the more disjointed his thoughts became.

Warner knew whatever it was, it couldn't be good.

The Dark Champion needed Mari.

Warner looked for her, but couldn't see her. Or Lenore.

And suddenly, the sound of helicopters roared against his ears. He looked up to see a swarm of hunters rappelling down into the battle. They were all dressed in black and carried the latest in werewolf killing technology.

Too bad it wouldn't do shit.

At least not long term.

They slaughtered the infected pack, taking heads and hearts. He watched in horror as the pack began to devour their own. Even as they were beheaded in the process. Other wolves would come along and restart the process.

Warner's guts twisted. An awful connection made itself known in his head, but he couldn't quite consider it.

A giant containment unit dropped from the sky, still attached to the cables and four helicopters hovered.

Of course, they would try to take them alive. To study them.

Oh Goddess.

He watched as what was left of the pack went willingly and one particularly shitty human began to shovel the remains into the cage with them.

Warner knew that when the wolves regenerated, they'd decimate the hunters, but these dumb bastards weren't really his concern at the moment.

His super hearing could hear what Lenore what was saying through the roar of the helicopters if he concentrated.

Strange scents drifted his way. Lies had a particular scent and he knew that they weren't coming from Lenore.

"What are you doing, Connor? This wasn't what we agreed on."

"It's what the high council wants."

"Goddamn it. When are they going to fucking learn?" Lenore scrubbed a hand over her face.

"Well, you'd have better luck if you weren't such a fur fucker, wouldn't you?" Connor sneered.

"Eat the entirety of my ass, Connor." Lenore turned to walk away from him, but he grabbed her arm.

"Where do you think you're going?"

"You want to keep that hand?" Lenore stared at him and jerked her arm away.

"I don't give a shit if you're Diana Breslin's daughter."

"The only part about who I am that matters is that since I am such a fur fucker, as you say, I'll chew your goddamn head from your body if you touch me again."

He laughed. "Fair enough. Where is the Champion? We need him too."

"That wasn't part of the deal."

"Deal? Lenore, you're a hunter. You know how this works. He's a danger to humans as well. Maybe more so than this pack. The witches say he can bring them back."

"Who?"

"The wolves we've killed."

Stupid fucks. They'd regenerate on their own.

Except he thought about the first of the infected he'd consumed. He thought about the evil. He thought about the thoughts in his head.

And the devastation it would wreak if Peter Breslin were somehow reborn.

That connection in his brain, the one he couldn't quite consider, couldn't quite bring to the forefront of his mind... it erupted in all of its foul glory.

Warner knew with a certainty now that the strange voice in his head, the one that was not the Dark Champion, it was Peter.

The hunter turned werewolf apocalypse lived inside of him.

And soon, he would want out.

Warner knew that somehow, the answer was Mari.

The thing inside of him cringed away from even the thought of her.

When he'd been thinking about marking her, and his thoughts had turned to the darker aspects, it had all been Peter trying to trick him into devouring his would-be destructor.

Warner crept forward, trying to gain Lenore's attention.

The helicopters dropped another cage and that's when Warner knew.

Lenore had been betrayed.

And so had the world.

He watched as a tranq dart hit Lenore's neck from behind, and he felt the prick in his own neck.

He went down hard, still able to see and hear, but he couldn't move.

For all of his superpowers, he guessed that the powers that be must be fallible if they hadn't counted on hunters with something as simple and rudimentary as a tranquilizer dart. Or maybe they thought he'd be better prepared.

They dragged him into the cage with Lenore.

The members of the infected pack went batshit at his nearness, trying to rip and tear into him.

Visions of them tearing his body apart to get at the one inside of him, to free him, assaulted him.

Warner knew that's exactly what was going to happen if they could reach him.

Mari. I need you.

The one called Connor spoke. "You love them so much, see how you feel about it when this one wakes up ravenous for flesh and you're all he's got to eat." He kicked at the cage.

Yeah, he supposed they would see, wouldn't they?

He and this Connor would have a reckoning when this was over.

If Lenore didn't get to him first.

He thought of Mari again. Of her sweet softness, of her voice, her touch.

And of the red ring around her eyes.

He called her to him with his mind, using the mating bond and all the power of the Dark Champion, all the while hoping against hope he wasn't wrong.

That he wasn't luring her to her death, her true death and the Wendigohe now believed was inside of her would end this nightmare.

He realized with a sudden awful clarity that he didn't want Arianna. She was long dead and Mari was here. Mari had stood by him, she'd come when he hadn't even know he'd needed her. She was loyal and brave, so much stronger than anyone had given her credit for.

Mari was the one.

❧ 15 ☙

Mari wasn't a killer.

But she knew if she wanted to be on this transport, she'd have to be.

She quickly considered her options.

She was dressed like a camper and she might be able to get them to lower her guard if she approached them like another human looking for help.

They'd test her with silver eventually, but she'd have to act before it went that far.

She'd be taking a chance they wouldn't recognize her. Hunters had to study all the major houses and learn the names and faces of the major players. Her father was a pack Alpha, but Mari hadn't really participated in politics nor had she Changed. She kept to herself.

It was possible the hunters had considered her not really a were-wolf, therefore below their notice.

Or she'd approach this hunter and get riddled with silver.

It was a chance she was willing to take.

She'd heard him. Warner, calling over their mate bond.

His voice had been faint, the signal weak, but he'd said he needed her.

And by all that was holy, unholy, and beyond, she'd answer that call.

She looked down at herself and rubbed some dirt on her face and mussed her hair. She banged around in the underbrush just enough so their dull human senses could detect her.

To her extreme luck, one hunter found her. He wasn't too terribly huge, but his fatigues would still be kind of big on her. Luckily, they tended not to bother getting to know the newer ones until they'd survived a few missions.

An unknown face wouldn't be cause for concern.

"Stay right there," he commanded.

"Who are you?" she whispered, hoping she sounded like a damsel in distress.

"Who are you?" he aimed a gun at her.

Mari gasped. She found she lied easily. It was supposed to be hard for werewolves to lie, if not impossible, but the words came as if they were true. "My name is Jennifer. I was hiking with my friends and we got separated and..." she forced her eyes to well with tears. "I'm lost and I think they're dead."

He reached for the radio on his belt and she launched herself at him, wrapping her arms around him.

"I'm so glad to see you."

The man was so surprised, he just held her. "It's going to be okay."

She knew he'd been trained for this situation, so she wondered why he didn't just shoot her.

Then she knew why.

"How glad are you?" His hand was on her ass.

Bastard.

She didn't feel too badly about tearing out his throat. If she'd actually been what she pretended to be, if she'd actually been in danger and afraid and he'd treated her like this, well... really, she was doing the world a service, wasn't she?

Mari realized this was what she needed. If she could get him out of his fatigues before she tore his throat out, well, it would just be better all around.

"So glad."

He unbuckled his belt and pushed her down.

He grabbed her hands and held them above her head and then he whispered in her ear, "I know you're a filthy wolf bitch, but I'm going to fuck you before I rip your heart out."

She laughed.

Mari didn't feel a single second of fear that he'd follow through on his threat. Oh, she knew he would try, but she'd take his head first.

She found a new voice inside of her. One that belonged wholly to the wolf she'd ignored for so long.

It wanted to take his head.

It wanted him to know fear and terror before she did.

Mari found that she wanted that, too.

Mari wasn't afraid of the new bloody thoughts, she reveled in them and this fucker deserved everything he had coming.

"I've always wanted to know what it was like with a human," she murmured.

"You're not going to trick me into letting you go."

"I'm not trying." That was a problem, wasn't it? Oh well. So the shirt would be bloody. She'd just have to spread it around so it looked like it belonged to the werewolf victims instead of him.

He tried to snap silver cuffs on her wrists, but that was when she showed him exactly what she was made of.

Teeth, and fangs, and everything grand. That's what wolf bitches were made of.

She tore him apart.

Ripped his head from his body and dropped kicked it out into the forest.

She hoped he could see her foot coming at his face in those seconds and knew his head had been removed from the rest of his meat.

Mari made quick work of stripping his clothes and squirming into them.

She experienced a level of control over her wolf that she'd never known. His boots were too big, so she transformed, just her feet to fill the boots.

The wolf part of her hated being confined inside the hot, restrictive leather of the boot, but the wolf part of her hated it more that they might get away with what they'd done to Lenore and Warner.

At least until the infected pack killed them, but then they'd have another problem that would have to be dealt with.

She approached the transport with an M16 slung over her shoulder, acting for all the world as if she belonged there.

The guy checking names off the list looked at her expectantly.

"Warner," she said.

"Goddamn it. Another one we didn't have listed. Home Office has to do better with this shit. It's all gone to hell since we lost Peter." Then he looked stricken. "Fuck. You didn't hear that."

She nodded gravely. "Of course I didn't. Snitches get stitches, am I right?"

"Thank fuck for that. Good on you, recruit. Good on you." He slapped her back heartily and she climbed onto the transport and buckled in.

The roaring of more helicopters filled the air and the transport was lifted off the ground.

Mari watched as they flew ever higher and covered a considerable amount of ground.

North, they were heading farther north.

When she looked down, she saw that they'd barely made a dent in the infected population.

Swarms of them had come from miles around to converge on the spot where they'd been.

"Holy shit, look at that," one of the other recruits pointed down to where Mari had been looking.

"This is a bigger problem than Home Office had anticipated."

"Yeah, that's why they had to catch the Woolven. He's the key to defeating them," another said.

"That was pretty fucking stupid, don't you think?" Mari couldn't help but say.

At the expressions on the others' faces, she realized she'd spoken aloud and wondered just what she'd do if they figured out who she was.

She rushed to add, "Why involve ourselves and send our guys to die when they can handle it themselves?"

They seemed to relax and the older one said, "Because we need to be able to defend ourselves. Warner Woolven is the key. Although, I'm surprised we took him so easily. We need to be on our guard and prepared for anything."

Mari was surprised by that, too.

Not just by how easily they took Warner, but by how easily they'd captured part of the pack. These hunters would be the best resource for that kind of information, if she tread carefully.

"Hey, so I'm new," she began. "I know we're not really supposed to ask questions, but I saw one of the others throw the remains in with the pack. I don't understand."

"You think it was cruel and inhumane?" The guy next to her snorted.

"No. They eat their dead to regenerate. Or weren't you paying attention?" Mari answered.

"That's just fucking nasty. Also, I guess it's going to suck to be on the ground when that starts." He shrugged.

"Don't you think you should tell someone?"

"They'll figure it out."

Mari sat back in silence for the rest of the ride.

It was hard for her to reconcile Lenore was part of this. She was nothing like any of these assholes.

Maybe that's why she was more pack than anything. Lenore didn't fit with these people. They were awful.

Awful humans who did awful things.

Lenore was a good person who did awful things for the right reasons.

That's what Warner was, too.

She had to get to him.

When the transport was about to land, the guy next to her said, "This is your first time, huh?"

"That obvious? Fuck." Mari looked down at her feet.

"You're gonna do fine, kid."

She nodded.

"I can tell you want to do the right thing."

The transport landed and noise from people on the ground drowned out anything else he would've said.

When they disembarked, he stayed by her side. "That's a lot of blood," he said, indicating to her shirt after he'd maneuvered her toward the warehouse.

She didn't like being herded, but it was taking her where she wanted to go anyway.

But fuck, what did she say to that?

"Is it? One of them got me on the ground so I had to take his head off."

"With what, your bare hands?"

Damn! She hadn't thought about that. She'd didn't think anyone would be looking at her hands.

"It's okay," he said. "Me too."

Him too, what? So she just rolled with it. She considered just taking this one's head before he could cause her any more problems but there were eyes everywhere.

"You killed one, too?"

He smiled at her and pushed her against the wall of the warehouse.

"Man is not man," he said to her.

She looked at him blankly. So he repeated," Man is not man."

Mari had read that somewhere before. Her brain scanned through the hundreds of thousands of books she read, but she kept coming up blank. She realized it was some kind of secret passcode.

Her brain finally alighted on the proper quote. It was from a Roman philosopher and it sprang to her tongue. "But a wolf to those he does not know." She finished the Plautus quote.

"Thank shit you answered correctly, or I'd have had to kill you. And you're too pretty to kill."

"That would've sucked," she agreed easily.

He laughed.

She wanted to ask him his name, but she had the feeling it wasn't the done thing.

"Tonight is going to be epic. These stupid fucks. Don't know how they survived so long. Am I right?"

"Totally. Stupid fucks," she parroted.

"To rebirth," the guy chattered on. "Stand by me for the frenzy?" he asked.

"For sure," she agreed.

A sick feeling twisted in her gut.

His tone changed now. He'd gone from being this commanding threat to almost child-like. "If he doesn't Turn me Himself, you will, won't you?"

She nodded absently.

"What's he like? I know we're not supposed to ask about him, but you've met him. Had his teeth in your throat. I can't imagine it."

Mari was going to be sick.

"I'll trade you stories. I don't know how it's going to go down and I need to. I want to be prepared so I honor him. We can trade deets. You seem like you're in the know here."

He turned to look at her with wild eyes. "Why don't you know? If you were worthy of his bite?"

"Oh, you know. He wants me to be resourceful. I came from the first he Turned back in Italy after he was infected by that De La Luna bitch."

"Fucking bitch," he agreed. "So, don't tell anyone I told you."

"Swear."

"Tonight, Peter is going to tear himself out of that guardian wolf. The new breed pack is going to devour the pieces so they take his power and there won't be anyone to stop him anymore. His sister is going to get what's coming to her, too."

Mari watched him carefully. "Not like you think."

"What do you mean?"

"It's an honor to be Turned. Even if she doesn't think so."

"He's going to eat her, not Turn her."

"No, I'm pretty sure he's going to Turn her. All he's ever wanted is for her to join him. He married her best friend just to be closer to her."

"He didn't."

Mari couldn't stop the smile on her face. "Oh, but he did. And now she's married to some werewolf."

"That's disgusting."

"If you think werewolves are disgusting, why do you want to be one?"

"New breed. Peter's breed. We'll hunt every last one of those fucking mutts until all that's left is us and we're going to rule the supes. We'll be immortal."

And Peter's everlasting bitches, she silently added.

One question kept burning hot in her brain. How did they know that Peter was inside Warner?

The simplest answer was often the easiest.

Would Lenore or anyone who'd been present at the picnic say anything?

No.

What did that leave?

Warner said he'd felt a darkness growing inside of him, something that seemed too evil to be the Dark Champion.

The only answer was that Peter lived inside of him and he'd been taking the reins.

Bile rose in the back of her throat. Had she mated with Peter?

No, no. That wasn't possible. Peter would never have... but wouldn't he?

She swallowed the bile down. No, she refused to allow it. When she'd looked into Warner's eyes, even when they'd been savage and red, it was always the wolf she knew looking back at her.

Mari wouldn't think about that now, anyway. It didn't matter.

All that mattered was saving Warner.

Peter was going to get out. She'd accepted that. Something about that knowledge was immutable. It had to happen. It was supposed to happen.

She wondered when the Wendigo would come. Mari hoped it was soon.

It was sooner she'd have to say goodbye to Warner, but it was sooner everything would be as it should be and her pack, and everyone else's would be safe.

Warner. Her heart splintered as she thought of him. She couldn't imagine what he was going through. The pain and horror he'd have to endure.

She needed a plan.

"We should get ready," he said. "The rest of the new breed will be here soon. The other hunters underestimated their tracking abilities. They should be here by dusk."

Warner could deal with Peter. Along with the Wendigo.

But he couldn't do it if the pack tore him apart.

She needed a diversion.

Blood.

She'd need a lot of it. That would be the only thing that would distract the pack long enough.

"Meet me back here soon?" the guy said.

"Yeah. I'll be here." She watched him go, and as she did, her sensitive ears caught the sounds of something happening inside the warehouse.

It was Lenore.

"Jesus Fucking Christ," was all she said.

And Mari knew it had begun.

16

Warner awoke in a cage, but that wasn't the part that really upset him.

It was the stabbing, slicing pain in his gut.

It felt like something was trying to rip its way out of him and when he turned to see Lenore in the cell across from him and the expression she wore, he knew it was more than a feeling.

By the powers, Peter Breslin was going to rip his way out of him.

Warner wasn't afraid of the pain to come.

He was afraid of his failure. Afraid for what it meant for the packs and for humankind. If he, the Dark Champion, couldn't keep Peter from rising again, who or what could?

He knew the answer.

The Wendigo.

An evil such as Peter's must be swallowed twice, the softer, quieter voice inside his head told him. First, by the daywalking world's defender—the Dark Champion. Then by the underworld's champion —the Wendigo.

"This is going to suck," he muttered.

Lenore had put her hand over her mouth, as if the act could hold back her revulsion.

The infected pack watched him with great interest and no small amount of glee.

He realized this was what they were after. If they could get Peter as soon as he was reborn... if they managed to stop the cycle before the Wendigo could do her part, he didn't know what would happen.

But it would be all bad, of that he was sure.

"Lenore, you should get your hunter friends in here," he ground out.

"I don't think any of them are my hunter friends any longer. And those left who are hunters, well... I think they're fucked. They can't help us."

"Damn right," one of the infected said.

"Shut up. Or I'll make you," Lenore threatened.

"What are you going to do from over there?"

She murmured words of a curse that made the bottom of their cage catch fire.

"It won't kill us," it said.

"No, but it'll hurt. And that's good enough for me." Lenore smiled a devil-may-care grin.

Then Warner's stomach twisted, and grew, billowing out to a horrific size and they could all see something moving inside.

"Jesus Fucking Christ," Lenore said.

Warner sensed Mari before he saw her. Her presence sent a cool, calming sensation flowing through his veins.

"You're here," he managed through grit teeth.

"Of course I am. You called. I came." She reached through the bars to hold his hand.

The burning wolves were strangely silent and much to Lenore's obvious chagrin, the flames died down much too soon.

"Have to work on the longevity of that one," she said, more to herself than anything.

"Has she come?" Mari asked him.

"*You* came," Warner said, drinking in the sight of her.

"You must be out of your head with agony. She'll come. Arianna will. I know it."

"It's not Arianna. It's you."

Mari closed her eyes. "No, it's not. That's okay, I will still do everything I can."

Warner was about to argue with her when another bolt of pain wracked his body and the shape inside of him twisted and claws tore at the flesh, but still couldn't quite break free.

"Hold on, I'm going to get you out."

"No, stop! Don't. The infected want me out."

"Because the rest of their numbers are coming. You can deal with them better out than in."

Warner cringed. "Word choice, Mari. Word choice."

She looked down to his distended stomach. "Sorry."

Lenore cackled and Mari wondered if the badass hunter had finally cracked.

"Goddess, you're worse than Parker. Now is not the time for a fart joke."

"It's just... my brother." Lenore kept laughing. "For all of his scheming, and plotting and evil... he's been reduced to... The Great and Terrible Peter Breslin. A fart in a cage."

The infected snarled at her and she laughed harder.

Mari scanned the room for a way to open the cages. They were high tech, the very latest in werewolf containment.

Lenore managed to contain herself long enough to point at the master console. "Over there."

"Would they really be so stupid as to use a code that you'd know?" Mari said.

"Fuck the code. Just bash the console. The doors will open." Lenore grinned.

"I don't want all the doors to open. Just yours and Warner's."

Lenore shrugged. "These fuckos aren't going to be a problem."

The howls that suddenly echoed from outside indicated that the fuckos would indeed be a problem.

Warner's whole body surged. It was as if his skin tried to crawl off his body. Or maybe just what was under it. The new version of Peter Breslin.

Mari knew they were running out of time.

And so was the Wendigo.

Goddessdamnit, where was she?

Mari shifted her claws and ripped out the console, and all three cages opened.

Mari expected an immediate bloodbath, but they were fixated on Warner. Lenore immediately headed over to the gun locker was loaded for bear.

Err... werewolf.

Although, nothing she did would make them stay dead. The Dark Champion had to devour them, but he couldn't exactly do that while hell on earth was ripping its way into the world from his insides out.

She had to get them away from him so he had time to regenerate.

A knot formed in the back of her throat and she went to Warner, helping him move from the cage to the corner of the room where his flesh began to tear and his bones shattered and tried to reform.

"Run, Mari. Get to safety," he said through grit teeth.

She looked up at him, love shining in her eyes. "I'll never be safer than when I'm with you, Warner Woolven."

"Mari, I don't know what you're planning, but don't."

She smiled at him. "But I have to." She kissed his cheek.

"Mari," he ground out and reached for her as she pulled away.

"Do you remember when you told me that I was too pretty to be of use?"

"Goddess, no. I was just..." he trailed off as another spasm ripped through him.

Mari's time was oh-so short.

"It's okay. I'm not reminding you now to punish you. It's important. Because I believed it then, but I don't now. I know what I can do. What my use is. It's to buy you time."

Warner reached for her, but she knew she couldn't be weak. She couldn't hide her face in his arms, or let her save her.

In this moment, it was her, or the rest of the world.

She knew what she had to do and what she had to choose. For him, for Lenore, for Noah... for the humans who didn't know about the things that went bump in the night.

For all the sacrifices who'd come before her.

She didn't understand why she'd feel the mating bond with Warner when his true mate would come back to him. Why would the powers do this to her?

Aside from the fact she must've burned down an orphanage and kicked puppies in a past life.

It was so she'd be willing to do this. To sacrifice herself in this moment. To give the Champion the time he needed to survive until the Wendigo came.

"I love you, Warner. Be happy."

Warner howled as the monster known as Peter Breslin finally tore through from the underworld, using Warner's flesh as the passageway.

Mari used her nails to tear open the skin on her wrists and the blood began to flow, hot and sweet.

All of the wolves' attention was suddenly focused on her. It was like flipping a switch.

The one who seemed to be the leader spoke. "Nice try, but it won't work," he snarled as a strange shift came over his face.

His teeth grew bigger, and more awful, somehow. As did the rest of him. They were adapting. Dear Goddess, she had to make herself run.

Lenore snickered. "No? I think it will. Look at you. You can barely contain your teeth. If you're not going to use them, put them away, big boy."

The wolf snarled at her, half-turning his face toward Lenore, but seemingly unable to break away from Mari completely.

"Uh, Mari. Mari?" Lenore questioned. "Your blood, it's not slowing. Your wounds aren't healing."

Mari knew that. She could feel it.

In truth, she'd known somehow they wouldn't.

When this plan had formed in her mind, she hadn't ever allowed that she'd survive. She'd never considered her superhuman healing ability. Her body had known before her conscious mind that something had changed.

"Come get me, fuckers." Mari forced her feet to move, to carry her to the door.

"I'll come for you. Stay alive, Mari." Warner lay, his sternum split open and a howling, ravening beast crawling from his body. "I swear it."

Peter roared and to Mari's intense dismay, he joined the hunt.

She could run faster as a wolf, but had less blood to spare. All that was left was her warrior form. It was always the hardest for her to attain.

Except now, it seemed to happen with a thought.

Her own howl joined the chorus of the damned and she ran. She moved at superhuman speed through the makeshift village the hunters had set up and many of them joined the chase.

The infected began to turn on each other, and the hunters who'd helped orchestrate Peter's return, Changing them to increase their numbers and to replace the comrades they ate to build their strength.

She had the vague notion that's what was going to happen to her.

Mari could only hope she'd be dead before it happened.

Which meant she needed to run until she had nothing left.

She grew cold first, her limbs beginning to become heavy and her lids weighted. Then the cold gave way to numbness. That numbness was the sweet spot she needed. It dulled her thinking, her fear, and let her move faster. Faster than she'd ever run before.

They were still on her trail.

The farther she ran, the more time she could give Warner and the Wendigo.

Peter gained on her.

She couldn't have that. Dear Goddess, not that.

But she was no match for the reborn devil as he ran her down. He tackled her to the ground, sending them both crashing down a rocky embankment. Mari kept waiting for the darkness to take her, but unfortunately, she was still all-too present when they came to a stop in the cool, clear water of a wide, shallow river.

"What a lovely birthday present," he said, his horribly twisted face so close to hers.

He looked like some caricature of a werewolf caught mid-shift. It was like really well-done horror movie makeup. Except it was all real. All him.

And all evil.

His red eyes were still shedding mucus and buried his snout at her throat, but the pain didn't come.

"You smell like flowers."

"You smell like shit," she managed. "If you're going to do it, just get it over with."

"I haven't decided how. Do I want to let you linger until Warner comes for you? Because he will come for you. The Dark Champion would damn the world for you. I could feel it in his bones, when I chewed through them."

"Don't be stupid." The darkness was closer now. The numbness was colder, somehow. "Even if he did feel that way, he would never put his own needs over that of the pack."

Peter snorted. "Is the world his pack now? Ridiculous."

Mari could see the truth in Peter's words. Yes, the world had become Warner's pack. Supe and human alike, and Mari thought it was beautiful. He was the savior the world needed.

So for these last few minutes, Mari could be the savior he needed.

She was honored to be part of it. To be of use.

"You're so pathetic. I don't know how to hurt you. You don't value yourself enough that I can take anything from you." He shook his head and spittle spattered her face.

"Or maybe I just know what's worth living for and dying for."

His teeth grazed her throat, tearing at the flesh, but not quite ravaging her. "Why aren't you pissed?" He peered closer at her, as if she was some kind of strange bug.

She was angry. Of course she was angry. She wanted to spend her life with Warner. She wanted to have pups with him. She wanted to have adventures with him. She wanted to help him bear the weight of the Dark Champion's mantle on his broad, strong shoulders.

She wanted more late nights with the other Woolven Brides. More of the sugar fairy's treats and trading secrets over wine at grown-up slumber parties. She wanted more family picnics where bone fairies sat with sugar fairies and vampires and dragons came to visit. She wanted to see her pups trailing after their Alpha, Noah.

She wanted to see her father again. She wanted to hug him so tight.

She wanted more days in Westwood's lab.

Mari wanted more of everything. She didn't want to give it all up.

Was it unfair? Massively.

But what could she do about it? Not a goddessdamned thing.

When she passed from this world, she'd be thinking about Warner. What he'd said. That he would still come for her, that he would find her.

That she was his one.

She'd take that with her and hold on it through the long dark.

Mari couldn't change the fact she was going to die her. She couldn't change that it would be Peter Breslin who took her life while inflicting as much pain and agony on her as he could. He'd drink it like a fine wine.

She was under no illusions that she was strong enough to keep him from that small, sick pleasure. No, Mari didn't handle pain well at all.

The only thing she really had a choice about was the memories she'd hold on to when her abused body surrendered.

And the satisfaction of knowing that Peter Breslin would breathe the air of this world just long enough to know he missed it before the Wendigo sent him straight back to the dark.

So she smiled at him.

"You won't be smiling when I finish tearing your throat."

Mari kept smiling.

"Fight me," he demanded.

The smile didn't waver.

As he tore out her throat, she hoped her death mask would remain a smile that would piss him off even when he rotted in hell.

❧ 17 ❧

Warner lay wrecked and miserable while his body knit itself back together.

"I'm going to kill him," he growled.

"Didn't you already try that?" Lenore said, as she shoved a headless body toward him. "Hurry up, eat this one before it can grow back. Plus, you need to keep up your strength."

"This is not somewhere I ever thought I'd be," he grumbled.

"Me either, boo. Me either. If I would've even suggested it during my hunter training, I'd still be looking for my teeth, but here we are." Lenore paused. "Do you still believe she's the one?"

"I was convinced," he said between bites. "But when she started bleeding..." he trailed off, stricken.

"The prophecy said she had to die to be reborn, too."

"I want to have hope, Lenore. I do."

"I understand. Wanting and having are two very different things."

"I have to get in touch with Blake. He needs to know this whole pack has been lost. If we don't survive, he and the Council needs an account of what happened. Otherwise, there will be war. Again."

"I'm mostly useless against these things. So I'll see if I can hack their comms. I can do that."

Lenore's words reminded him of Mari.

The way she'd said she could be of use.

His fingers curled up into fists.

She was the best thing that had ever happened to him and he hadn't gotten the chance to really tell her, to make her believe it.

The pain that throbbed and radiated throughout his body was nothing compared to the pain in his heart. The empty, gaping hole of nothing that was an ever-widening chasm.

The Dark Champion felt her loss acutely.

It was a strange and awful thing to love a woman with two hearts, and feel the loss of her in two souls.

He'd never felt this for Arianna. What he'd felt for her was a tiny, flickering tea light candle. It was warm, soft, and more like decoration.

This thing that burned for Mari, it was a cascade of fire, it was volcanic, it was the sun. It was utterly vital.

There was no way Mari wasn't the Wendigo.

And he wouldn't let her rise alone.

Warner struggled to his feet, and Lenore offered her arm to help him.

"That's my Dark Champion right there. Hell yeah."

"You're not going to tell me I need to heal?"

"You'll figure it out." Lenore grinned. "And you're gonna go get our girl, right?"

"Damn right."

"In all this One Mate, True Love stuff, don't forget you've got to wipe the rest of this infection off the face of the earth and stuff. Okay?"

"I mean, I guess." Warner shrugged and gave her a half-grin. "Damn hunters. Always wanting something."

"Fuckers. Every last one." She shook her head. "Swear to Goddess, I'm hanging up my guns after this."

Warner watched as the last bits of flesh on his gut stitched themselves back together, then said, "Wait, what?"

"I'm over it. Dark Champion has this hunting rogue things down."

"What are you going to do if you're not hunting? Take up knitting?"

"I might." She made a stabbing motion with pretend knitting needles. "I can still stab things with the needles." A soft look crossed her face. "I might take a vacation. With Luchtaine."

"You should."

Lenore looked around. "I can't believe I said that out loud. I can't believe I said it out loud and he didn't materialize like a fucking ghost stalker."

"Too bad he didn't. That would've actually been helpful."

"I can call him."

"If you want." He stretched, feeling his body move to accommodate his commands. The pain was gone. He was ready. "Let Blake know what's going on first, though. Report your fuckwit hunters, too, if you've the time. I'd love to see your mother's face."

"No, you really wouldn't." Lenore snorted. "Meet back here for cake and ice cream after the party?"

It was Warner's turn to snort, but his was much louder, and much wetter because his muzzle had erupted from his face and his warrior form was ready for the fight.

He could smell the pack. They smelled like a herd of cattle, but if they shat sulfur. The stink was rotten in his nose.

His senses honed in on them, those who walked, but should not be.

He could no longer see Lenore, or sense her. Part of his rational mind knew she was still there, but the Dark Champion had blocked her out.

Warner followed the trail of their stench, registering another scent, more delicate, and somehow more awful because he knew it was Mari's blood.

He followed it for miles.

She'd run so far, and so hard, his little mate.

His teeth elongated in his mouth, stabbing into his gums as rage filled him. Warner raged that she'd had to fight so hard. Raged that she thought that her only purpose in this life had been to buy him time. Raged that it was possible Peter had taken her from him.

He refused to allow that thought into his head. He pushed it out like the poison it was. Because he was going to find Mari, he was going to hold her close while she healed, and together, they were going to take down these abominations.

That was his plan for the immediate future.

For the long-term, he just wanted the time to love her as she deserved to be loved.

He leaped down the embankment easily, his powerful legs pushing him forward, and absorbing the shock-force as he landed and leaped again.

He smelled her death, it still hung in the air over the water.

Warner knew it had to happen if she was the Wendigo, but it still tore into him with sharper claws than Peter's had been trying to get out.

He threw back his head and howled his pain and his grief into the sky.

At the sound of his howl, the most base and primal sound of sorrow, the clouds gathered and crashed together to blot out the sky. Lightning bloomed in giant flashes and thunder split the atmosphere.

It was as if all of nature felt his grief, too.

He noticed that while he could scent the loss of her, that it wasn't stained with fear. Warner was so proud of her. Hope burned in his chest like a tiny sun.

He picked up Peter's trail again and he knew from the other wolf's gait, that he carried Mari with him. Warner followed him through a grassy field and into the woods. Warner realized the trail was leading back to the small village. They were probably crowning Peter king with Mari's body on display like some kind of trophy.

As he approached the outlying edge of the tiny settlement, sentries howled the alert, but Warner wouldn't be turned away.

He expected them to charge him, to try to take him down, but they didn't. They only howled. Until he neared the entrance to the town, the single road going in and out.

Then, braver wolves ran up to him, snapping with their teeth and slashing with their claws.

He'd get them all in turn, but if he stopped now to devour each one who came at him, it would make him full to bursting and it would slow him down.

Also, he never wanted a past-full stomach again.

Warner kept pushing forward until he'd moved into the town square, surrounded by infected wolves.

He finally saw her—Mari.

She'd been posed in the square on a throne of hay bales, like a macabre May queen. Her throat torn out, the skin splayed like curtains at a peep show to reveal her now bloodless insides. The sight of her, unmoving, her wounds unhealing, snuffed the burning flame of hope in his chest.

It left nothing behind but darkness.

Part of Warner was prepared to lie down next to her and go wherever she was. That was where he wanted to be. Where he needed to be.

But that would make her sacrifice for nothing and he wouldn't allow that. Not on any plane of existence.

"I'm curious," a voice echoed from a small storefront behind Mari. "Do you hunger for all the dead, or just infected dead?" Peter nodded to Mari.

"I'm taking her with me," he said.

"I'll allow it. I just want to know what you're going to do with her. Make a statue of her and worship her like you did Dead Saint Arianna?"

Warner knew that Peter was trying to make him angry, but he didn't understand why, where was the benefit?

"What's it to you, Breslin?"

Peter shrugged. "I don't know. Seems pretty important for you to come in here all alone."

"You can't hurt me any longer. Mari saw to that."

"She did, didn't she?" Peter's mouth turned down in a frown as he cast her a look. "Interesting. It's almost like she thought it mattered."

It did matter, but he wasn't going to waste his time arguing about it.

"I've been waiting for this mythical Wendigo to come and all I've got is a corpse and... you."

"I'll tear you apart," Warner promised.

"Mmm. There is that. You'll eat me again, too, I suppose? Do you think it'll work this time? Do you think I'll stay dead? Because I don't." Peter stepped closer to him. "But by all means. I kinda like it when your teeth tear into my meat. It's intimate. More intimate than I've ever been with a woman. Unless you count my teeth tearing into her." He jerked his head in Mari's direction. "It's not the same, though, after they're dead. Don't you think?"

Warner put aside his fury and went to Mari. He gathered her up in his arms and studied her face. The expression she wore in death was at utter odds with the now bloodless wound at her throat. It was all calmness and serenity.

If Warner didn't know better, he'd even call it a smile.

He pressed his lips to her forehead, oh-so-gently and he carried her back toward the way he came.

"You should devour her, Warner. Maybe your body will be her passage back from the land of the dead, too. Won't you try it? Even if it doesn't work, you'll get to keep her with you forever if you do."

He'd keep her with him forever anyway. She'd always live in his heart.

"Why are you so obsessed with this idea, Breslin? You're a sick fuck, you know that?"

"Says you, the eater of wolves."

"Jealous?" Warner tossed back.

"Obviously."

The other wolves began swiping at him again, taking tiny bites out of his flesh. He didn't care. They'd heal. As he carried Mari, he couldn't resist pressing his lips to hers one last time.

After he pulled back, he saw that the tiny split in her lip had healed.

So he pressed his mouth to a secondary wound on her throat and it too quickly healed.

Elation bloomed through him and he knew he had to get her out of there. They'd never let him resurrect her. They'd tear her apart first and she needed a body to come back to.

That was why Peter wanted him to devour her.

He suspected Mari was the Wendigo and if Warner devoured her, she'd no longer be a threat.

"Aw, the great Dark Champion doesn't want to play? Why not?" Peter called out and began walking after him. "Too bad, because I'm not done."

"Yes, you are."

Warner felt him approaching from behind and he closed his mouth over her wound, his teeth elongating into the cool flesh.

He hoped against hope this was what they needed. This would heal her and bring her back to him.

⚜

M ari awoke to a strange landscape.

It looked like the wilds of Nevada, if they'd been on Mars.

She was alone.

She sensed no animals, no small creatures, no insects. Nothing that lived was present. She'd never felt so incredibly alone.

The desolate landscape seemed to amplify that feeling. It was beautiful, but harsh and strange and filled with reds and oranges and browns. She'd give anything to see something green.

Being dead was every bit as awful as she imagined.

More so, because she thought when creatures passed from the daywalking world, they forgot their troubles. She did not leave hers behind. They came with her and Mari wished desperately she could see Warner, just to know he was okay.

That he won.

She wished again for something green and suddenly, a meadow burst to vibrant life before her and in the very center of that green meadow dotted with periwinkle and daisies, she saw a woman.

A woman she knew somehow, her presence so very familiar.

The woman sat with her legs crossed wearing strange looking leathers, and a bow slung across her back. Her hair was like a waterfall of midnight down her back and her chestnut skin was smooth and unmarred, except for the scar at her throat.

It bore the shape of claws.

The woman motioned for Mari to join her and she didn't hesitate to cross the soft, fresh grasses that felt so real beneath her bare feet.

"Maribella," the woman said, her voice low and husky. "Come sit with me and let me see your face."

She realized if she'd survived, her scar would've looked much like the one that this woman bore.

Maribella sat down next to her and allowed the woman to pull her head into her lap and she stroked Mari's hair in a familiar rhythm.

"My sweet little Maribella. What a powerful woman you've become. I'm so sorry I didn't get to see you bloom, but that was the tradeoff, I suppose. I get to be here now."

"I know you, but I don't," she said honestly.

"I'm your grandmother, child. My people called me Tala. I am here on behalf of the Great Mother. You know her as the Goddess."

The name struck a chord of recognition inside of her and it echoed like a golden bell.

"I did it, then? I saved Warner in time? Is everyone safe?"

Tala continued to stroke her hair. "Oh no, my child. Your work is not yet done. You must go back."

"Back?" she murmured. "I have nothing to go back to."

"You have your destiny."

"Me?" Mari swallowed the hope that rose up inside of her. "Am I..." she was almost too afraid to give it a voice. It was her greatest hope.

She wanted to be the Wendigo. She wanted not only to shoulder the responsibility with Warner, to make the world safer, but she wanted to live. She had so much she wanted to see, do, experience.

"Your fear isn't of the Wendigo." Tala sighed. "I wonder if it's because you haven't been told enough of the old stories to be afraid."

"I'm not afraid of Warner, and he's the Dark Champion. So why should I be afraid of the Wendigo?"

"The Wendigo has walked the earth much longer than any Dark Champion. Warner *is* the Dark Champion. It's as much a part of him as his wolf. The Wendigo is much different. She is a holy thing, and we are but the chosen to be her vessel."

She sat up and looked at her grandmother. "You were Wendigo?"

"Yes, and so are you. It's why you couldn't access your wolf. When I had your mother, I had already become the vessel and while she wasn't granted powers, you were. A gift for my service from the Great Mother, but your father, he didn't understand. He was afraid for you as all fathers are." Tala nodded as she spoke. "Doesn't make it okay, but he did for you what he thought would keep you safe."

"I know he did." She looked around. "Safe? I guess it doesn't get much safer than dead, does it?"

Tala gave her a gentle smile. "Do you hear him calling your name?"

She heard nothing. "No."

"Listen, child. Listen for the voice in the dark."

Then she could hear it, so faint, barely audible, but there. Warner, begging her to come back to him. Begging her to stand by his side.

Begging her to get the fuck up because he didn't want to do this without her.

He didn't just need her.

He wanted her.

There was magick in those words.

Tala's hands began to Change, and she held them out to Mari. "Take my hand, child, and with it, the gift of the Wendigo. Take her back to your world." Then she smiled, and didn't look the least bit grandmotherly. She looked all wolf with her sharp teeth bared. "And kick Breslin's ass back down to the pit he crawled out of. I'll be waiting. Along with the soul of every Wendigo vessel." She gnashed her teeth together.

Mari reached out and took her hands in her own.

The power of the Wendigo poured into her, filled her up and before she knew it, she flew through the sky like a rocket aimed at the sun.

Only it wasn't the sun, she knew she was flying from the world of the dead back to the world of the living.

She brought the Wendigo with her.

The first thing Mari felt was Warner's tongue on her wounds, and they stitched themselves up tight.

Air dove into her lungs, and with that breath of life, the Wendigo stretched inside of her, filling her arms, her legs, her eyes, her ears, and even the deep recesses of her heart.

The Wendigo bore an eternal love for her Dark Champions and was gentle with him, when she opened her eyes and touched his face.

Then she exploded to action.

On her feet, the world got a lot smaller. Or maybe it was just that she got a lot bigger. The infected were nothing to her. Ants scrambling from their little hill away from her foot.

A great roar echoed throughout the trees and Mari realized with a numb shock that the terrifying sound had come from her.

"Oh fuck me," Peter mumbled. "I never thought it would be you."

No one did, she supposed. She focused solely on him and her vision honed in on the pulse in his throat.

She knew before this day was done, she'd bathe in the fountain of his blood and devour him whole.

For she was the Wendigo, the vengeance of the Great Mother made flesh.

Mari ran him down and while he fought her, and the infected tried to make their stand, she tore through them as easily as a warm knife through butter.

She devoured a screaming Peter with one giant gulp. She'd wanted to make it last, to make him suffer, but she remembered her grandmother's promise.

And really, that's how the bad guys always lost. They tried to rhapsodize about their evil plans, or they hesitated.

Mari did nothing of the kind.

She simply opened her jaws and a hurricane from hell sucked him in and she swallowed.

Warner followed her into the action, obviously trusting her to do what she needed to do while he wreaked his own carnage.

They decimated the infected together, ensuring none escaped and none survived.

Infection contained.

After all they realized they'd won, their eyes met. She could see Warner swallow hard as he seemed to look for the right words.

She didn't need them, but she wanted them. So she waited for him to speak.

"Helluva first date, I guess." He grinned.

She ran to him and he swept her up in his arms.

"Goddessdamn, Mari. I thought I'd lost you."

"Me too. But I found me, and so did you."

He squeezed her tight. "Guess I was right, huh?" He was smug, but playful. "Told you that you were the one."

"I guess you did. But it's funny how no one can tell you your own worth, you've got to figure it out for yourself."

"And did you figure it out, my Mari? Do you know you're the world to me? That I love you?"

She pressed her lips together tightly. "I do."

His neck looked so appetizing, she just had to take a bite. Mari wanted her mark there for all the world to see. To know that Warner Woolven, the Dark Champion, was all hers. Not her puny human bite, but the bite of a powerful bitch. Her Wendigo bite.

Her teeth emerged, long and aching and she plunged them into his neck and shoulder.

Warner tightened his grip on her so that his nails became claws that dug into her back. "Keep doing that, and we're not going to make it home."

She licked at the place where she'd marked him. "We have important Wendigo/Dark Champion business to attend to, Warner, before we go home. We need to get started on our happily ever after."

"The werewolves never get a happy ending."

"That's why we're writing our own fairytale, Warner. A fairytale where no one is too pretty to be of use, or too old. A fairytale where—"

"—an old, curmudgeonly gray tail steals a beautiful young heiress but he's the one who ends up with his heart stolen? Yeah, I'm good with it."

"You better be. Because that's what we're doing."

He laughed. "Good to know. I think you need a bath first." Warner swiped his tongue against her neck.

She broke away from him.

"I don't know. I think maybe you have to catch me, first."

He growled low in his throat. "Woman..."

"Wendigo," she said with a grin. "Or maybe, just maybe, *I* want to catch *you*."

Warner gave a great, deep belly laugh. "Hell yeah."

And he took off running into the woods with Mari not too far behind him, ready to ravage him in all the ways they both wanted.

❧ 18 ❧

It was a midnight picnic with the whole Woolven Pack.

A great, long table had been conjured out on the south lawn overlooking the small town that sat in the protective shadow of Aphelion.

Westwood was busy fussing over various dragonlings, fairies, goblins, and Noah, while her new husband, the goblin-king Enoch looked on with a self-satisfied smile.

Gin, the sugar fairy sat much closer to the giant terror of a bone fairy and he showed her a new skull he'd affixed to his belt. This one had tried to kidnap a broom full of sugar fairies for his own nefarious purposes and Kasadya had stopped him. And cheerfully plucked his head from his body to bring to Gin. Gin, for her part, gave him another cupcake he couldn't eat. She thought it was a trade, but his black, fathomless eyes shone with something Mari would've called devotion. The little sugar fairy would realize it soon enough.

Drew and Emmie laughed together, his hand on her waist and their attention mostly for each other. After all the darkness and horror, it was good to see. They were talking about going back to Greece where they'd met.

Parker and Belle were elbowing each other under the table and

Parker couldn't stop smirking. Until Belle licked her finger and shoved it in his ear. "Gotcha, fucker." Parker was rather displeased by this turn of events, but he wouldn't be outdone. He didn't hesitate to pounce of her and shove her to the ground, tickling her mercilessly.

Noah and the other children decided this was a must-do activity and joined in.

Belle showed her vampire teeth, but that didn't stop anyone.

Tirigan, her terrifying vampire-god father looked on. "You okay down there?"

"Help," she cried.

"I think you're fine. You've got this," the scary bastard elbowed his current squeeze, Randi's father, David.

"I don't know. She's turning kind of red," David said. "When Randi turns that color, someone is pretty close to death."

Tirigan shrugged. "Eh, Parker likes to live dangerously, don't you, boy?"

Parker growled playfully, but when Belle nipped his finger, all the playfulness left him and something else altogether came over him.

"Gross, not at the table, Uncle Parker," Noah said.

"Then we should leave the table, eh?" Parker waggled his brows.

"I ought to smack your nose with a newspaper, Parker Woolven," Westwood interrupted. "There's cake."

"Cake?" Parker's attention was back on the table.

Belle just rolled her eyes.

Blake sat at the head of the table with Randi by his side. "It's so good to have all of my family here to celebrate our peace. As long as it lasts."

"I'm here to make sure that it lasts a long time," Alpha DeVaughn said, approaching the table.

"So glad you could come," Blake said and embraced him.

Mari was frozen in place. She hadn't expected to see her father. She'd missed him, she'd wanted his counsel, but she hadn't known quite what to say.

Alpha DeVaughn turned to Mari and he didn't say anything. Instead, he held his arms open and Mari flew into them, hugging him tight.

He wasn't an overly affectionate creature, her father. So his public display meant so much to her.

She missed the comfort of him. The way he smelled. The way she felt like the whole world had to obey his commands when he held her tight.

"You channel her well," he said quietly. "Did you get to see your mother?"

"No. I saw Tala."

"Ahh. Tala. A terrifying wolf if there ever was one. I had to run her gauntlet to win your mother's hand even though we were mates. She wouldn't tolerate anything less. I wish you could've known her."

"She spoke... gently of you."

"Did she?" He laughed. "I'm surprised."

Oceans of things passed between them in that moment. Regret, sorrow, and loss, but on the heels of those things came joy, hope and love.

"If you have time soon, I'll tell you about all of it. If you still want to hear it."

"I do." Mari nodded and hugged him again. "I'm so glad you're here."

Alpha DeVaughn held out his hand to Warner and Warner shook it with a very serious expression on his face.

"I knew you were the one for her."

"Then why did you betroth her to Parker?" Warner blurted.

"Eh, I had a dream. These things in our family have a way of working out, you know."

"I can see that." Warner shared a look with Mari.

"In the future, if anyone cares about my opinion," Blake coughed, "I'd like to be kept in the loop. When things happen."

Randi waved him off. "Yeah, yeah." Then her eyes went wide.

Mari was sad Lenore wasn't with them, but she knew she'd see her soon. She was on the first vacation she'd ever taken.

With Luchtaine.

They'd gone to Antarctica. Mari couldn't wait for pictures.

"What, what is it?"

"The baby is coming."

"What?" Blake asked. "Right now?"

"No, in two weeks. You said you wanted to be informed. I'm informing you. Baby is coming."

Westwood clapped her hands together and let out an evil wicked witch cackle. "Oh, perfect." She got up and ushered Randi toward the house, with Blake, the Woolven Alpha, big, important wolf that he was, trailing alone behind them managing not to look like he was about to lose his shit.

Warner looked at her. "He's totally freaking out."

"Can we do anything to help, do you think?"

"Nah. She'll do all the work. Westwood will ease her pain, and there'll be a new Woolven at the table soon."

"Maybe more than one," Mari said with a grin.

Warner looked like he'd been punched. "What?"

"Why not? It could happen."

He exhaled heavily. "It could, but should it? I mean... what we are."

"Our pups would be amazing. But I want to practice making them some more, just to make sure we get it right."

Mari got up from the table. "Wanna play Stealing the Heiress again?"

Warner pushed back from the table and got up to follow her. "That's your favorite game, isn't it?"

"It's kinda hot when you rip the roof off the limo with your bare paws." Mari licked her lips.

"You're not going to make it to the limo, pretty one."

"Wanna bet?" Mari's eyes flashed red and she ran, thinking the whole way this was better than anything she could've imagined.

This was her fairytale.

he End.

THE WOLLSTONECRAFT LEGACY

Welcome to my new series Love in the Time of Monsters. Enjoy this free novella.

When Dr. Elizabeth Wollstonecraft kicks off what could be a zombie apocalypse, she discovers the legacy of her name isn't the shame she thought it was, but the ultimate weapon that calls a monster of legend to her side, and reanimates her heart.

PATRON SAINTS OF IMPERFECTION

"Since childhood I've been faithful to monsters. I've been saved and absolved by them because monsters are the patron saints of our blissful imperfections."-Guillermo del Toro

CHAPTER ONE

Kythnos Island, Greece
Bureau 7 Kythnos Installation

Dr. Elizabeth Wollstonecraft almost jumped out of her skin when the door to the lab buzzed.

"Hey, it's Margie. I brought you some lunch since you didn't make it to the mess."

She pressed the access button and the young, fresh-faced girl brought in an aluminum tray with a lid.

"It's that smoked salmon with the pineapple mango salsa you like so much. I knew you wouldn't want to miss that." Margie offered her a wide smile.

"Thanks." Elizabeth's stomach rumbled, reminding her that she hadn't eaten yet. "I was really caught up in my work. I think we're close to something big."

Margie leaned over and put her chin in her hands. "I can't wait until I get to play with diseases, too."

"Do you want to see?" Elizabeth offered her the electron microscope.

Margie pressed her face to the eyepiece. "I have no idea what I'm looking at, but it's cool."

"If it's what I think it is, then I'll tell you all about it." Elizabeth grinned back at her.

"Thanks." The girl smiled. "You're the only one who takes me seriously."

"Bureau 7 takes you seriously. Otherwise, they wouldn't have paid for you to move to Greece and agreed to pay for school. You just have to finish your tour in 'work study.' All of us working class folk have to do whatever we can to pay our way. I believe in you."

Margie hugged her. "Don't forget, this weekend you're coming to the mainland with me for Tony's birthday party."

"I wouldn't miss it."

"Ah, we have company?" Dr. John Polidori emerged from his office and into the lab, smiling his too wide grin.

Margie shivered. "I was just leaving."

"No tray for me, I see? I feel you just don't love me anymore, Margie, my love."

"We both know you wouldn't eat it." Margie turned to her. "I'll let you get back to work. See you Saturday."

Elizabeth smelled the salmon and took a bite. She saw that Margie had tucked a couple gyros and pita chips with saganaki inside as well. Luckily, the saganaki wasn't still on fire. The flaming cheese dish was one of her favorites.

"I get the feeling she doesn't like me."

"I get the feeling you like that she doesn't like you."

"You may be right there." He peered over her plate and wrinkled his nose. "You know, you really should go eat in the mess. Get away from the lab now and then. Nothing will happen without you. I promise."

"I know," she answered, but Elizabeth had been too fascinated by the war being fought under the electron microscope to stop for lunch.

She'd been working with prions, proteins that were thought to act as a protector for cells in the central nervous system. When these proteins became misfolded, the end result was damage to cells that culminated in neurodegenerative diseases like Creutzfeldt-Jakob in humans and bovine spongiform encephalopathy, or "mad cow," as it was more commonly called.

Her work had reached a brick wall until she'd been tapped by Bureau 7 to work for their science division. Since coming to Kythnos, she'd seen results. Elizabeth supposed working for a secret government agency that handled ghosts, goblins, and everything that went bump in the night had to have its bennies.

With Bureau 7 resources, she'd managed to reprogram those misfolded proteins. Basically, to remind them of their purpose, so they'd continue doing their job. Instead of interfering with synapse function, they'd cause new pathways to be built.

Right now, the newly programmed prions were attacking cells she'd taken from a glioblastoma, a malignant brain tumor. They weren't just attacking, they were consuming, devouring, and what they left in its place were healthy astrocytes, the cells that formed the glioblastoma.

Euphoria washed over her in waves. Making this kind of discovery, it was better than sex. Better than anything. It was why she worked in the field that she did. She wanted to make a difference.

And she wanted the Wollstonecraft name to bring more to the table than visions of a tragic girl who wrote about an even more tragic monster. Her mother was a noted activist, but no one remembered her name. Not until interns went digging to come up with "10 Facts You Didn't Know About XYZ."

Elizabeth was determined to make her mark, to create something the world couldn't ignore. The headline wouldn't read "Mary Wollstonecraft Shelley's Descendent Cures Disease." It would be "Dr. Elizabeth Wollstonecraft Cures Brain Cancer."

Most anything would be better than that. Especially going into the medical field, she'd taken her share of jeers about her name. For med students, they hadn't been very bright. Elizabeth had corrected them on more than one occasion that it wasn't a "Frankenstein." That was the name of the doctor, not the monster. And of course, it had been tossed back at her that she would know.

And she did know. She knew a lot of things.

Success was so close; she could taste it on the tip of her tongue like spun sugar.

She peered down into the electron microscope again.

"From the look on your face, I'd say we have some new data," Dr. John Polidori said.

"We do! Those vampire stem cells have had an amazing impact. Look!" She offered her place in front of the microscope to John.

A year ago, she'd never have thought to say anything about vampires in conjunction with science. Vampires weren't real. Or so she'd believed then.

Yeah, no. Wrong. They were as real as she was. It hadn't taken her long to accept it as fact because, as a scientist and a doctor, when one was faced with an inconvertible truth, one adapted. It was the only logical answer.

She'd seen vampires, met them. Elizabeth was sure the doctor she worked with now was one. She'd recognized his name. Elizabeth hadn't called him on it, because he hadn't said anything about her name. So, why bring it up? His dead or undead status didn't make him any less of a man of science.

The commlink buzzed and Elizabeth and Polidori exchanged a nervous glance.

"Seems they do keep up on things here." His hand hovered over the button. "Ready?"

"As I'll ever be."

Executive Director of Science and Tech, Mae Lin's face loomed on the gigantic screen in front of them. "On behalf of Director Roanridge, we send our congratulations. This was the breakthrough we've been looking for. We'll be moving to human and inhuman trials immediately."

This was unheard of. It was unethical. They needed to reproduce these results again and again, they needed years of data before moving to human trials. But this was Bureau 7, and they operated outside the laws of men or gods. She knew this was wrong. She wanted to say so, but found she couldn't move her mouth with the cold, sharp eyes of the Executive Assistant Director boring through her.

"Is that a problem, Dr. Wollstonecraft?"

She debated how best to answer. "Protocol—"

"We don't have time for protocol. The cells you're working with right now are from Isla Roanridge."

The Director's wife.

"Your volunteers will be arriving within the hour." EAD Lin smiled at her. "We've been waiting for this. I trust you won't disappoint us?"

EAD Lin didn't really want an answer. If she had, she'd have stayed on the comm and waited for one.

Elizabeth scrubbed a hand over her face. "This doesn't feel right."

"What did you think you'd signed up for when you took this job?" John asked her. "Just look at it like this. Usually, you present your results to a board. You apply for funds, for grants. You have the money. The board said yes."

"We don't have enough information to move to human trials. We both know what these neurodegenerative diseases can do. If we infect people with this, and what happened just now was a fluke, we've murdered them."

John took her hand gently, as if she were a child asking about the monsters in the dark. "It's a better fate than whatever else Bureau 7 has in store for them. Or ugly death waiting for them with these other illnesses. I guarantee that half of these people don't know their own name, let alone where they are or what's happened to them. You'll be the cure for their pain one way or another, Dr. Wollstonecraft."

This wasn't what she wanted. "How are our supplies?"

"You mean do we have enough pentobarbital to put them down if it fails? We do." Polidori began gathering files. "You should know, the other half of our experiment group? The ones who do know what's going on? They're all dead men walking."

"What do you mean?"

"Death penalty cases slated for execution. Don't get too soft in your feels over them. They've done terrible things." John smiled. "Terrible, terrible things."

That didn't mean they deserved this, but Elizabeth didn't speak. Instead, she peered back down through the electron microscope and saw that the glioblastoma had been obliterated. All that was left was healthy, functioning, living cells.

Cells that should've been long dead.

Elizabeth wasn't sure anyone was ready for the effect this would have on a human being. Her gut knotted with fear, but coiled around that fear was something she was ashamed of.

Excitement.

The curiosity that had pushed her toward this field and the drive to succeed that made her accept this job also had a dark side. The end should not justify the means, but sometimes, it did. She didn't like to stop and examine that in herself, but she had to.

If this went sideways, she couldn't claim ignorance. She'd have to own her part. It was her hands administering the drug. No one could force her to do it. There was always a choice.

Elizabeth would like to say that it was a hard choice, that she was going to wrestle with it and ultimately decide that her ethics were more important, but they weren't. She knew the Director's pain. Her own mother had died of a brain tumor.

"Having a bit of a crisis, are you, Elizabeth?" Polidori fixed his predator's eyes on her and, for the first time, she felt like prey.

"Maybe I am."

"Did you think we were the only team working on this project?" His tone was gentle—too gentle. Almost as if he pitied her and she was a child wandering in the dark.

Maybe he was right, because she had thought this was her project. "Of course I did. I'm the one who pitched it to EAD Lin."

"Who knows how many little research facilities like this Bureau 7 has? How many minds they have working on the same problem? You may have pitched this version of the idea, but they've been working with prions for years. Since the 60's and Gajdusek. You're the one who managed to reprogram them, though."

A cold sense of betrayal washed over her, but she stuffed it down. It wasn't on Bureau 7 to give her the rundown of every project they had in development, even though it felt like Polidori had been laughing at her. This wasn't about her. It had to be about the science.

His regard didn't seem so remote or condescending anymore. He was just John again. "Hey, chin up. You've made strides where no one else has. You're still the one who gets to move forward with the research. Don't let something as silly as human morality keep you from accomplishing something great."

She pressed her lips together. "Why didn't you tell me?" Elizabeth saw something in his face and spoke again. "If you tell me it's a need to know basis and I didn't need to know, I'm going to kick you."

John laughed. "It's like many things between us, I thought it was understood. You're a brilliant woman, Elizabeth." He left the rest unspoken, just like the knowledge that passed between them.

Warmth suffused her at his praise. In his position, she wondered if she'd still be able to see the world as he did. As something to explore and discover. Part of what made her job hard was lack of time. There was never enough time to do everything that needed to be done, or everything she wanted to do. The hands on the clock always seemed to be spinning. But what if they weren't? If she had nothing but time, what would she do with it?

"Did I render you speechless, dear Elizabeth, with my compliment?" His smile was warm and genuine, no trace of the predator, only John.

"I was thinking of other things unspoken. Those that I know to be true." She referred to the fact he was a vampire.

"Shall we speak of them now, in this moment before the fall?"

She knew exactly what fall he spoke of. This moment, it was brand new. It was a beginning. It was infancy. It was innocence. What came next was... something else. Something that would make this time inaccessible, even in memory because it would change them irrefutably. "No, I don't suppose they matter any more now than they did then."

"I must. Just this one thing. You remind me of her." His regard was keen, as if even now, he was stacking and weighing her merit.

"Of Mary?" Something in her rebelled. She was so tired of being compared to her by people who didn't actually know either of them, but this creature who did? A million times worse. She wasn't a silly little girl running off to marry a tragic, aged poet twice her age. She was a doctor, a scientist.

"I know that's not what you want to hear, but yes. She had an insatiable curiosity. A certain fire. Once she set her sights on something she wanted, there was nothing that could stand in her way."

"But all she wanted was a man. I've got bigger plans."

"Are you sure about that?" Polidori eyed her. "Maybe she'd be just as disappointed with her legacy as you are."

"Really?"

"She wanted to be a doctor for the same reasons you did. Her mother died of a brain tumor. Seems the Wollstonecraft line is rotten with them."

He was a master manipulator. She knew his words had been designed to push her forward, to jump into this aberration with both feet. Elizabeth had made her choice, but not because Polidori told her to. Or implied that if she didn't, she'd be the one with the brain tumor.

"Then why wasn't she? Why she did she spend her holidays at debauched house parties and chasing after a married man?"

"I'm surprised at the moral judgment in your tone."

"She was a child. A silly child that wrote a silly book."

Polidori seemed all predator again. "There are things you don't know about that night. Things no one knows. Mary trained as a doctor in secret. That's why we were all together that night."

"And the orgy, don't forget that part." Elizabeth rolled her eyes.

"So we engaged in a bit of fun, the four of us. What does that matter?" Polidori smiled, his teeth too white, too perfect. "I wanted to change them, you know. Bring them with me on the rest of this journey, but George wouldn't hear of it and Percy was taken from us much too soon." Polidori was silent for a long moment before casting a sly glance in her direction. "And Adam. He wouldn't allow me near Mary with those thoughts in my head."

Who was Adam? But she didn't ask, because she could see how badly he wanted her to. He was so eager to share this information with her, to make her dig it out of him. She refused to indulge him.

She began gathering her papers. The subjects from the mainland would be there any moment.

"Don't act as if I haven't caught your interest. Come now, Elizabeth. Ask me. You've seen the scars on my biceps. You know you're curious."

"Of course I am, but you'll tell me in your own time. Or you won't. I'm not going to dance for you."

"But you do it so prettily."

"How does anyone not know you're a vampire? You're textbook." She shook her head.

He laughed. "My apologies, my dear. It seems I can't help myself from taking advantage of your good nature. You must forgive me."

Elizabeth rather liked his old world manners, even if he could be a bit of a shit. "I guess. Tell me." She sighed.

"Hmm." He inspected her again. "Now that I revisit the subject, I don't know that you'll believe me."

She narrowed her eyes, and he laughed again. "You're too much fun." He removed his lab coat and began unbuttoning his shirt.

She'd seen his scars, yes. Never up close, only in passing. She'd been curious as to what could've possibly made them, because it was obvious they'd been inflicted post-transformation. All of their human ills were obliterated when they were turned. Their skin was like an infant's, perfect. Unmarred.

As he revealed his flesh to her, she was able to see the scars under the harsh fluorescent lights of the lab. Twin marks showed on each side. It looked for all the world as if the giant hands of God had gripped him there, and it had been seared into his flesh for all eternity.

Burned and bruised, purple and raging. If he were human, she'd have guessed whatever happened to him had only occurred last night. They weren't scars in the traditional sense.

"Do they pain you?" She reached out a hesitant hand to touch them, but dropped it to her side.

"Only if I think about things I shouldn't," he said cryptically.

"Like what kinds of things you shouldn't?" She wondered just what exactly would register on John Polidori's list of restricted things. It didn't seem like he denied himself much.

"Things like you. What your blood would taste like."

Before her eyes, the marks on his arms began to glow as if they'd been lit from a fire that burned beneath the skin.

"Why are you thinking about my blood, Dr. Polidori?" Had she mistakenly as*sumed she was safe with him?*

*"Just to pr*ove a point." The flares died down.

Her brain suddenly made the connection. Adam wouldn't let me...

things I shouldn't... The only thing she had in common with Mary Wollstonecraft Shelley was a name and a bloodline.

The pathway that lit inside her head was impossible, yet it seemed to be the only logical answer.

The silly little book was more than a book. The Modern Prometheus was real and tied to her through blood. It would explain why Bureau 7 had been so keen to get her. She was good at what she did, but there were those who were better. She wasn't well-known, or a sought after name. Not in the academic sense.

She couldn't figure out exactly what she brought to the table that had caused them to agree to her salary requirements when they could've had someone just as good for less money. Someone with even looser ethics than her own.

That was what made it real: simple fiscal logic.

It was something she'd suspected when they first came knocking—that their recruitment fervor had something to do with Mary and the monster.

Only, right now, looking at Polidori, she wondered who the real monster was.

"Figured it out, have you?"

"Maybe."

"They want him, you know. Bureau 7. You've always been bait. Beautiful and brilliant, but bait." Polidori slid into his shirt and buttoned it.

"What's your role to play, Doctor?"

"Only what I've been doing. To work with you on this project. To lure Adam. I told them they should simply tell you. That if they gave you project head, you'd get him here of your own volition."

Elizabeth didn't know how she felt about that and wasn't sure she wanted to examine it. "What do you get out of it?"

"George, of course. Your work with Adam coupled with this project? Reanimation and immortality, my dear." He advanced on her, but his touch was gentle when he squeezed her arm. "You're going to give me back the love of my life. With these prions, you've unlocked something that's defeated me for hundreds *of years*. I'm not sure if I'm jealous or in awe. Perhaps a bit of both."

The comm buzzed. "Subjects inbound. Code Blue, Dock Five."

Shit. Code Blue meant death. "Link us to onboard medical."

Static buzzed over the comm, and the raging sound of the helicopter. "Middle-aged white male, unknown cardiac event. Unable to resuscitate."

Elizabeth didn't know what to do with him. They weren't prepared for this. "Put him in Lab 2."

"You'll want him in a containment unit," the voice over the comm said. "He's already been dosed with PrPM3."

PrPM was her synthesized refolded prion.

Just what the fuck was PrPM3?

Nothing good.

She looked at Polidori who shrugged. "Bring him to the main lab."

"ETA in five."

CHAPTER TWO

Trieste, Italy
Miramare Castle

He'd spent his days in the bowels of the castle, in secret passages that time, architectural plans, and modern man had forgotten.

But it wasn't like it used to be. He wasn't hiding, not really.

He hadn't been chased into the pit of hell by an angry mob of villagers carrying pitchforks. No, he had a job looking after the castle, making repairs, and keeping everything in working order for the tourists that wandered the halls.

Adam enjoyed his work. It was simple, but fulfilling. These days, if someone caught sight of him, they didn't scream or run. People smiled at him and told him he'd done a good job. If they saw the scars on his wrists or around his neck, or any of the other things that made people fear him in the past, they said nothing.

What Adam especially enjoyed about Miramare was the long evenings on his boat. Fishing for his dinner, preparing it. Eating it while the gentle waves rocked the boat and drinking one of the many

SARANNA DEWYLDE

bottles of wine people had given him in exchange for his masonry or other skills.

He didn't have much use for money. Even this boat, he'd taken it in trade. He wasn't a man, not anymore, and therefore had no use for most things in the world of man.

This new age made him wonder if perhaps he'd been mistaken. Until hunters for various groups found him, wanted to study him. If only they'd ask, and not try to take his freedom, he'd share the knowledge of his flesh.

Only they didn't ask. They wanted to take. Just like his maker.

No, he'd stay in the dark until the world forgot about him again.

He both feared and yearned for the day the bloodline was extinct.

Adam knew they were the reason for his existence. Perhaps when they expired, so would he, but he didn't fear death. He feared slavery, imprisonment. The theft of his free will.

He'd done horrible things in service to the Wollstonecraft bloodline, murder perhaps not even being the worst.

For the last month, the tingling at the back of his neck that always precipitated the loss of his freedom, the call to arms to defend, protect, and serve the Wollstonecrafts had become an ever more intensifying itch.

Adam hadn't thought little Elizabeth would be a problem.

He'd been there the day her mother died. He'd sensed her distress, her need of him. He'd gone, only to find the small girl child sitting alone in the hospital waiting room, sobbing into her doll's hair.

She'd been so small then, her blue eyes large and luminous. Corn silk hair in two ponytails. She could've been a doll herself. "My mama is gone," she'd said.

He'd sat down beside her, unsure of what to say. For someone such as he, immortal, the ages passed. People changed. People died. He stayed the same.

She didn't need him to speak. She'd clambered up his massive lap, and planted herself there, tugging on his arm—wanting him to embrace her. So he had. It was what she needed and what he was bound to provide.

He kept thinking someone was going to see him with this child and

168

think all the wrong things. Someone was going to come and rip her away from him, but they didn't. No one came.

Little Elizabeth Wollstonecraft was all alone in the world. The last of her line. He'd known a kind of relief then. He'd been heartsore for her, the little lost girl, but a kind of peace bloomed inside of him to know that this was almost over.

He'd checked up on her a few times—whenever that tell-tale tingle on the back of his neck made itself known—and he'd always arrived just in time. When she was a student at Carnegie Mellon attending a mixer, he'd arrived just in time to see a young man add something to her drink.

Adam hadn't seen Elizabeth as the grown woman she was, because in his eyes, she was still very much the small, helpless, big-eyed child with no one in the world but him.

That was a murder that he carried no guilt for and when he thought about it even now, it gave him a sense of satisfaction. A job well done.

His fingers curled into fists. No one would hurt Elizabeth. She was the last and he wouldn't fail.

He thought about her again. She'd seemed so different than all of the others.

Flashes hit him *hard and fast*. If *he*'d been human, they'd have been called "migraines." But he was just a monster who inflicted pain, he wasn't supposed to feel it.

She was in a lab with John Fucking Polidori.

Adam snarled past the discomfort, the electricity crackling around his head like lightning. He forced himself to be calm. She was safe with Polidori, at least from his fucking leech teeth. The burns on his arms would make sure of that. Even with all the distance between them, the lightning would find him and turn him to ash if he tried to drain Elizabeth.

But that wasn't the only danger.

He could see the paths unfolding before them, and perhaps that was his purview as a monster and not a man, but if she chose to continue what she was doing, Elizabeth Wollstonecraft could unleash an armageddon unlike anything this world had ever seen.

She and Polidori were meddling where mortals ought not to trespass.

Adam himself was evidence of such things.

For a moment, he considered sitting back in the bowels of the castle and letting the world spin as it would. After all, why did it fall to him to save the dumb, lumbering, cruel beasts from themselves? They'd never done anything for him.

The world would be a much more beautiful place, the planet so healthy and green, if the talking apes who liked to play God were obliterated. No more hunts, no more fear, no more war. No more starving children. No more torture. No more oil spills, or whole species of animals wiped from the face of the planet that was meant to nurture them.

None except one, the parasite known as man.

But he couldn't get the memory of little Elizabeth out of his head. The way she'd turned to *him for safe*ty and comfort without hesitation. Without fear.

She wasn't a child anymore; she was a woman grown who made her own choices. She didn't need a champion or a defender.

Goddamn it.

It was the small things that did him in. The helpless things. The pitiful things.

He sighed. Adam could never turn away a stray—and that's what she was, a stray trying to make her way in a world of those who belonged.

Alone.

He knew what it was be alone. To be lost and searching for something.

The human race was lucky he was bound to this particular human. For her, he would save them. For her, he would change the tide.

All because of the kindness she'd shown him once, a very long time ago, when in her moment of grief, a child could've forced his hand. A child could've forced him to give his gift and raise the dead.

Instead, she hadn't asked him for anything but the comfort of his arms around her while she cried.

Yes, for that, he'd save the goddamn world.

Lightning flashed and crackled, tearing through his body and bringing with it images of exactly where she was.

The island was beautiful, but the signage on the impossibly high stone walls, the electrified razor wire behind it was not.

Bureau 7.

He'd be walking into the lion's den. They were chief on the list of those who hunted him, who wanted the secrets of his flesh. Who thought nothing of taking what they wanted. He'd killed more than one of their bounty hunters.

That extra sense told him she was on the isle of Kythnos. If the wind was with him, he'd make it in less than a day. That would be cutting it close.

If the wind was against him, it would take two.

Perhaps he'd leave it up to the great mother, if she wanted to shake off the human parasites like fleas?

Part of him still wanted to give this choice over to a higher power. He wished he believed in that, but he didn't. He'd seen no evidence of the divine in all his long years. Only the earth beneath his feet, the sky overhead, and man, a talking ape throwing his own shit at the wall in the dark.

Adam needed to gather his supplies, mostly making the boat ready for human occupation. He didn't need the creature comforts, but Elizabeth might. She'd need a new identity as well, because if this went down like he feared, she'd be number one on Bureau 7's shitlist. He wasn't going to go to all this trouble to stop the apocalypse just so they could decide she was a liability and take her out.

Adam put in a call to his employer, leaving a message that he would be *gone for* several days for a family emergency and proceeded to outfit the boat. The sooner he could set sail, the better. He wouldn't wait for the tide.

As soon as he'd gathered what he needed aboard the No Stars, he started the engine on the oceanvolt, an electric and solar powered generator that harnessed the energy he created sailing—just enough to propel him out into the open sea and then he'd be using wind power all the way.

He wondered if she'd remember him, because it seemed through all these long years, he'd never stopped thinking about her.

Adam was sure, if she remembered him at all, it would be gray and fuzzy. Perhaps she'd already dismissed it as a dream.

Or a nightmare.

Those had a way of coming true.

Because it occurred to him that this was a ploy, a plot to get him to Kythnos. Polidori knew what 7 wanted from him and he could've filled Elizabeth's head with all kinds of nonsense.

The monster Polidori spoke of in his ever so reassuring tones might not have even registered as the same one who'd held her hand as a child.

Not that it mattered.

He was going.

Soon, Bureau 7 would have more on their plate than they were prepared to manage, he was sure.

A zombie apocalypse would put a strain on anyone's resources.

CHAPTER THREE

T hings that Dr. Elizabeth Wollstonecraft was prepared for while conducting an autopsy: strange sounds, strange smells, odd variations in what people thought the human body should look like, and all the nitty gritty parts of being human—including bowel and bladder evacuation upon death.

Those things had never affected her.

The corpse on the table in front of her was something different, mainly because of the erection.

Most death erections were caused by a violent death that damaged major blood vessels causing priapism—the most common of these to cause the condition being hanging or strangulation. Her John Doe shouldn't have been subjected to either.

She'd been led to believe that it was the injection of PrPM3.

Elizabeth examined his throat and found ligature marks.

What the actual hell was going on?

Polidori leaned over his work and moved quickly, scraping under the John Doe's fingernails, drawing a blood sample and preparing the bone saw. "We need to get a look at his brain as soon as we can."

"Wait, he's been strangled. He was murdered," Elizabeth said.

"Was he?" Polidori looked as if he already knew that.

"Just tell me what's going on. Stop with the surprises. I can't do my job effectively without all the facts." Elizabeth gripped the side of the table, the cool metal grounding her and reminding her to breathe.

"Get a load of his Angel Lust." He nodded to the erection.

"Yes, I saw that. That's why I was checking for ligature marks, and I found them," Elizabeth said, exasperated.

The hand on the table jerked.

Elizabeth wasn't fazed. While muscle movement after death was rare, it wasn't unheard of. Neither was the sudden vocalization. The long, dry, death rattle that was simply air leaving the lungs.

What was unheard of, however, was when she pressed the scalpel to his chest, his eyes opened and he grabbed her wrist.

Elizabeth wasn't ashamed to admit that she almost shit her pants.

She shrieked and Polidori grabbed him, pried his fingers from around her wrist, breaking them as he did so.

PrPM3 had done something to this man, something that made him not living and not dead.

His eyes were all white, yet not sightless. They tracked her. His jaw creaked and cracked as it separated, much like a snake's as he dove for her arm. Venom dripped from newly sharp teeth—he had a mouth like a buzz saw.

"Elizabeth, if you'd please exit using Strategy A, I'll follow. The manacles will hold him until we're free."

As he spoke, the manacles in question clamped around the struggling cadaver's wrists and ankles, even his neck. The dead man turned his head at an unnatural angle to look at her. There was a rage in his unseeing eyes, something dark and unholy.

Fear knotted around her, and she found herself frozen to the spot.

This, what they'd made, it was wrong. "The phenobarbital," she began.

"You have to understand, we need to study these specimens in real time. I thought you understood that now."

"Goddamn it, Polidori."

"I thought we agreed I didn't need to read you any more nursery rhymes? Now, please. Do as I've asked. This one is stronger than we anticipated, and the manacles won't hold him long."

She pressed her lips together and looked between the escape and Polidori. "I won't leave you alone with him."

"Oh, my dear, I'm dead. He can't hurt me. But you... he could hurt you very much. He's obviously venomous, but I don't know if he's infectious. I don't believe that's how you imagined the end of your day."

He was right. She did as he asked, trying not to think about what else he hadn't told her or what other horrors awaited them. Elizabeth could do that later. Right now, she needed to get herself to safety, to the room beyond this containment unit.

They'd known what they'd done, what was going to happen. It was why the transport team had left so quickly. They'd dropped their parcels and evacuated the island like it was...

She got herself on the other side and, as soon as she was secure, Polidori released the thing.

He broke through the manacles as if they were nothing more than paper.

Jesus, it was strong. She wondered if the containment unit would be able to hold him. She ran back over all the exit routes from the installation, the safehouses and hiding places they'd shown her on the tour.

This was all supposed to be worst case scenario, something that happened due to forces beyond their control—not something they'd engineered on purpose.

She cringed at her own naiveté. Had she ever really believed such a thing? Deep down in the dark places of her heart where only truth could breathe?

No.

Now was the time for protocol.

She watched as it ignored Polidori, as if he was inconsequential to the thing. It followed in her steps, like a dog sniffing out her trail, and tracked her to the door. It dropped to all fours and licked the floor, venom and spittle pooling at the corners of its mouth. It gnawed on the doorframe with those horrible nightmare teeth. Not getting the result it wanted, it lifted its nose to the air, scenting.

Polidori eased his way around the room, edging toward the door. Waiting for it to explore some other avenue.

It seemed like hours they stood there, frozen. In reality, she knew it had only been seconds. Her fingernails had cut half-moon wounds into her palms and, when Polidori moved toward the exit, she held her breath.

His fingerprint opened the door and suddenly, the creature turned its head and darted for him, moving faster than she thought possible.

Her idea of what a reanimated corpse could do had been shaped by Hollywood, and this was a thousand times more awful. It seemed as if he was more sentient than she would've thought, with deductive reasoning.

The idea of a mindless hungry automaton was terrible, but put human cunning behind it with only a primal need to feed, and the possibilities were the stuff of nightmares.

It knew she was there. It still had no interest in Polidori, only that his fingerprint could open the door.

John made it into the decontamination sally port and, after he'd been rendered safe, he stepped through to the observation room where she waited.

With dawning horror, she watched as the creature put his finger up to the door as Polidori had, mimicking his actions to open the door. He splayed one hand on the window while he pressed the buttons with his other.

"He's trying to talk!" John exclaimed.

Elizabeth fumbled with the controls on the comm and set it to record. This would all be transmitted back to the Bureau 7 mainframe for study and observation.

Proof, really.

His voice echoed with a death rattle, long drawn out exhales of what had to be putrid breath from dead lungs.

What he said made it all the more horrible.

"Help me," he hissed in that singular voice. "Help me."

"You know there's no help for him, right?" John looked at her.

"Of course there is. It's a one-two shot to the back of the head."

He laughed. "I'm glad you're not on about putting him down humanely. I don't know that anyone should get that close."

"I don't know that it would work." She wasn't sure if it was fear or bile crawling up the back of her throat. "And a bullet to the cerebellum is pretty humane."

He pressed himself more fully against the glass, his dead, white eyes fixed on her. They seemed to bore under her clothes, under her skin, and deep into the meat—meat he wanted to mash between those awful jaws.

As they watched, he began to bash his head against the door with all the supernatural strength in his reanimated body.

Smash after smash against the door bloodied his head. There was an audible crack to his skull, but it didn't stop him. He licked at the gore on the window, devouring those bits of himself with a manic glee. All the while, he continued to watch Elizabeth.

She could practically feel his teeth tearing into her.

And he smiled. He grinned, a stretched maw, as if he knew exactly what she was thinking.

For all she knew, maybe he did.

"What's going on with the other subjects? Were they all injected with PrPM3 before transport?" Elizabeth tried to pull up the vid feeds on the comm.

"No, only three of them. They were part of another study at the installation in Athens. Or that's what it's showing in the file."

"So can we pull up the vids of what happened on transport? Why was this man killed?"

Polidori began typing, entered his clearance code and the vids from the transport came up. They showed nothing out of the ordinary until she saw a woman she recognized from her case files.

"Oh my god, stop it. Stop it there!" She pointed at the screen. "Zoom in on her. Dressed like security detail, but look, just there at the back of her neck."

"Fuck," Polidori hissed. "If that tattoo is any indication, she's X."

X was a group of paranormal militants that wanted to lift the veil, wanted to stop hiding in the shadows. They wanted to bring all of their kind out into the light so to speak.

That would induce a mass panic and anarchy that the world wouldn't survive. At least, not the world of humans.

Leaving a vacuum for the paranormals to step in and take over. Humans would be used as slaves and livestock—the various secret organizations who worked within this world to protect humankind fought a constant battle.

They continued the playback and watched as the woman injected their test subject with something and then broke his neck with a quick snap. She looked up at the camera and smiled before injecting three other subjects.

She'd still be in containment with them.

How many others had she injected? What was that shit?

"Damn it," she growled.

"We have to get a sample," John said what they were both thinking. "I'll go back in. He's not going to hurt me."

"I'm going to call security and let them know we have a breach."

"Let me get the sample first. Whatever this stuff was, we need to know. If we call for a lockdown, we'll never know, but that crap will still be out there, a ticking bomb."

"You're right." Elizabeth scrubbed a hand over her face and sighed. "Okay, so you're going back in. What can I do?"

"There's a secret compartment behind the cabinet." Polidori pointed. "Open it."

"Can't you?" She narrowed her eyes.

"There's a weapon in there that will key to your biometrics. You need to open it so it will key to you. I don't need it. I have my own weapons." He clicked his teeth together to accentuate his meaning.

He stood precariously close to the entrance, and there was something about the situation that felt wrong, but against her better judgment, she opened the panel.

Instead of the weapon he'd promised, a hidden door opened revealing a secret room, and from what she could see of it from the outside, it looked to be a panic room.

Polidori was abandoning her.

"I'm sorry, Elizabeth. If you'll recall, I tried to talk you out of coming in today." Polidori gave her a smile that was more pity than anything.

"So you're part of this? Part of X?" She refused to acknowledge the panic rising in her chest.

"No, not at all. I'm part of Team John. See, your monster is coming. I can't be here when he arrives. It would probably be better for all involved if you never met him." He shrugged. "This way, the rest of us have a fighting chance."

"What are you talking about?"

"No time to chat, Elizabeth. I'll miss you." He slammed his palm down on the door to the containment unit and the snarling, slavering creature was free.

It charged toward her just as the saferoom door closed and left her alone with the revenant.

"I'll kill you, Polidori. I don't know how, but I will kill *you,*" she cried. Jesus, she didn't know what had possessed her to say that. She wasn't a killing kind of person.

Of course, being cornered by a flesh-eating zombie could change one's constitution.

There was an ax encased in glass on the wall—goddamn it, why hadn't she seen that sooner? Polidori with his—oh shit!

She slammed back into the wall and put her elbow through the glass. Elizabeth was suddenly grateful for the self-defense class all employees of Bureau 7 had to take. She grabbed the ax just in time to put it between them.

He was strong, so incredibly strong, and his breath and body were fetid. He smelled as if he'd been dead for days, not hours.

Elizabeth wasn't sure how long she could fight him off, and if he was infectious...

A horrible flash played out in her mind's eye. There was no way out of this. He was stronger than she was, faster than she was...

And she was alone.

Alarms blared and a calm, recorded voice came over the comm. "This is a Code Black. Prepare for containment and cleaning protocol. Please secure your stations and proceed to the nearest safety pod. This is a Code Black—"

She shuddered to think what was going down outside their lab. Even if she defeated this one, how many more were there?

"Safeeeeeety pod..." he hissed in her face.

Suddenly, he was ripped from her by Barton Smith, head of security on Kythnos. He was just as strong as the revenant, fighting him with his bare hands. When Barton wrestled him down, Elizabeth didn't hesitate.

She swung the ax in a mighty arc and brought it down on the creature's neck, severing the head. It rolled from the body, those razor teeth still clacking together as if still searching for meat.

The body jerked and twitched, but finally stopped—even as the teeth continued snap and chatter, the head chewing on its own lips and tongue now as it died.

She shuddered with revulsion.

"You okay, Dr. Wollstonecraft? Did it bite you?" Barton checked her over, turning her this way and that with his big hands.

"I don't think so."

"Let's hope not. We lost Sector 4."

"Sector 4?" That was the housing unit. "All of Sector 4? How the hell does that happen?" Her voice hit a higher pitch than she meant. She was trying like hell not to freak out, but she was losing ground rather quickly as the world around her went to shit.

Yeah, that was the scientific term: going to shit.

"This infection spreads quickly. I need to get you to a safety pod. Where's Dr. Polidori?" Barton asked, rubbing his arm.

"Polidori took the pod and locked me out."

"Bastard. Just for that, when I get back to the central command center, I'm popping his door."

Elizabeth wouldn't deny the idea held appeal, but she was more concerned about what was going on with Barton and all the scratching. He seemed to be working something pretty awful on his bicep.

"What's that? Were you bitten?"

"Just a scratch. Itches like a motherfucker, though." He hadn't stopped scratching and his uniform shirt was bore a dark stain that grew as she watched.

"Let me see it."

"Doc," he began.

"Barton, let me help you."

"I guess you are pretty handy with that ax." He unbuttoned his shirt and peeled it off. "Fuck," he said, when he saw it.

It was obviously so much more than a scratch. The flesh around the wound had putrefied, and it was spreading.

"Jesus Christ, it feels like there are bugs under my skin." He started scratching again, and this time, he tore into his skin, beneath it.

Elizabeth didn't want to know, didn't want to see. But she couldn't turn away, she had to help him. He'd saved her.

And if she didn't do something, he might be the one to end her. The whites of his eyes were tinged with red. It wouldn't be long now.

"I'm changing, aren't I?" He shook his head. "Goddamn it." Barton couldn't stop scratching and tearing at himself. "Take my sidearm."

"I can't."

"Take the goddamn sidearm."

She pulled the gun from the holster. It was heavy in her hands, foreign. She'd never shot a gun before, and she didn't want to have to start, but unless she was hatcheting her way out of this place, she was going to have to.

"The safety mechanism, push it to the right. Right is right and left is dead. Go on, now." He said this as if he were speaking to a recalcitrant child.

But they both knew how this was going to end. She wasn't a little girl who wanted to stay up past her bedtime. She was a grown woman, a doctor and scientist who had given an oath to help people, not... Though she supposed that she would be helping him now.

A bullet to the head was the only thing that could.

CHAPTER FOUR

When the Bureau 7 installation came into view, urgency surged and with it, adrenaline. Adam could feel the chemical changes in his flesh as the body prepared for war.

A visible change came over him. The network of veins under his skin expanded, giving the appearance of some vine-like infection spreading across his body. This allowed for increased blood flow to all of his muscles that in turn increased in size. He could feel his bones expanding, hardening.

It was sheer agony.

But it was pleasure, too. It had been so long since he'd felt this primal strength, a sense of purpose. He hated that part of it, that he didn't feel whole, or real, without it. He was a shadow, a spirit, drifting in the ether until the Bloodline called him. Then he became corporeal, the only real thing in a pit of shadows.

Electricity crackled around his fingertips, which only happened in cases of immediate threat to life.

Adam docked quickly and, as soon as the boat was secure, he ran for the fence. He didn't hesitate to grab hold of it, the electric charge in his hands stronger than the voltage of the fence. The gate slid open for him, but if it had slid open for him, it was open for anything that wanted in.

Or out.

Fuck it. Containing the infection was not his circus or his monkey. He was there for Elizabeth, and he was pretty sure even if humanity wiped themselves out, he could keep her safe.

Images of a man—a genetically modified man—burned in his brain. He was with Elizabeth now. He'd tried to help her, but he'd been infected. He'd demanded she take his gun.

The woman who'd once been that sweet child raised the weapon with shaking hands.

He could feel her fear, her sorrow, and her guilt.

Adam was torn between wanting to change that for her, to take that weight from her, and wanting her to feel every second of it. What had she been thinking agreeing to come to work for Bureau 7?

It kept coming back to that, and he supposed, if he was able to get her out alive, he could ask her.

Hopefully, she wouldn't be too stubborn. The Wollstonecraft women were a breed apart, and getting any of them to do anything he wanted took more effort than he had the time or inclination to expend.

Surrendering to the instinct he knew would guide him to her, he ran. He ran hard and fast through the formerly sterile intuitional halls that had once been pristine, but were now covered in the gore of what used to be men.

Decidedly unsanitary.

When he finally saw the architects of the carnage, they were like one snarling mass of teeth. Some wore lab coats, security uniforms, others wore jumpsuits. But there was nothing left of what had once made them human.

The current flowing through his hands seemed to have little effect on them. It would move them, but only enough to draw their attention. He had to pop their heads off like so many undead dandelions to get any real results.

Several sets of those stiletto-like teeth tore into his arms, but they barely broke the skin. Adam wasn't worried about infection. Only the living had that concern, he was sure. Of course if he was wrong—well, if he was wrong, he'd be past caring.

And those who meddled where only gods should trespass would get their just desserts.

He fought his way into the lab, eliminating the revenants that stood between him and Elizabeth just in time to see the genetically modified unit turn.

And the bullet that exploded out of the weapon in Elizabeth's hand.

Her aim was true and the force of the specially modified ammo knocked the newly turned revenant back ten feet. What was left of his brain exploded against the wall in an artistic spray that reminded Adam very much of a flower.

She focused all of her attention on him, determination in her eyes.

"Shoot me, if it will make you feel better, but I'm taking you out of here."

She didn't ask who he was. She simply lowered the weapon and nodded.

That was so much easier than he'd anticipated. He had to wonder, was she infected?

"Are you bitten or scratched?"

"No." Her eyes were drawn to his arms.

He looked down and realized he'd definitely been bitten more than once, but the wounds started to heal even as he watched. "Doesn't matter. I'm immune."

"Really? I'd love to look at your blood." She bit her lip. "Um, maybe not here. But... somewhere."

"Goddamn it. You've unleashed a zombie apocalypse, and you're still trying to play God."

"No, that's not it at all. The zombie apocalypse is here and it sucks, but you have a cure in your veins. Why wouldn't I want to study it? Maybe it doesn't have to be an apocalypse?" Her tone implied he was stupid for thinking otherwise.

"The cure is in your blood, too. Although, a bite would most likely kill you. But hey, you wouldn't turn." He shrugged.

"How do you know so much about it?"

"Because our blood is... similar." He spun just in time to catch another revenant as it launched itself into the room. Adam caught it midair and beheaded it.

"You're very strong. I wish I was that strong." She tucked *the* gun into the waist of her slacks and swung the ax up over her shoulder. "Lead the way, big guy."

He narrowed his eyes. "Do you know who I am?"

She nodded. "Well, I don't generally run off with strangers, although in the middle of this shitstorm, I'd probably leave with most anyone. But Polidori told me you'd come for me, if you're Adam?"

"I am he." He scanned the room. "And where is John?"

"I don't know. He locked himself in a safety pod." She pointed to the wall.

"I can't believe he left you here to face this alone," he snarled. Adam was completely disgusted. "I'm sure he's immune to the infection as well."

"He said you were coming. That I'd be fine." Elizabeth lifted her chin. "It seems I am. Let's go. I don't care where he is."

"I do." He ran his hands along the wall where she'd pointed, the electric current shorting out the door on the safety pod. It whooshed open, but he was not all surprised to find it vacant. A hole had been torn in the steel of the ceiling and that was likely how Polidori had made his exit.

"I told him I was going to kill him."

Her need for revenge, or maybe it was justice, it didn't matter, but it was still a heavy weight that settled like manacles around him.

"Do you want me to kill him for you?" he offered casually, as if her answer was of no real consequence.

But it did matter. It mattered so much he could taste it.

"No." She shook her head. "I just want to get the hell off this island. John will get what's coming to him, I'm sure. He abandoned his post in a crisis. The people I work for have... rules about that."

"Isn't that what you're doing?"

"No. You're going to help me get to a safehouse on the other side of the island."

"My boat—"

"I have to get in touch with the mainland before I do anything. I'm not putting my neck on their chopping block, too, for abandoning my post. It'll be safe. Just get me there."

He sighed. He didn't think it was the right choice, but what did he know? She was the one who worked for Bureau 7. She seemed confident that Polidori was going to be punished ugly for what he'd done, and maybe she had firsthand experience.

"How far is it?"

"About eight kilometers through dense forest. There's a trail."

"That all of the staff working here know and so, too, probably, do the revenants."

"So we need to move fast and hope we get there first."

"Then let me carry you."

"Excuse me, what?" She eyed him.

"I didn't stutter. I can move much faster than you can. I'm immune to their bites. You need to get there fast, and I can get us there fast. I don't need to stop to breathe. I don't need to worry about rocks or uneven ground."

"So, should I just climb on your back, or what?"

She looked so doubtful, he couldn't help but smile. He didn't want to smile. This was serious business and there shouldn't have been anything to smile about.

But smile he did.

"Well, it is a bit ridiculous, isn't it?" She smiled back.

By the angels in heaven... or perhaps it more like by the demons in hell... The smile transformed her face. He'd never liked looking at one of them so much as he did this one—humans. Women.

He wanted to keep that smile on her face always because she was the most beautiful thing he'd ever seen. She was enough to make him believe in the divine.

"Come, like this." He swept her up, taking her ax, and pressing her against his chest.

"I can't see what's coming now."

"You don't have to see. Leave that to me. Just hold on." Adam had never understood what it was like to hold something he found precious. He was careful with the antiques in the castle, he was aware of the power in his body, the strength. He knew he had to be careful with small things, but this was different.

He didn't have the words to explain it.

Yes, she was definitely enough to cause him to believe in the divine because it would take the hand of such a being to wrest her from him now that he had her.

She was so soft, but he didn't he didn't get the sense that she was fragile. Perhaps human, breakable in a singular way that only humans were, but she was strong, too. She didn't need coddling, didn't need saving. Not really.

Adam tried to quell the disappointment he felt. If he was honest with himself, there was part of him that wanted to be her knight. Her savior. It was a role he'd hated and despised, but resented for all of her ancestors since his birth.

But for her, he wanted to fulfill his purpose.

He couldn't, because she didn't need him.

Taking a revenant's head from his body with a one-handed swing of the ax told him that maybe that wasn't entirely true.

She turned her face against his chest and hung on tight.

Adam felt guilty he was so aware of her—of the way her body fit against his. He'd been with prostitutes, but he'd always had to pay them extra and it was always from behind. None of them had ever wanted to look at his face or his scars.

He'd stopped paying for pleasure when he'd stopped trying to be human. He wasn't like them; he wasn't like anyone. He could find the same pleasures with his hand. The warm, soft flesh wasn't worth the price he had to pay—not in coins, or in his dignity. Even a woman who sold her body as a product didn't want to do business with him.

That was telling when a hungry mouth and an outstretched hand would withdraw when he passed.

Fuck, but he was twisted up in all the crap he'd thought he'd let go of so long ago. She brought back so many ugly things.

But beautiful things, too.

The arc of the ax as it delivered a swift and deserved death, once upon a dark time, it had been his weapon of choice.

And the memory of a woman's body, her sweet lemon scent...

Damn, but he loved lemons. He loved them because they were bright and sour. He loved them because in their unvarnished, unprocessed state, they were unpalatable to so many.

But he loved them.

He took head after head with his ax as he fought his way back to the outside. He should've already worked his way through the staff and inhabitants. Adam knew in his gut there were more people, more subjects, at the installation than what Elizabeth or anyone else was aware of.

Otherwise, he'd have stayed and cleaned up their mess, but he couldn't risk exposing Elizabeth.

They moved through the security gates and out into the open forest. It felt wrong to him to be running away from their only method of escape. Some enterprising undead might have enough muscle memory to remember how to operate the damn thing.

Some of them were talking, there was awareness in those dead eyes.

For a second, he'd felt a twinge of remorse at killing them, because for these single moments, he wasn't alone in the world. There were others like him—not living, not dead, and had once been human.

If the master directive to protect the bloodline hadn't been instilled in him, he wasn't sure if he'd have killed any of them.

Strange images of a world where he was king played in his mind, but he didn't stop running, didn't stop fighting.

There was something unspoken between them. She didn't have to verbalize where she wanted him to go. Somehow, he just knew. He pushed as hard as he could and covered the ground so fast, it was like he was flying. Adam never felt the earth touch his feet.

He didn't breathe and the twin hearts beating in his chest never changed their steady rhythm. Adam slowed when he saw the edge of a cliff approaching. There was no more ground, only the sea beyond.

When they stopped, she looked up at him. "Did we make it?"

He eased her to her feet. "I'm here. At the picture in your mind. Now, where do we go?"

Elizabeth looked around and for a moment, seemed lost, but he watched as she squared her shoulders and then sank to her knees, digging in the dirt for something.

"What are you looking for?"

"The lever. There's a staircase down to the cave."

"That doesn't seem very bright." Not that anyone asked him.

"It can be deactivated once we're inside." She pulled a lever and the sharp sound of creaking metal pierced the air. "Look, there." She pointed toward the edge of the cliff.

A gleaming metal staircase had emerged. From where, he wasn't sure. It seemed as if it had materialized from nowhere.

"I remembered. Oh, thank God."

"Again, I don't think God had anything to do with it."

"You know what I meant."

"Did I? It's a thing you humans say when things are good. Or some random chance works out for you because you needed it to. But you don't say it when the bad things happen. Like when your mother died from her brain tumor. There was no thanking God, for surely, if there is one, that is his realm too, as are all things. Or so humans believe. No, instead, you're trying to do things to thwart his plans. The illnesses he allowed."

She eyed him and was ready for the fight he and his maker would have on this topic, the fight that he and Mary had... Even the fight he'd had with Elizabeth's mother when she'd found out she was sick.

Instead, she said, "That's too deep a conversation to have while running from zombies."

She, in a word, delighted him.

He found himself smiling again.

She headed toward the staircase.

"Wait, I should go first."

Elizabeth held out her hand. "By all means."

CHAPTER FIVE

The monster.

He wasn't a monster at all. Not really. He looked like a man, but that wasn't what made him human. It was the wealth of emotion in his eyes.

She found herself incredibly curious about him, about his life. About who he was at the cellular level.

The way he'd covered the distance between the institution and the safehouse had been insane.

Inhuman.

But he already seemed to be the most human being she'd ever known.

Elizabeth found him strangely compelling, no more... attractive. She didn't date, she'd always been more interested in what was going on in the brain in a literal sense than actually engaging with the opposite sex.

Granted, she'd had her share of relationships, but they always ended badly. She never had enough time or attention to give them. Even when they'd both agreed to no strings.

She wanted to see his flesh, yes. For scientific purposes, but he was so big and strong she couldn't help but wonder if it was everywhere else, too. Her lips and mouth were suddenly dry as she watched him descend the newly revealed spiral staircase down the side of the cliff.

It was only a moment before he called up to her, "It's safe."

She was glad for his presence. The only thing that could make what was happening worse would be if she had to try to survive it alone.

Elizabeth followed the steps down the side of the cliff, and paused, looking out over the Aegean. The blue, it wasn't like any blue she'd ever seen before. It was at turns midnight and midday sky. The tang of salt in the air was a welcome one, and the wind whipping her hair against her cheeks until her eyes stung was worth it.

It occurred to her this might be the last view, her last glance at this world. She inhaled deeply, filling her lungs and holding it there until she thought her chest was going to burst.

"Elizabeth, are you okay?" His big body blocked the entrance to the cave.

There was something about seeing him there. Something that silenced all the guilt, all the fear, all the doubt in her head. She believed that everything was going to be okay.

"I'm fine."

"The view is quite beautiful," he said, but he wasn't looking out across the sea as she had been. He was looking at her.

"Do you like the sea?" she asked, finishing her descent and following him inside the mouth of the cave.

"I love the sea. I prefer to always have her in my sights."

She wondered about him. Where he lived? Did he hide himself? Elizabeth tried to picture him in a house or an apartment, and she simply couldn't.

"I came from Trieste. I was working at Castle Miramare, living in the dungeons."

That she could picture. "Do you always know what I'm thinking?"

He turned to study her. "Not always. Enough. If it's something that's much on your mind, some need you have that I can fill, then yes. It's part of how I was designed."

Oh hell. She needed to not think about his shoulders. Or his biceps, or how much she'd liked being cradled against his chest while he fought off the zombie horde with one hand. That was the kind of man she'd dreamed about. He didn't need to know that.

He wasn't a man—he was a monster.

Guilt crashed over her as soon as the thought formed. He was no more a monster than she was—no, that was a blatant untruth. If anyone in the cave were a monster, it was her. For what she'd done. What she'd allowed to happen.

"I can see that, you living in a castle. I've always wanted to see Trieste."

"I could take you there now. It's a little more than a day on my boat."

If only... But she knew what she had to do. "Perhaps someday. Can I ask you something?"

"You have already asked me something. Many things." He nodded.

"I will ask you another something, and I suppose you don't have to answer, but—"

"If you ask, Elizabeth Wollstonecraft, then yes, I must answer."

"How did you know to come? You arrived just in time to save my life."

"You saved your own life. You didn't really need me."

"But I did. I needed you to get this far." She studied the walls of the cave, looking for the next passage, running her fingers along the rock.

"Check in with your masters, then I will answer all of your questions if you're still of a mind to hear them."

"You know what they're going to say, don't you?" She pressed her lips together. "Yeah, me too. But I don't want to." Elizabeth sighed. "I don't want to go back in there."

"So, do not."

"You know it's not that easy. They'd send a bounty hunter after me. Or worse."

"I will protect you, if that's what you wish."

"Polidori said they want you."

"I'm sure they do." He shrugged, but continued to stare out of the mouth of the cave.

"You'd fight them for me?" She inched closer to him, her search temporarily forgotten.

He turned to look at her, intensity burning in his mismatched eyes. "I'd do anything for you. All you have to do is tell me what you want."

Elizabeth needed to touch him. She reached out and put her hand on his shoulder. His skin was so hot, he felt feverish, but she didn't pull back. "For me, or the bloodline?" It was stupid that she wanted him to make the distinction, that she wanted to be the one he'd fight for. Elizabeth didn't need drama or faux alpha male macho bullshit. She didn't want anyone to fight over her or for her, but somehow, it was important that he would.

"The bloodline. I'm bound, but yes. For you, too, Elizabeth."

"Why?"

"I doubt that you'll remember, but once you were a little girl crying over your mother all alone in a hospital waiting room."

That memory was sharp as a blade slicing into her awareness. It was strange how she remembered even the color of her mother's ponytail holder, the exact number of frayed edges on the embroidery of her favorite sweater, but him... she'd believed the big man who'd come had been a dream. Something she'd made up to comfort herself in the darkest times when she'd been so very much alone.

Only it hadn't been.

"You asked me what I needed," she said, as the memory became corporeal in the being in front of her. Her hand, of its own volition moved to his cheek.

He closed his eyes against her touch. His face was burning up, on fire. Like the rest of him. "And I didn't say anything. I wanted to ask you to bring my mama back, but I knew it was wrong to ask. How did I know that?"

"I don't know." His voice was a jagged whisper, but the words seemed to have been torn from him. "But I'll fight for you. I'll save the world. For you."

His words were a balm and a wound. Being so close to something she'd thought was a myth, a legend, but somehow he was so very real, so very... him. It twisted up her insides, and she couldn't think straight.

All she wanted in that moment was to get her hands on him. She couldn't get close enough to all that hot skin.

The circular stairway began to retract and the sound of the scraping metal startled her. She lurched against him.

He caught her easily and, the moment they touched, something changed. Some electric charge crackled between them.

They were in the middle of an apocalypse. They couldn't do this, even if he wanted the same thing that she did.

But why couldn't they, a voice in the back of her mind asked. Why? They could ride out the storm and let the Bureau 7 SWAT handle the carnage. It was what they signed up for. Elizabeth had simply wanted to cure cancer.

She was dizzy being this close to him, on fire, her knees were weak. She'd never been so affected by a man.

He looked into her eyes, and it was like drowning. No, like he could see what she looked like underneath it all, not just her clothes, but like he could see deep into her bones and knew exactly what made her Elizabeth.

It was intense and awful, being so bare, but it was kind of wonderful, too. Because he didn't look away. He saw her for every horrible thing she was, and he didn't flee her. Didn't break this dark thing between him.

And she could see him, too.

Elizabeth could see all the darkness inside of him, the shadowed place where humans had souls. His wasn't empty. He was fire. He was lightning. He was everything.

He was part of her, somehow.

She gasped on an intake of breath, her heart thudding against her chest, and she wished for all the world that he'd kiss her. Her hands slid up his back to his shoulders and she wondered if he'd ever kissed a woman. If he felt desire.

"I will keep you safe," he swore. "You don't..."

A shaky laugh escaped her. "You think I'm trying to pay you?" She swallowed hard. "I've never felt this before."

"What do you want from me?"

The way he said it sounded so... broken. "What do you want?"

"I want to take you away from here and sail somewhere beautiful. I want to be free from these chains that bind me."

"That's it?" Jesus, he wasn't experiencing what she was at all. She'd never thought someone could feel something that intense and have it be utterly one-sided. Elizabeth tried to gather her senses, but had little luck being so close to him. He hadn't released her, and she wasn't inclined to be released, even if he wasn't going to kiss her.

Taking a deep breath, she said, "How does this work? Your chains?"

That seemed to shatter the moment. He released her, almost as if she were something he didn't want to touch at all. Her ego might've whimpered just a bit.

"I must protect you. I must do what you say."

"What happens if you don't?"

"Pain until I comply, unless I'm refusing the order because it's dangerous to you."

"Can I release you?"

He spun back around, gripping her arms. "Don't say that unless you mean it."

Electricity crackled, and his touch carried with it a bit of a current. Nothing uncomfortable, but surprising. "Of course I mean it, Adam."

"Then say it. Now."

She opened her mouth, but for a single second, knew doubt. If she released him now, would he leave her here to fight this alone?

He shook his head. "I knew you wouldn't. Mary promised she'd release me too, but instead of the release she promised, she forced me to murder one of the kindest women I've ever known," he snarled.

"Hey, shit. Give me a second to process, okay? I'm scared. I'm alone."

"I said I'll protect you. Trust my word."

"And I should trust you won't leave me? If you're free, you'll have no horse in the race. You can't blame me for thinking of my own survival." That was the only reason he was there, because he'd been compelled to be. He didn't want to kiss her, touch her, his skin didn't ache with the need to be touched like hers did.

She steeled herself, because fuck this. Elizabeth had always had to fight. She'd always had to fight alone. Why should this be any differ-ent? She didn't need him. Not if he didn't want to be here.

"I release you."

Elizabeth turned away from him to renew her hunt for another passage. Bureau 7 must've had a safety pod or some means of commu-nication and survival gear hidden in the cave. She simply had to find *it*.

She could berate herself later, while she was waiting to be rescued.

A roar was torn from him, and she found herself hoisted against him, and she didn't know what it was in his eyes. Fury? Fear? Grati-tude? Whatever it was, she liked seeing it on him. She liked looking at his face, the hard angles of his jaw. Even his one gold eye, and one blue. She liked the scar around his neck...

"Why do you think of me this way?"

"I don't understand what you're asking." Perhaps some part of her did, but he'd already made it clear he wasn't interested.

"This desire." He tightened his grip on her. "You've freed me, but I still feel it. You can't want this."

She understood now. Elizabeth leaned her head against his chest, pressing herself as close as she could get, returning the firm, almost painful embrace. "Of course I do. I won't say I'm not curious about you in all ways, that it's not at *all a sci*entific interest. That's just how my mind works, but I can say, we'd have to do many, many things before I could even focus on that aspect. You make me dizzy." She pulled back to look up at him again. Elizabeth wanted him to see the truth of her words in her eyes. "You make me hot."

"Why?"

"That's the question that any two people could ask, don't you think? Why? Because our genes are compatible?"

"I cannot... that is... I do not..." he spluttered.

"Does it matter? If you want me, take me."

"I swore I'd never touch another Wollstonecraft woman this way."

Another? "So you've been with one of us before? Was it not some-thing you wanted?" She couldn't imagine the horror of living, bound as he was, to another's whims. To be forced...

"She was woman-shaped." He shrugged. "It wasn't a hardship. Not that part of it. It was the other things she made me do. The murders."

"Mary, you mean. She was a child when she married Percy."

"No, it was after he died."

"The woman you spoke of, the kind one." Elizabeth searched his face and found the sadness she'd hoped to see. She was on the right track. "That was Percy's first wife, wasn't it?"

"Yes, and hers is the only death I've regretted."

Elizabeth wished she had some words to make it better, to ease his guilt and pain, but she didn't. So instead, she offered him the same thing he'd offered her all those years ago. A quiet touch, the simple knowledge that he wasn't alone.

"Come with me," he said. "Leave this place, leave Bureau 7."

He'd dipped his head now, and his words were a feather-light whisper against her lips.

"You know I can't. Not yet. Maybe not ever."

"Why?" He was still so close to her.

Jesus, but he was intense.

"Because of what I want. What I need. 7 has resources I won't have access to anywhere else. With 7, I have a real chance of curing brain disease. Of making a difference so mothers don't leave little girls to cry alone in waiting rooms in the arms of strangers."

"Goddamn it." The epithet was torn from him, as it seemed was his *next* action.

His mouth crashed into hers.

That faint crackle buzzing between them exploded, and there was nothing left in the world but him. The scent of him, like the storm, the brand of his hands, and the slant of his mouth over hers.

Everything was ash and it didn't matter one-third of a damn because of this moment.

He pulled back, breaking the kiss slowly. Elizabeth didn't want him to stop, didn't want him to let go—only more of this.

"Is this really want you want? To be fucked against the wall by a monster while the world burns?"

She paused. Were there people who didn't want this? "Hell yes." Elizabeth bit her lip. "I mean, if that's what you want. I released you, Adam. You don't have to be here with me. Not like this. Not even at all."

"I want to be here, more than I thought possible."

"Can I touch you?" she dared, her fingers going to the strangely banal t-shirt. What did monsters wear, after all?

His eyes fluttered closed as she peeled the shirt off of him. She didn't know why he was always portrayed with green skin—perhaps it was something to do with death. He wasn't green at all, he was golden. Perhaps it was from all the hours he now got to spend in the sun on his boat. Perhaps because he didn't have to hide in sallow darkness.

And he shouldn't, *he had* a body that was like art—no, it really was art. It had taken an artist to put together a man so beautiful. To stitch him from the bits of others and integrate them so perfectly—creating a whole new being.

She traced over the scars at his neck, her fingers fluttering like butterfly wings against the marred flesh. Then down to the scar on his shoulder where his left arm had been attached to his torso.

"That's the arm of a killer." He embraced her again. "A priest," he shifted to indicate his right arm, "and a condemned murderer. My maker believed in duality."

"It's beautiful. You're beautiful," she murmured and continued her exploration. His chest was a mass of scars, but two determinate marks over his heart. "And this, what happened here?"

"It's where he gave me another heart."

"Why?"

"I'll never know." His massive hands circled her wrist, but he didn't try to stop her. He simply held her and waited patiently.

With her other hand, she dared to touch down to his waist where he bore another scar, one that circled all the way around him. Then another at his hip. She pushed her hand down past the waist on his black fatigues and gripped his cock.

A low groan was drawn from him. "It's been so long."

"For me, too." She pressed her lips to his shoulder, and down his collarbone, while she moved her hand over him.

"You're so soft," he said, peeling her bloody lab coat from her shoulders. "So breakable, but not. Strong in the way only soft things can be."

His hands on her felt so good, so right. "You promised me fucking against a wall," she said breathlessly.

"That I did, Doctor." He hoisted her up effortlessly, and she wrapped her legs around his hips.

She regretted not being able to play with his cock anymore, that gave her more power over him *than* any curse or binding ever had—the power to give pleasure or deny it. But that meant he was going to fuck her, and she knew it would be good.

He made short work of her slacks, tearing them from her. That was one way to try to keep her from going back to the facility, but she found she didn't care.

Adam kissed her again and pushed his length inside of her as he pressed her back into the wall. There was little preamble, but she didn't want it or need it. She just wanted him—hard and fast.

As soon as he began to move, that lightning snapped between them and sparked deep inside, almost as if—oh god!

"Elizabeth!" he growled against her ear. As if that spark was something she'd done, and not him. Or maybe she had, or he'd turned her into this primal thing that could only feel. Could only want.

Could only gorge herself on need.

She liked how the cold, craggy cave wall felt against her back, the contrast of the heat of his skin, but it too was like rock. So hard everywhere. She loved touching him, raking her nails across his back because of how much he liked it. It made his hips piston a little faster, a little harder.

He was so deep inside of her, and she felt impossibly stretched to allow his girth, but she liked that too. She wanted more.

So she told him. She dug her nails into his flesh, "More, Adam."

"More what?" he rasped.

"Everything."

Her demand spurred him on, and he gave her exactly what she wanted—more of everything. He gripped her thighs harder, lifted her higher, and thrust into her again and again. He seemed indefatigable.

There were definitely benefits to sex with non-mortals.

She locked her ankles and moved with him, clenching her walls to pull him deeper, hold him longer, almost as if she fought his thrust.

Elizabeth could feel his twin hearts beating fast and hard against his chest.

His muscles were all tensed, even though she knew it cost him zero effort to hold her up. Her orgasm snarled and clawed at the edges of her awareness, but she didn't want to surrender to the pleasure. She wanted it to last, needed it to. She wasn't ready to be back in the world.

The choice was taken from her when suddenly, the wall moved and slid open to reveal a hidden room.

Before he could say anything, she whispered, "I don't fucking care."

"Me either." He drilled into her, kissing her hard.

It was his kiss that pushed her over the ledge to tumble down into the mindless storm of sensation. She was so lost in him it was like drowning, but she didn't want to be saved.

His culmination arrived just after hers and he spilled inside of her, with his power*ful body* spasming against her.

Elizabeth clung to him even as he softened, her face buried in his neck. She didn't want to look at the room. Didn't want to report to Bureau 7 and receive the orders she knew were coming, but didn't want.

Right now, consumed by him, the world and possibility was infinite. If she allowed the outside world to intrude, this would become nothing but a memory she was sure would pass to the realm of fevered dreams.

The idea of ever being parted from him twisted something in her.

Fucking shit, she'd caught something worse than a zombie infection.

She'd caught feelings, or obsession, or something for an immortal who had better things to do than drag her through eternity.

CHAPTER SIX

He didn't want to look at the room. He didn't want her in there, at the whims of men who claimed to be apostles of science but cared nothing for the lives they meddled with. He knew voicing that opinion would get him nowhere.

"Are you going to wait out there?" she asked, after she'd wrapped her lab coat around her, bloodied as it was.

He knew it would be best for both of them if he did, but the idea of that wall closing between them was unthinkable. Adam tugged his fatigues up and put on his shirt before stepping into the cold, sterile room with her.

"It looks like there's a bathroom. All the luxuries. Maybe you want to go in there while I activate the emergency comm?"

"I don't give a shit if they see me."

"Adam, this is already hard enough."

Hard enough because she was embarrassed? He hated that voice in his head because usually it was right. Except not this time. He knew that she simply didn't want 7 to get their hands on him. Or order her to—she was right. This would put her in a bad and possibly dangerous position.

"Yeah, okay." He dropped a kiss on the top of her head before locking himself behind the door in a space that he was sure had been designed for human toddlers. The walls touched him on all sides and the ceiling caused him to hunch over. He was pretty sure the edge of the sink was going to ask for a second date.

"Executive Director Lin," she began.

He heard something soft, quiet.

"My errors?" He heard the pitch rise in Elizabeth's voice. "No, this situation has nothing to do with any error I made. It has to do with Bureau 7 pushing protocols that were put in place for a reason and—no, let me finish. I just chopped the head of our security team's head off with an ax. An ax! Those subjects had been injected with another bastardized version of my prions. Without my consent or my permission. That, and X's sabotage. You should've gotten the playback from the transport."

Damn it, why did Lin speak so quietly? He hated only catching half of the conversation.

"Yeah. What? I don't want to go back in there. Why don't you have SWAT deployed for that?"

He didn't hear anything else for a long time, not until a soft knock on the door, and Elizabeth stood pale and shaking in the doorway.

"I knew she'd want me to go back. They need the research."

"I heard. Why can't SWAT go in? You know, the people they've trained and employ for this kind of thing?" It didn't make any sense, not unless they hoped to eliminate all the evidence of what had happened here, including Elizabeth.

"Polidori locked down the satellite comm. A parting gift, I guess. The uplink has to be reset on site and manually sent."

"SWAT can't do that because?"

"They're already on the way. Apparently, some of the subjects are trying to walk to the mainland. This thing with X was a coordinated attack. Several other facilities were hit with other things. The installation in Siberia was hit with a carnivorous form of anthrax. Everyone has to do their part. I guess this is mine."

"I'll go with you," he offered.

She touched his arm. "You've already done your part. Now, you're free." Elizabeth exhaled heavily. "And I don't want them to catch you. I think Lin knows that you're here."

He nodded. "With all the tech on the island, I'm sure this place is wired with heat sensors and everything else you'd need to survive an apocalypse. Doesn't matter though. I'm going with you." He grinned. "And you can tell me not to all you want, but I'm going anyway."

The look on her face was something akin to pain. He hadn't wanted to hurt her. "Hey, it's okay, Elizabeth. We'll get through this."

"It's just... you didn't leave me, Adam. Everyone leaves me, and it sounds so overdramatic to say, but I'd rather you do it now."

"As opposed to when?"

"As opposed to when I've come to depend on you."

"Yeah, well, I already depend on you. Maybe you're not sure about what happened between us, but I am. I don't want to give that up. Do you? And I may be a monster, but I'm not a piece of shit. I wouldn't leave you here to fight by yourself. No matter if I wanted something more from you or not."

"You can't mean that. It's just chemistry. Science. People who experience trauma together—"

"Maybe this will disturb you, Dr. Wollstonecraft, but today was not trauma for me. I killed what needed killing. That's part of who I am. What I am. This isn't trauma. It's a connection."

"A spark?" she asked hopefully.

"It's a goddamn electrical storm. I'm not letting go of you." For the first time, he'd gotten something he wanted. Adam hadn't known how badly he wanted her until she'd been in his arms. He hadn't reconciled the little girl she was with the woman she'd become.

He was now her creature in all ways. In giving him his freedom, giving him the choice to serve her. He'd follow her into Hell.

Or a Bureau 7 facility infested with zombies.

Whichever came first.

Adam still couldn't believe she'd given him his freedom. It had been like dropping one-hundred pounds of chains that had been wrapped around his neck for the whole of his existence. Now, they were gone. His purpose wasn't to serve; his purpose was whatever he wanted it to be. He'd never felt like his life was a gift, not until this very moment.

She pulled several pairs of fatigues and boots, t-shirts, and other essentials from a storage bin. "Hey, look at this. You're right. They were prepared."

Elizabeth shrugged the lab coat off and dressed.

He liked watching her slide those fatigues up her long legs. He liked looking at her body, her face. He even liked watching her tying her boots.

The idea of her going anywhere near the facility twisted him up. He was afraid for her. He'd never felt that for another creature before.

"I'll do it for you," he blurted. "Just tell me how. You can stay here. Safe. I can do the rest."

"You'll need a staff fingerprint to access it."

"I can take it off one of the dead."

"Adam, I'm going. I need to go and help set this right."

"I knew you were going to say that, but I had to try." He had this insane urge to tranq her, put her on the boat and haul her back to Trieste and chain her up in the deep, dark, secret places of the castle so no one could ever hurt her.

So no one could ever take her from him.

He knew that was completely unreasonable, but it didn't stop him from feeling it. Adam grabbed the ax and handed it to her. "You're going to need this."

"You know just what a girl wants." She grinned. "I wonder if there are any more weapons stashed in this place. If I'd been thinking, I'd have grabbed that laser scalpel from the lab."

"We're probably better off with old faithful." He patted the handle. An ax was pretty much the final solution to most problems.

"Are you going to make me walk back or can you run?"

"I'll go with you. I'll run to get you away from danger. But toward it? No. That goes against my prime directive."

She laughed. "I'm not changing my mind."

"I know."

"We could possibly sail around to the other side. I thought I saw an emergency raft in one of those bins."

"That would be safer," he agreed. "Did you see rappelling equipment, too? The face of this cliff is sheer. I can jump." He shrugged. "You, not so much."

Elizabeth went to the bins and riffled through them, but found only the emergency raft and a pack of flares.

"They seem to be big on secret passages." Adam pressed his hands against the walls. He could jolt them like he had in the lab, but he didn't want to take the chance it would activate some unwanted failsafe.

"There are instructions." Elizabeth held up a booklet. "Apparently, when one is at a loss, one should read the directions."

Diagrams within the pages made him think that he'd much rather jump off the side of the cliff. He was right, there was another secret passage, but it was beneath him. A freshwater river that connected the various safehouses with the main facility. The door could only be accessed from inside the safehouse.

But he didn't like it. Of course, there wasn't much about any of this he did like. Just Elizabeth, really. "You don't think they've found their way into the river yet?"

Elizabeth looked from the raft to him, and back to the raft. He knew what she was going to say.

"Listen, if we go overland, we'll be out in the open, but that also means there are more places to run. If we take—" he motioned with disgust "—that thing, we'll be singularly vulnerable. There won't be anywhere to run, we'll be underground. We also don't know what kind of life has developed in this river. This installation has been here in one incarnation or another for a long time. Do you think this is the first incident to happen here?"

"The river would empty into sea. Surely..."

"No, look at the diagram. It's self-contained. Fed by various creeks and underground pools. There are falls here." He pointed on the diagram. "The water goes into a pool that eventually wraps around to feed the mouth of the river again."

Her eyes brightened. "Now you know I have to go down there. This was not the way to change my mind. When I read about the independent ecosystem in the Movile Cave, a place where animals have no eyes, and they live off carbon dioxide, not oxygen, I almost wanted to become a microbiologist so I could go in the cave."

"There are probably leeches the size of my arm."

"I guess we'll just have to take care not to fall in." She grinned. "Come on, let's go."

He helped her unfold the raft and, when they'd gathered everything they needed, he pulled the tab to activate the self-inflating mechanism.

The floor dropped out from beneath them and they careened into a sulfuric darkness. The raft didn't hit the water though. They'd been caught by some sort of lever mechanism that lowered them into the water gently and didn't disturb the flow. Yeah, leeches. "It stinks like someone's asshole in here," he muttered.

Elizabeth held up the lantern, the soft sallow light illuminating their surroundings. The walls were stone and moist, algae growing up over them just until the cavern ceiling. Something about it the algae couldn't tolerate and he was grateful for it. There was something about the red-tinged growth that told him it was no regular algae.

Something dark darted through the small rapids. Several some-things. It was too much to hope for that they were dolphins. As if to display itself, one leaped up and crashed back down into the water on top of another, its tubular mouth of teeth, just like the zombies', closed over its prey. Others latched on to the one that was bleeding and took it down, thrashing.

One of them didn't join the others. No, instead, it turned its eyeless face toward them. It sensed them, even if it couldn't see them.

Shit, the blood on her hands. Shit, shit.

"Elizabeth, I need you to stay very still."

"If I wanted you to catch one of those—"

"Not a chance." He was torn between relief that she wasn't afraid and fear because she wanted to catch one and study it. "It can smell the blood on your hands."

She peered over the edge of the raft with the lantern.

It was promptly smacked from her hand and they were plunged into darkness. Electricity crackled around his fingers and he upped his voltage. He wondered how much it would take to fry the entire river— charge it all with electric current.

"Stop that," a strange, silky voice said.

He'd never known a voice could sound...slimy. It reminded him of the algae somehow. Moist. Slippery.

Wrong.

"Hello?" Elizabeth said. "I'm a doctor from Bureau 7 and I'm trying to get back to the main facility."

"I know who you are, silly girl. And you didn't follow the directions, did you? It said to bathe before you came down here. To bind all open wounds with the laser and rinse all blood from your body. It's not nice to taunt my children."

Elizabeth leaned further over the boat, obviously trying to get a better look at the creature talking.

"And you better not try to catch one, or I'll tear you apart."

Scaled hands gripped the edge of the raft. It would be so easy for her to use her claws on the raft. They were long, and sharp, like knives. She pulled herself up so that she was face to face with Elizabeth.

She flicked her tail at him, the long scales flickering with her own electric current. She was like some kind of mermaid, electric eel, zombie hybrid.

But the creatures moved for her as she passed.

"I'm sorry." Elizabeth apologized. "May *I see one?*"

The creature laughed. "You want me to show you my children? You aren't afraid?"

"I find fear is easily allayed with knowledge."

"I suppose, then. Put out your hand."

No way in hell. Adam put out his hand. "I will hold him first."

"No, you won't."

"Let her wash her hands, first."

"My children will not hurt her." The creature seemed offended.

"Is it rude to ask," Elizabeth began, "what you are?"

"Only slightly." The creature's eyes were visible in the shadows. They were white orbs with no iris. "But I like you, human. I am a Rusalka. I guard this river. Below Bureau 7 is mine. Above is all theirs."

"I have to warn you, there's been an accident," Elizabeth said.

"I know. We've eaten many of your accidents." A wet sound that could've the smack of lips echoed.

Adam didn't like how close she was to Elizabeth. In all the stories of Rusalka he'd heard, they were like sirens, luring men to their deaths.

"What do you want with us?" Adam asked.

She laughed again, the sound horrible. "It is you who have come to me, dead man. Not the other way around."

"Will you allow us to pass?" Elizabeth asked.

"Yes," the Rusalka agreed. "But with your promise to send me more of your tasty accidents."

"They're infected with a virus. You don't know how it will affect you."

"Aren't you sweet? Just sweet enough to eat, if I didn't like you." A fork in the river appeared and the Rusalka guided them to the right, toward the frothy waters that contained ever more of her young.

"Wait!" Elizabeth cried. "Look! It's Polidori's lab coat!"

Adam looked to the left and saw John's blood splattered, shredded lab coat.

"You know him?"

"Yes. I worked with him," Elizabeth answered.

"I hope you didn't like him. I sent him the wrong way and there are worse things in these waters than me."

"Have you been topside?" Elizabeth asked.

"You're just full of questions, aren't you?"

Adam stayed silent.

"I'm a scientist. I'm curious about everything."

"No, I am much like your Poly-dor, in that aspect."

The canal narrowed and the scaly hand disappeared from the side of the raft.

"This is as far as I go. See the light up ahead? Make sure to grab ropes or you'll go over the edge of the falls."

She sank beneath the swirling black waters and her children followed.

Adam decided he was definitely anti-Rusalka.

Elizabeth, on the other hand, was excited. "That was amazing."

She was probably going to be the death of him. Literally. His hearts would stop in his chest, but he decided that was mostly okay.

The fire in her eyes was worth it.

The ropes came at them quickly and they were pulled up into the light. Into a room where everything was sterile and clean and bright. It was completely different from the subterranean world they'd just left.

It appeared that none of the infected had been in this room, either.

There was a keycard and thumbprint apparatus on the only door out and the ax and other weapons had stayed in the raft. There'd been no way to grab them and hold on to the ropes.

Now, the only thing standing between Elizabeth and infection was him.

For the first time, it mattered if he was enough.

For the first time, he doubted himself.

Whatever it was that gave him that extrasensory perception about the Wollstonecraft bloodline also told him that it was Elizabeth who was going to pay the price.

CHAPTER SEVEN

The Rusalka had been terrifying, but one of the more interesting creatures she'd gotten to interact with since taking the Bureau 7 job. She'd thought for sure the thing was going to eat them, but was pleased they'd made it to the ropes.

She looked to Adam and instinctively knew he was wondering how she was going to fight with no ax. Elizabeth still had the gun, but she had limited rounds and she wasn't that experienced.

She supposed the zombie apocalypse would be the mother of invention. Experience. Whatever.

Part of her so desperately wanted to take Adam up on his offer to let him carry her away to his boat and sail to warm waters where none of this mattered. But if she didn't stop it, who would? She couldn't abdicate her responsibility for what happened here. Sure, they could blame X, but they couldn't blame them if she abandoned the mess they'd made without trying to clean it up.

"Are you ready?" she asked him.

"Would it do any good if I asked you to stay behind me?" He sounded tired, like it was an exhaustion that went deeper than the body. Soul-tired, if one believed in such things.

"Yeah. I can do that."

He pulled her close and kissed her hard. "I knew fear once, when I was first made. The first time the villagers came for me, the first time they burned me, I was afraid. But never since. Not until now. I'm afraid for you." He said this as if he didn't understand the feelings.

She cupped his cheek. "I'm afraid for you, too."

"And still we press on." He nodded. There was no recrimination in his words, no accusation. Only fact.

"We do, because it's the right thing to do." She allowed herself to lean against him for a long moment before she approached the door. "You ready?"

"Hit it."

She pressed her finger against the scanner and the door whooshed open. It was like pulling back a curtain in a slaughterhouse. Blood and meat was splashed on the walls like modern art and there was a pack of them feeding on another. They'd already started on their own.

One lifted his head from the meal, backed away from the throng of feeding and turned his attention on her.

No, it wasn't a him. It was a her. Margie, from the cafeteria. Margie, who brought her lunch when she forgot to feed herself. Margie, with her pretty hair, a handsome poet husband, and a young son on the mainland. Tony. His birthday party was Saturday... Margie, who was working for Bureau 7 so that she could go to medical school.

She didn't want to look, didn't want to see how the infection had changed her. How it had done things there was no going back from. The skin hanging like dried leaves from her face, that once pretty hair all white, thin, with patches missing. Her hands curled into red-stained claws.

"Margie," she whispered.

All seven of them turned their attention from their still struggling meal to her.

"Goddamn it, back inside. Right now!" Adam commanded.

But there was no going back inside. There was only forward. There was no keycard or fingerprint module to open the door from that side.

Terror knifed her. There were too many of them.

Adam was strong, and he was fast, but he only had two hands. She drew her gun. Elizabeth tried to stay behind Adam, but snapping teeth and claws were everywhere.

And most importantly were the deadly jaws right in front of her on the face of her friend. She knew what was coming at her wasn't Margie anymore, but she couldn't shoot her.

Except, didn't she owe her that?

No, what she fucking owed her was to have thought about these kinds of outcomes when she agreed to move forward with testing on live subjects.

Her heart clenched and tears welled. Fuck, she wasn't going to cry. There was no time for tears. Only survival. She could cry later.

Margie launched herself and, even though she swore she wasn't going to cry, tears streamed down her face, hot and acidic. But that didn't stop her for doing what she had to do.

She took the shot and dropped the creature that had once been her friend in a pool of her own blood.

The other revenants didn't try to claim the meal. They took off down the halls, running as if the hounds of hell were at their heels.

And maybe they were.

Adam looked like a demon, his face and hands covered in blood, and the rage in his eyes was something only the damned could know.

But it died when he saw her.

It was a physical change in him as all that ferocity left his body. His eyes were hooded pools of shadows, no longer the fires of hell. He seemed smaller somehow. Yet, he'd fought so bravely. He was so strong. She didn't understand what looked like the weight of defeat on his shoulders.

Until she looked down at her wrist and saw it.

The bite.

She was infected.

Part of her raged at how unfair it was. She wasn't supposed to be punished for doing the right thing. She still had work to do. She had to fix this.

But she never would fix it, would she? It was all going to be over in a matter of minutes. There was so much she still wanted to experience. She'd only just now found Adam, and she had to leave him.

For a moment, she felt a wash of cold guilt for thinking of herself. Margie hadn't wanted to leave her life, either. Especially not her son, who was turning four...

A cry was wrenched from her, and even she didn't know if it was grief, rage or some toxic sludge of both.

Because she knew what she had to do.

"I don't know how long I have," she began.

"No."

She'd already learned to recognize that hard set to his jaw. "You don't even know what I'm going to say."

"Yes, I do. You're going to tell me to go to my boat. You're going to tell me to leave you, and I won't do it. I'll never leave you."

Her heart swelled and cracked, broken for what they could've shared. "What are you going to do, Adam? Take me back to your castle and chain me in the dungeon and feed me tourists?"

"A monster just might."

She gave him a watery laugh. "What if I got free? Then what?"

"Woman, don't you understand yet that the only reason I came was for you? I don't give a flying damn about the rest of the world. They can all rot."

"No, Adam. They can't." She shook her head. "My friend Margie... her son is going to be four on Saturday. Would you leave him to this?" She motioned at the carnage before them.

"Don't ask me to leave you."

"I'm going to ask you, because it's what I need you to do. Help me get the rest of the way to the lab to initiate the failsafe. Then you have to leave. If Bureau 7 finds you here, you won't go home, and you won't be able to stop them from putting me down."

"I'll kill them all," he snarled.

"I don't want you to. I'm part of the contagion now." She shivered as her body temperature began to drop. "It's happening. We have to move."

"Wait!"

"Adam—"

"No, that one."

He pointed to where Margie's body lay. She didn't want to look, didn't want to see the aftermath of what she'd done.

"You have to look."

Slowly, she turned her eyes toward Margie's body. It was so much worse than she thought. Margie's eyes had returned to normal, except for the empty stare of death. Her hair was still white, and patchy. But her face... oh God, her face. It was all too human and the bullet hole in the center of her forehead much too surreal and bright.

"She's the one that bit you, isn't she?" Adam asked.

"I think so."

"You might not turn. We need to get to the lab. Which way?"

Elizabeth gave him directions as a certain numbness spread through her. It was highly unlikely that she wouldn't turn with her symptoms. But she didn't tell him that. She had to get to the lab, no matter the cost.

Even if it meant letting Adam have false hope.

The revenants didn't bother them now, they could smell death on her and could sense that Adam would be no easy meal, even if they were turning on themselves. That didn't stop him though, didn't crush his hope like it should've. No, he kept moving so fast—she couldn't keep up.

When she was sure she was going to fall, Adam caught her and carried her the rest of the way.

"I'm turning, Adam. You have to go," she murmured.

"Shh. Rest. Just rest. We're almost there."

"If they find you here—" Elizabeth didn't get to finish her sentence. Darkness filled all the noisy places in her brain, that need for survival screaming in her head was silenced as it drowned in shadow.

All she could do was surrender.

CHAPTER EIGHT

A dam refused to believe this was the end for them.

When Elizabeth's eyes closed and her heart stopped, a roar was torn from him the likes of which no creature had ever heard before. It rattled the very foundations of the walls around them. Walls that he would tear down with his bare fucking hands if his Elizabeth had been taken from him.

The electricity crackled around his fingertips, and he didn't try to hold it back. He let it flow from his body, into hers. He'd give her everything he had.

He'd give her the gift she hadn't asked for when her mother died.

Her body spasmed in his arms and the current was like alchemy, binding them in a way that curse never could.

Two long, white streaks appeared at her temples and the wound stitched itself back together, but left a scar, much like his own where his body had been cobbled together from spare parts of dead men.

When the lightning storm passed, she lay limp in his arms and he sank to the floor, holding her close.

Without her, nothing mattered. Not humanity. Not the infection. Not the new pack of revenants that seemed to sense his surrender that were coming for them. He'd let them tear him apart—anything so he didn't have to face the long, endless eternity without her.

Only, when they crept close to them, they didn't attack. They slavered their venomous drool, and snapped their teeth, but they didn't bite. It was as if they were waiting for something. One reached out a skeletal hand, and he slapped it away.

The thing howled.

Adam bared his teeth. "Mine."

"Ours," one hissed. Then another and still another until it was a chorus. "Ours."

A loud thump startled them all. Then another. And still another.

It was her heart! It had found the rhythm! Her eyelashes fluttered, and she opened her eyes slowly—so slowly.

He waited to see if this world had earned its apocalypse or its redemption.

If she'd become one of those things that now reached for her, that tried to claim her as their own, the world had signed its own death warrant.

Her eyes were brown, not the pale white of the undead.

Yet in them, he still saw the yawning stretch of eternity. In them, he saw the same Wollstonecraft eyes that had witnessed his beginning, and in what about them that made them uniquely hers, he saw those that would witness his end.

She reached up and touched his face. "I'm okay."

The revenants seemed intrigued, also reaching forward to touch him. Again, he slapped them off. "Stop."

"Mother," they whispered and reached for her.

"They're evolving," she whispered.

Her interest was suddenly consumed by the unnatural creatures before them, and it was if she'd never been in any danger.

Adam felt a sudden sharpness at his leg and saw one of them trying to bite him, so he crushed it like a bug.

The rest of them shied away from him now. She was right, they were learning. They were evolving past their hunger. Or perhaps, they'd only become more efficient hunters? Why had they called her mother? He supposed she'd had a hand in their birth, but how would they know that?

Perhaps the same way he knew without even looking at her that she was of the Wollstonecraft bloodline.

"Do you think they'd go with me to the lab?"

"Elizabeth—"

"I need to get all the information I can. There's a SWAT team on the way to help put them down, but if X has the prion, they could unleash this anywhere."

Adam sighed. "You're right."

He stood and followed behind the group as they moved through the bloody halls toward the lab.

Not all of the revenants were evolving, only the few that walked with them. They picked up two others as they made their way through the labyrinthine halls. Some watched them warily while they continued their grisly meals, but it was as if the ones who knew they were different, knew to join their motley group.

If one tried that wasn't like them, they quickly ripped him to pieces. They protected their small tribe, and Elizabeth, even though they gave him the side-eye.

Once they got to the lab, Elizabeth took samples from everyone, except him. She loaded them into the centrifuge and led them into a holding area. They did everything she asked. As the minutes ticked by, it seemed they became more familiar. They lost the white film over their eyes, they began speaking in coherent sentences. With every change, they seemed more and more human.

"Adam, look!" She pointed. "They all have a bite mark, just like mine."

They were all scarred in the same place.

Except for one. One he'd seen start on Elizabeth's friend, the one who'd bitten her.

"It's in your blood, Elizabeth. The cure for this disease, is in your blood."

She ran to the data terminal and began typing furiously. "I need to upload all of this information. Hey, I have a jump drive in the second drawer. I'm making copies."

He handed her the jump drive and in truth, had never felt more worthless. He didn't know how else to help her. Killing, he could do. Fighting, he could do. Science... He could hand her a jump drive.

She laughed. "Oh my God. I look like the Bride of Frankenstein. Have you seen my hair?" Elizabeth ran her fingers through the white streaks that had appeared at her temples.

"Frankenstein was the scientist, not the monster," he corrected with a smirk.

Her mouth curved into a smile that reached her eyes. Even soaked in blood, that smile was the most beautiful thing he'd ever seen.

"I never date other scientists." She moved her fingers over the keyboard, and it looked for all the world like she was weaving some magic spell.

Adam still thought technology was a kind of magic, anyway.

She stopped, hit a few more buttons before she looked at him. "But I find that I might have a penchant for monsters."

"This monster?" he teased. "Or those?" He indicated to the holding area where the zombies seemed to be recovering their senses.

"Both of you, actually. They feel like my children, so I'm going to go with it."

"I used to dream of a big family."

"There's not enough Turducken in the world for that holiday dinner."

The comm buzzed. "Attention in the compound. Attention in the compound. This is Commander Whitman. Stay where you are. Do not activate the failsafe. I repeat, this is Commander Whitman with Bureau 7 SWAT. Stay where you are. Do not activate the failsafe. We will come to you."

All the playfulness was gone from Elizabeth's face. Her face had gone chalk white. "You can't let them catch you."

"I don't want to leave you," he said, knowing that he had to. For now.

"Find me. You can, right? Even though you're free?"

"I'll never be free of you." He wrapped his arms around her. "And I don't want to be."

"That's so the right answer." She looked up at him. "Kiss me."

He didn't hold back—not his strength, not the electric current that lived inside of him, and not everything that he felt for this woman.

His woman.

She kissed him back. "Don't be gone too long."

Adam thought he'd done hard things before. Killing Harriet Shelley had gone against everything in him he knew to be right, and it had ripped him apart to hurt her. But the curse made it impossible to deny.

Walking away from Elizabeth, no curse compelled him to put one foot in front of the other. To not look back and walked away from her and left her in the middle of a crisis. Perhaps the immediate danger had passed, but no one could protect her like he could.

He knew he was protecting her by walking away. If the Bureau wanted him badly enough, and they realized *she was* like him, they'd lock her away, too. They'd take her apart and put her back together all to dissect the divine.

He tried not to think about the taste of her on his lips, the way she felt in his arms, or the simple, pure joy he'd felt knowing that she lived.

The only peace he'd ever known was when she touched him.

He would find her again, when it was safe, and hope that this horror hadn't all been a fevered dream. Adam would take all of it, all the long years, the loneliness, even the first time they burned him—it was all worth having Elizabeth.

When he exited the compound, helicopters buzzed above like shiny wasps, darting here and there, and an army of what looked like tiny ants swarmed down rappelling lines. The SWAT team they'd been promised. They were armed to the teeth and outfitted in body armor.

He watched them for a long moment and wondered if they'd notice the No Stars drifting away from the dock. If they did, he could always lose them in the sea. He could walk to the mainland if he had to, but Adam had decided maybe he had use for some human things after all. He really enjoyed his boat and, someday, Elizabeth was going to be naked in the sun on that deck.

Adam crept aboard, and it seemed all attention was on the facility. There were a few stray revenants, and they were quickly put down. He supposed he blended in, as well as a monster could, in his fatigues and combat boots. They must've assumed at a distance, he was one of them.

Sloppy work on their part.

He was half-tempted to turn around.

But he kept hearing her say, "Find me."

Adam untied his boat and let the wind and waves do as they wished with him. At least until he got out of sight of the island.

He grabbed a bottle of wine he'd been saving. It was the last from his maker's cellar. Adam knew it was probably pure vinegar swill by now, but it was the end. It was a beginning.

It was time.

"I assume you have another glass for me?" John Polidori climbed up from below deck.

"You piece of shit," Adam said with a sigh. He didn't bother to ask what the bloodsucker was doing on his boat. It was obvious he was trying to escape.

John waved him off. *"Oh,* you say the sweetest things. It's positively poetry."

"I should rip your arms off."

"If you were going to, you would have." John reached for the bottle of wine and took a long pull. "This is piss. Why are you drinking—oh. That's why." He inspected the bottle.

"Aren't you even going to ask what happened to Elizabeth?"

Polidori looked up from the bottle. "I rather thought you wouldn't want me to." He narrowed his eyes. "You Tarzan, Her Jane?" He rolled his eyes. "I'm sure she's fine."

"She was bitten."

"I know. Rather clever of me, don't you think?"

Adam considered murder. Popping his head off like a dandelion in summer and making a wish while he sprayed the vampire's guts all over the Aegean.

"Oh my God, you're so boring." He handed Adam the bottle. "Silly little Prometheus. It's not like you were going to kill her just so you could give her your gift. You wouldn't have been able to do it. I helped you. Now, you just have to get her bone marrow to do what yours does and it's happily bloody after."

"How do you propose I do that?"

"Must I do everything? You graft one of your bones to one of hers. Rib is the easiest, I hear. Downright biblical, if you ask me." He smirked. "Ironic, isn't it? The creation of man, bitter at his creator playing divine, must now play the game himself or lose the woman he loves. Personally, I like it."

"You left her alone, John."

"And is she not just fine?"

"That's not the point." Adam advanced on him. "You let her be afraid. That's not something I'm willing to let go."

"Oh, for fuck's sake. Seriously?" Polidori put up his hands, as if that would ward him off. "Let's be civilized about this."

"There's nothing civilized about abandoning a woman who trusted you."

"I didn't ask her to trust me. I mean, if we're dissecting particulars."

"Oh, but you did. When you agreed to work with her. When you signed your contract with Bureau 7. Elizabeth says they'll put a price on your head."

"As if that's anything new." He rolled his eyes. "Back up, sir. You are decidedly in my space."

"I'm going to do a lot more than be in your space," Adam promised.

"How rude." Polidori sighed as Adam picked him up by his arms. "Those take forever to regenerate. Don't tear them off."

"I have something better."

Polidori didn't squirm in his grip or even try to get away. "Don't hurt yourself. You get those gears in that skull turning too quickly, something important might catch fire."

"Indeed, Doctor. Indeed," he agreed jovially.

He hurled John Polidori over the side of the boat.

"You're not really going to leave me here, are you?" John said when he surfaced, treading water.

"It is fair. You left Elizabeth drowning in a sea of death. I will leave you here." He nodded.

"I can't drown." John looked smug.

"No, but you can wish you could." Adam called on the electric current and stuck his hands into the water. "There is a little-known species of eel—"

"Oh for fuck's sake. Electric eels are freshwater, air-breathing—"

"Let me finish. There's a little-known species of eel that lives in the deep ocean. It tolerates both the darkest depths and the surface surprisingly well. Most animals that live that deep die on the surface. Not these guys. They grow to lengths of twenty to fifty feet. I discovered them after Mary had me hammered into a coffin and dumped at sea. They were drawn to my electricity. They think I'm one of theirs." Adam laughed as he watched the terror wash over Polidori.

"You're immortal. They could drag you down so far, the pressure of the water could crush even your bones. And they'll keep you there. That's where you'll spend your eternity, in the bellies of eels. Unless you start swimming now."

Polidori composed himself and raised a brow. "You sir, are a motherfucker of the lowest caliber."

"No, I don't abandon helpless women during a zombie apocalypse of my own making. That is a motherfucker of the lowest caliber." He cocked his head. "Oh, what's that? They're coming. I can feel it."

"Damn you, Adam. I saved her! I helped you!" he snarled.

"Perhaps you did. And that's the only reason that I didn't tear your limbs from your body and reattach them with your own intestines. Enjoy your swim to shore, Doctor." Adam winked at him and went to engage the engine.

He couldn't go back to Trieste, not now. So it was on to warmer waters and maybe a beach where he would dream of Elizabeth and wait until the time was right to find her.

Even though she'd released him from the curse, she was part of him still. He'd always know where to find her.

"Find me," he replayed her whisper in his ear as sailed away from Polidori, from Bureau 7, from all the darkness that had always plagued him.

He may have left her behind, in a way, he was still sailing toward her. Toward their future together.

Toward home.

* * *

Elizabeth was in a helicopter next to "Mad Dog" Whitman when the installation lit up the night sky. Fireworks exploded around them in a bright, colorful display. The populace had been told it was a planned entertainment, but it was to mask the utter and absolute destruction of the compound.

"It just came over the wire, Dr. Wollstonecraft." The SWAT commander nodded. "They've captured the X operative in Turkey. I thought you'd like to know."

Elizabeth nodded. "After the mayhem she caused, I hope they throw her in the deepest, loneliest, blackest pit."

"And if they gave you the key to this pit?" The corner of her full mouth turned up with a smirk.

"I'd give it to a Rusalka."

Mad Dog laughed. "Hardcore. I respect that. I'm sure the information extraction process will be painful for her, if that makes you feel any better."

"I wish I could say it did. I mean, you know, kind of." She gave the other woman a lopsided grin. "But it doesn't undo all the harm she did. The people's lives she destroyed. The resources we've lost."

"Maybe it's not all bad. You've got the survivors who were able to be evacuated." Her dark brown eyes narrowed. "What's that scar on your arm? It looks like a bite."

Elizabeth smiled at her. "It is."

Mad Dog lived up to her name, and she pulled out her Glock and held it to Elizabeth's head. "You better start talking."

"I'm immune."

"You could have a secondary infection. You could—"

"I don't. My last name is Wollstonecraft."

"I don't give a good goddamn what your last name is, lady."

Elizabeth tried to think of a way to distill the information without revealing too much about Adam. "The people who are in those cages recovering? It's because one of them bit me. The cure is in my blood."

She eyed her. "Should've known you had some shit, what with your stripes in your hair like Frankenstein's Bride."

Elizabeth smiled. "Exactly like Frankenstein's Bride." She didn't bother to correct her that Frankenstein was the doctor, not the monster. Because in truth, he was the monstrous one. It was the monster who was noble. The monster who was good. The monster who was... Adam.

"You're a strange one. You're the only woman I've met to go anime-eyed over Frankenstein." She holstered her weapon. "But I can't blame you."

"Oh? A supernatural crush of your own?"

"You wouldn't believe me if I told you." Mad Dog eased back and looked out at the fireworks as they disappeared in the distance.

"I probably would. A little girl-bonding couldn't hurt."

"We went all this time without talking about men. Let's not ruin it."

Elizabeth laughed. "Come on. I'm dying to know."

"Your monster is real, though. Isn't he? He was the big, dark shadow on the security footage."

Elizabeth had a split second to make the decision whether or not to trust Mad Dog Whitman, SWAT Commander and fellow Bureau 7 employee. She knew full well she could be a plant to ferret out any information about Adam.

Elizabeth had some otherworldly perception about the woman. She knew instinctively, that as long as she wasn't trying to hurt anyone with her secret, she would keep it to herself.

"Yes."

"Well, don't worry. I erased the tapes."

"Why would you do that?"

"Call it a hunch." She shrugged. "In all the years I've worked for 7, I've never heard *of this* monster. If he was the kind of thing I hunt, I'd have heard about him."

"So tell me," Elizabeth prompted.

"Oh, for shit's sake." She sighed. "His name is Karl. He's not real. He was my imaginary friend when I was a kid. I'm probably just wired wrong. Most people who do what I do are."

"No, you're not getting off that easily."

"Okay, I've never actually said this out loud. If I tell you this, that's it. We're friends. You're coming at the holidays to meet my family and it's a forever thing." Whitman took a deep breath. "Karl Prinzehausen is his full name and he's the Headless Horseman."

Elizabeth kept her face neutral. "Seriously? Like, Sleepy Hollow Horseman?"

"Yeah. My parents own a B&B and an orchard just at the edge of town. Wanna come for Halloween?"

"Can I bring a date?"

"Sleepy Hollow won't know what hit them." She grinned. "Since we're best friends now, or something, I guess you can call me Mads."

"If you call me Lizzie, I'll kill you."

"Fair enough, Elizabeth." Something came over the radio and Mads answered. "10-4. I'll escort her myself."

"What's happened?"

"Roanridge wants you stateside for debriefing. There's a private plane in Athens waiting for you."

"Do you know where my patients are going?"

"Don't worry about them, Doc. We've got no orders to terminate. They're headed to the Shetland Islands. I'm sure you'll be there shortly. I guess you'll have to come home with me next Halloween."

"I hope you weren't kidding about that because I'm coming."

"Good."

"Good." She laughed. But her stomach was unsettled. She was not looking forward to debriefing. Why did he want to do it in person?

She guessed she'd soon find out.

CHAPTER NINE

S hetland Islands, Scotland
        Bureau 7, Roanridge Island Installation

T he cold wind whipped at her face as the boat forced its way
        through from St. Magnus Bay to the Norwegian Sea.
            Elizabeth was headed home from the Roanridge Island
Installation. She'd learned her lesson about living on site. She had her
own tiny island and, like Roanridge, it was on no map. She'd named it
Legacy. It had craggy desolate shores and tall, ancient trees. Just being
there instilled a sense of rightness in her, and she knew what to ask for
when Director Roanridge had offered her a bonus to continue working
on the project.

It was either continue the project or become part of it, anyway.
That had been the Director's ultimatum. So she'd moved to the frigid
north, closer to Norway than to Scotland. It was different here than
Greece, the island living. It was more rugged. Harsher. Living alone on
an island here was like waving your middle finger in the face of Mother
Nature and daring her to strike you down.

But that was in the Wollstonecraft blood, too, apparently.

SARANNA DEWYLDE

If Elizabeth hadn't had the survivors of Kythnos quarantined in Sector 4Z, she might have wondered if it had all been a fevered dream.

She rubbed the scar on her wrist absently, and thought about him—Adam.

Had a man made of death really come to save her?

Her logical mind said it was the fever as her body fought off the infection, but the infection itself, the fact that she was immune, that was enough to remind her that she was something else. Something different.

And that he had happened.

He was more than a figment of her imagination.

Tears stung her eyes as the frigid salt spray splashed her face, but she kind of liked it. It reminded her that she was alive.

It wasn't too long before her dock came into view, and she was disappointed to see yet again that hers was the only boat in evidence. He said he'd find her when the time was right and so she waited.

She hoped.

And sometimes, hope was a miserable bastard. Nothing could be so sharp a blade as the yearning beh*ind hope.*

Elizabeth guided the boat into the docking system, and it was locked down into position. If she wished, she could use the system she'd installed to carry her all the way to the secret lagoon under her house and from there, into a decontamination room.

Kythnos had inspired her, and Roanridge hadn't given her a limit on her spending. Not that she'd gone crazy. Her home was made of old shipping containers, powered by the sun and the wind. Gray water and rainwater systems, the whole works.

Technically, she could survive an apocalypse, zombie or otherwise. She hadn't neglected a panic room, a bunker, or an extra layer of security. She'd found herself a cold water Rusalka who was more than happy to play guardian.

Everything was as she wanted it, except for Adam.

After she disembarked, she hiked up the rocky incline, breathing deep and enjoying the air.

She carried a package in her bag, and she couldn't wait to get inside and open it.

Inside, were the original three, hand-written installments of Frankenstein.

In the months following Kythnos, she'd become obsessed, collecting everything about her family that she could.

Her study contained some gruesome, yet fascinating items. Percy's calcified heart, wrapped in his poetry. Mary had kept it after it had refused to burn when he was cremated. Mary's mother's secret journal, and the bone of her left pinkie. This, and many other items were said to contain the key to the true alchemy behind life ever-lasting.

The spark that made Adam.

If Roanridge was aware of her new proclivities, it wasn't addressed.

Unwrapping the books from the pouch, she carefully laid them out side by side and turned to chapter seven in each volume.

There, in the chapter heading were alchemical sigils.

The same elation she'd felt watching PrPM attack that glioblastoma flooded her. She'd found it. She'd found the keys.

Now, all she needed was Adam and his willingness to rip his chest open and give her a rib. Elizabeth didn't doubt for one second that he would.

She watched the door, half expecting to see him there. He'd said when the time was right, and it had never been more right.

But life didn't happen in perfect plot arcs. It couldn't be wrapped up so neatly. She sank down in the chair.

"It's not like you to give up so easily."

There he was. Just as he'd promised. When the time was right.

She ran to him, and he swept her up into his arms. "You know how to do this?" He whispered against her lips.

"I have a lab we can use to operate. It's ready."

"Then so am I, because I want to give you forever."

The monster carried his bride to the lab where he did, indeed, give her *forever with his* rib bone grafted to her own that caused a second heart to grow in her chest and electricity to crackle around her fingertips.

THE EVER AFTER

Dr. Elizabeth Wollstonecraft still works for Bureau 7. She plans to cure brain cancer someday and still believes reprogrammed prions are key. Under interests in her company biography, she's no longer ashamed to list "reanimation" as one of her hobbies.

Adam is a content house monster and lives to care for Elizabeth and, after writing his memoirs, has decided to pursue a career in fiction.

Dr. John Polidori washed up on an uncharted island populated by sirens. The giant electric eels have taken up patrols to keep him from leaving. He contemplates his life choices and decides that perhaps he should've turned left at Albuquerque.

Mad Dog Whitman officially returned home to Sleepy Hollow for some R&R, but she's really there on a secret mission for Bureau 7. There's a killer loose in Sleepy Hollow, but it's not the Horseman. It's something much worse. Read her story in The Horseman's Lady coming soon and enjoy a sneak peek at the first chapter.

C

hapter One

After neutralizing a near zombie apocalypse at the Kythnos installation, Bureau 7 SWAT Commander Madelyn "Mad Dog" Whitman was looking forward to some serious R&R. It had been nonstop action since the series of possessions in Guatemala, a serial killer ghost and his cult at that abandoned asylum in Maine, and now a zombie apocalypse. Yeah, using about a month of her ridiculously large cache of vacation days and living the high life on her hazard pay sounded like just the thing.

Too bad this trip home to Sleepy Hollow wasn't it.

Honestly, Deputy Director Colin Roanridge probably thought if she had a chance to breathe, to remember what life was like away from Bureau 7, she wouldn't come back.

As if. Mads loved knowing things other people didn't. Working for a secret government agencies that operated in concert with other secret agencies worldwide fit the bill a little too well. She was B7 for life.

Although, who knew how long that was going to be? Being a SWAT Commander had its perks, but B7 SWAT members tended to live hard and fast, and she'd like to say they left good-looking corpses, but that was a lie.

Dying horribly tended to leave a mark.

She was addicted to the adrenaline rush now, too. There was no way she could go back to civvie life. After all, she knew what made the sounds in the dark. The things that squirmed in shadows.

And goddamn if she was going to let those things out into the world.

No, this was her gig, for better. For worse. For life.

For death.

She shouldn't open the case file while she sat in the back of a civvie vehicle on her way to her parents' B&B, but Mads couldn't wait to get another look at the case.

Mads was on a secret mission for the Bureau, and surprise of all surprises, it didn't have anything to do with The Horseman.

At least, nothing in the brief mentioned him, but she knew that was part of why she'd been recruited to the Bureau. They liked to collect people with certain connections. But Madelyn was proud to say she'd earned her spot as SWAT Commander, as well as her nickname, all on her own.

No Horseman required.

But there were bodies and the M.O. matched a big bad that had topped the Bureau's wanted list for a long time. A dark magician named Parrish Fade who had aligned himself with a paranormal terrorist group called X. They believed that it was time to lift the veil, for all paras to become not only visible, but to establish a para domi- nated government where humans were either servants or livestock. And Parrish was doing his best to get them there.

She fingered the heart charm on her necklace. It was supposed to render her immune to magic, but whenever she crossed the border into Sleepy Hollow, the thing made her itch.

"This your first time in Sleepy Hollow?" The driver asked her.

She smiled. "No. I'm actually a local. My parents own the only B&B within city limits."

"Little Maddy Whitman?" He looked up into the rearview mirror and met her eyes. "Last time I saw you, girl, you were no bigger than a bug."

Mads narrowed her eyes, trying to place him. But she couldn't. Nothing about him was familiar, but that wasn't *cause for co*ncern. Everyone knew everyone in Sleepy Hollow. At least, the locals did. "I'm sorry, I don't remember you."

"It's been a few years. Chris's dad."

Warmth filled her. "Mr. Knickerbocker! I'm so sorry."

"Eh, well, they keep you busy at the FBI, don't they?" He flashed her a wink in the rearview mirror. "And you're grown. You can call me Bill."

"I'm just an analyst with a desk job." That was her cover.

"Don't lie to me, little girl. Your gun show says you're more than an analyst. The way you watch your surroundings? You forget, I was a cop in NYC for years before I came to Sleepy Hollow. But it'll be our secret."

"My gun show?" She laughed. "I just like to be fit and it's part of keeping the job. Even a job behind a desk."

"That's too bad. I'd hoped you were here to help with these murders. We may have a serial killer on our hands."

"I don't know what I could do, but I will if I can," she promised.

"We can't have some crazy man running around and hacking off body parts. Our schtick is the Horseman, not the green guy with bolts in his neck."

He's not green, she wanted to say, thinking of her new friend, Dr. Elizabeth Wollstonecraft, and her... he wasn't a monster. He'd helped contain the outbreak on Kythnos. But what did Knickerbocker know about that?

"You're right about that." She shook her head. "Is that what people are saying? That this guy is harvesting body parts?"

"That's what it looks like."

"Damn. He's going to scare away all the tourists. Then where will we be?"

"You know that's right." He turned down the small lane that led to the B&B. "You know Evie would love to have you for dinner, if you have time. I'm sure you'll be seeing Chris tonight."

"I hadn't planned—oh. My parents planned a thing, didn't they?" Mads sighed. She loved them. She was happy to see them. Even her friends she hadn't seen in so long, but what she really wanted to do was hole up in her room and sink her teeth into this case file.

After she'd helped catch that serial murdering ghost, they seemed to think she knew something about this profiling gig. That had been her original area of study when she'd applied to the FBI. She wanted in on their profiling program, but Bureau 7 had snatched her up and she'd ended up leading raids instead of shrinking heads.

Which she knew was mostly for the best.

"You know they love you, and Chris can't wait to see you. He's missed you."

"I've missed him." Mads hadn't talked to Chris in a long time. He was so pissed when she'd joined what he thought was the FBI that it had caused a deep rupture in their friendship. She wondered if Kat

Crane was going to be there, too. Last she heard, Kat and Chris had been dating.

Once upon a time, Mads had thought Christopher was the guy for her. But then she never would've left Sleepy Hollow.

Or her imaginary Horseman.

She pressed her lips together. The imaginary part was still, as of yet, to be determined.

He'd been so real. Until high school. Until she'd asked him to take her to the homecoming dance. Really, all she'd wanted was for him to dance with her in the orchard under the stars.

And she'd never seen him again.

The B&B rose up in front of them, a familiar stranger, as the car slid to a stop.

"Looks like Chris is already here. They must be waiting for you." He nodded toward the small parking area that was filled with cars.

It seemed like the B&B was at capacity and that was great news for her parents. Her gaze flickered up to the attic window in the Dutch-style farmhouse. A wave of nostalgia washed over her, both warm and welcoming but somehow sad at the same time.

Almost against her will, her eyes were drawn to the orchard behind the house. The place where some say the Horseman was betrayed. The place where he was buried.

The place where when the leaves began to turn and the fruit was ripe and plentiful on the tree that she saw him. Spoke to him.

Where she'd spent long nights under the stars eating apples and making wishes with him.

There was nothing there but the trees. The grass. The bright sunshine in dappled rays through fat cottony clouds sailing on a blue sea of sky.

"Would you like to join us tonight?" she asked him. "I mean, since I guess it's a party."

"I've got to hustle and pick up a few more fares. Evie and I are spending New Year's in the Bahamas. She needs some spending money." He flashed her a grin and a wink. "But I'll see you soon."

The car slowed to a stop and Mads took a deep breath. She loved her family, but she always had to put her mental shields in place before she faced them. She hated lying to them about what she did, but they could never know.

It would only put them in harm's way.

And there was a rift that had grown between them that came not from the distance, and not even from the Top Secret work that she did, but from the way her parents dismissed those experiences that had seemed all too real.

She remembered the way she spoke about the Horseman at the breakfast table with their guests. Her parents had thought it was cute, a bit of kitsch for the tourists. Until Maddy had insisted, even after their guests were gone, that the dead mercenary plucked her the ripest, juiciest apples from the tops of the trees. That he checked her closet for monsters until she was ten.

That when she was sixteen, it had turned into something else.

The breath of a kiss that had died on her lips before being born.

"You all right, Little Maddy?" Bill asked her. "See something there in the orchard, just like in the old days, did you?"

Mads looked up at him and met his regard in the mirror. "Not a single thing. Just like back then, right?"

"If you say so. Although, I wouldn't be saying it too loudly. Not until your boarders have gone. After all, they're here for the Horseman."

She pulled out her phone and used the app to add a ridiculously generous tip. Bureau 7 wasn't footing the bill for her lodging, so they could suck it up for Evie Knickerbocker to enjoy her New Years. Mads owed the woman for more than one evening of homemade chocolate chip cookies and hot cocoa. "For spending money. Thanks, Bill."

She got out of the car and grabbed her bag, heading up the walkway to the house.

It was odd how even though she was long grown, his first name still felt strange on her tongue. In her mind, he'd always be Mr. Knicker-bocker, or Chris's Dad. As if that was his given name.

It was different with Evie. Evie had always been... just that: Evie. From when she was a little girl. Katrina, Mads, Chris and Sean had all played together in the Knickerbocker's backyard, gotten otter pops from their freezer and the kind woman with a gentle hand and sweet voice had always had time for them. She'd never been too busy to put a dress on a doll. Or to tell Chris and Sean that "action figures" were still dolls and it was okay for them to play with too.

She remembered Evie's house always smelled like those chocolate chip cookies.

The B&B always smelled like apples. Like a good apple cinnamon candle with the underpinnings of the orange oil they used on all the wood. Especially the staircases. Maybe a hint of clove that her mother boiled in a teakettle on the stove.

As she pushed open the front door and stepped into the entryway, she was hit with scents and sights. The warm orange clove beneath the apple. The gleaming rail on the staircase. The dark, smooth wood floors and the sound of her mother's voice in her ear telling her not to run in the front room. Tidal waves of memories that she'd forgotten.

It was stranger still, to be standing in the place she'd once called home and to have a tsunami of homesickness wash over her.

Only Mads knew it wasn't really homesickness. It was a mourning for a loss of innocence. For the time before she'd seen what was behind the veil, and before she knew what it was like to ride beside the pale specter of death. She wouldn't trade what she had now for anything, but that didn't stop her from missing the way she'd once viewed the world. The way she'd once interacted with it.

No, if she were being honest, she really missed the way she interacted with him. If he were real, if this Horseman were more than a figment of a heated and youthful imagination, it wouldn't be the same if she saw him now.

She'd have to slap him in a containment unit. Turn him over to 7. Wouldn't she?

Except she hadn't forced Elizabeth's hand, so why force her own?

It was silly to think about, she admonished herself. Except, it wasn't, was it? She'd been taught to always be running scenarios. No matter how unlikely. So why not run the scenario? What would she do if she saw him again?

"Madelyn, is that you?" Her mother called out from the kitchen, her voice dulcet and soft, carrying with it the kind of comfort only a mother's voice can.

She took a deep breath. "Yeah, Mama. I'm home."

Mads would have to run the scenarios later because she was suddenly face to face with Christopher Knickerbocker.

"Hey, Mads. You got a hug for me?" He opened his arms.

She stepped into the embrace and found herself dwarfed by him. Mads hugged him tight, focusing on just how good it was to see him. Not the part where it felt good to be in his arms. To be touched.

To feel like he was the one who'd keep the dark things at bay for once, and not her.

Christ, but those were dangerous thoughts and they had no place in her head.

Except in her secret heart of hearts, there was just one corner where she hid that desire. To be a pretty princess. A lovely bird in a cage whose only concern was her song.

Or maybe the Horseman's lady.

She realized she'd been clinging much too long. "I guess you've been drinking your milk."

God, what a stupid thing to say. Why did she say that? She was an experienced, professional—

"Yeah. You were taller than me when you left."

"My biceps were bigger, too." Mads grinned up at him.

"Care to compare now?" He lifted his arm, showing off his bulk.

"I'll still kick your ass, Knickerbocker."

He laughed. "You know, I want to argue with you, but I'm pretty sure you could."

They were back in familiar territory, and she wanted to hug him again. Not because he'd gotten hotter, even though he had, but because he was home, too. Just like this B&B. He was part of her child-hood, her family, her tribe.

"Still wrestling in the dirt with the boys I see," Katrina said as she came in for a hug with a smile.

Mads hugged her just as tightly. "It is so good to see you."

"You think?" Katrina cocked her head to the side. "Because you know, you could FaceTime a girl."

Yeah, when would that happen? When she was exorcizing demons, or disposing of cursed bones, or hunting rabid werewolves? "You know how it is. Work. Work. Work."

"Your fancy FBI job," Katrina teased.

And the other member of their little crew, Sean Van Crane swept her up in a giant hug. He'd always been a bear of a kid, and now he was a gentle giant of a man.

But that didn't stop her from shrieking like a kid when he picked her up.

"Looks like the only one missing from this reunion is your Horseman," Sean said.

"Hush up with that, child." Her mother said from the doorway, looking every inch like she just stepped out of a fairytale. Her hair was pulled back into a gray, wiry bun. Her face didn't have any new lines, and she liked it that way, but there was a kind of ragged exhaustion in her dark brown eyes behind her wire-rimmed spectacles. There was an orange polka dot apron wrapped around her generous hips and her mother wiped her perfectly manicured fingers on it before reaching out to Mads.

"Mama," she whispered.

Her mother hugged her so very tightly, as if to make up for every day she hadn't been there in person to hug her. To give her a gold star. To tell her everything would be okay.

How she'd missed this woman.

And the apple tart she shoved in Madelyn's mouth.

"I know how to keep my baby quiet," Roz Whitman said.

Madelyn could only nod and chew, while looking pointedly for her father.

"Your favorite person to ever walk the earth is in the kitchen."

She mumbled something, then swallowed, and tried again. "He's not my favorite. You're both my favorite."

"Oh, run along with you, child. You've always been a daddy's girl, and that's okay. Go hug him now before he pops like an overfed tick waiting on you."

She'd been expecting recriminations. Madelyn hadn't been home in years. That's not to say she hadn't seen her parents, but they'd come to visit her, and it had been a good long year and a half since the last one. She'd been too busy with work.

"There's my girl, finally taking a break from keeping the world safe."

"It's just a desk job, Dad."

"Yeah, yeah. But you're making a difference. You must be, if it's kept you from us this long."

"Ah, Dad. Just go in for the kill why don't you?"

"You'll understand when you have kids of your own."

"I hate to break it to you, but I don't think that's going to happen." She tried to imagine it for a moment. Run the scenario.

Like hell.

How would she rappel down into a jungle village of a possessed tribe with a baby on board? Nah, she couldn't see it.

"Everything in its own time, Maddy."

"Ah, well, with everything in its own time, then that's when I visit. In my own time."

"You got me there, kid." He handed *her a m*ug. "Cider?"

"Always." She brought it to her lips and just inhaled the scent for a long moment before actually taking a sip.

"What do you smell in it today?"

"Christmas," she said without hesitation. "Snow. Fleece blankets."

"If your cider smells like sheep, you probably ought not to drink it," he joked. "But good call. Farmer's Almanac says it'll snow in a fortnight."

Everyone filed into the kitchen and sat at the family table. They usually ate meals with the boarders, so this was a surprise.

"Remember when we used to try to tell our fortunes with the first cider of the year?" Katrina said.

"Or who we were going to marry with an apple peel?" Christopher added.

"It was spot on for me," Roz said. "I got a 'w.' For Whitman."

"I never got anything," Katrina said. "Not a fortune. Not an initial. Nothing."

"You always said it was because you were too good to stay around here," Christopher said.

"Well, what was I going to say?" Katrina shook her head. "What did you get, Maddy? Didn't you get a 'k'?"

"Did you really?" Christopher's gaze was suddenly intense.

"It's not for Knickerbocker," Sean said, adopting a helpful tone. "Karl. Prinzehauzen. The Horseman."

"Oh my hell, you guys. Let it die." Mads was suddenly uncomfortable.

"I seem to recall you said he was taking you to Homecoming. I will never, ever let that die," Sean said, gleeful.

"Then we should go let him welcome you back, too, Mads. What do you say?" Katrina asked. "Maybe you can have a waltz in the moonlight."

"How are you going to waltz with a man with no head?" Chris snickered.

"If you are going out in the orchard tonight, take your shoes off on the porch before you come back inside. And for landsakes, can you wait until after dinner?" Roz fussed.

"This is why I don't come home," Mads replied, deadpan.

A flicker of movement outside the window caught her eye and as she turned to look, she could've sworn she saw the flicker of moonlight on a bright flash of something blue.

Something that could've been a Hessian soldier's uniform.

ABOUT THE AUTHOR

About the Author

Saranna De Wylde has always been fascinated by things better left in the dark. She wrote her first story after watching The Exorcist at a slumber party. Since then, she's published horror, romance and narrative nonfiction. Like all writers, Saranna has held a variety of jobs, from operations supervisor for an airline, to an assistant for a call girl, to a corrections officer. But like Hemingway said, "Once writing has become your major vice and greatest pleasure, only death can stop it." So she traded in her cuffs for a full-time keyboard. She loves to hear from her readers.